W9-CLM-598

The Man of My Dreams

The Man of My Dreams

Stories by
Diane Schoemperlen

Macmillan of Canada
A Division of Canada Publishing Corporation
Toronto, Ontario, Canada

Copyright © Diane Schoemperlen, 1990

All rights reserved. The use of any part of this publication repro-
duced, transmitted in any form or by any means, electronic, mechanical, photocopying, recording, or otherwise, or stored in a retrieval
system, without the prior written consent of the publisher is an
infringement of the copyright law.

Canadian Cataloguing in Publication Data

Schoemperlen, Diane.
   The man of my dreams

ISBN 0-7715-9973-0

I. Title.

PS8587.C48M3 1990   C813'.54   C90-093023-3
PR9199.3.S393M3 1990

1 2 3 4 5 GP 94 93 92 91 90

Cover design by Gordon Robertson
Cover illustration by Nicholas Vitacco

Typeset in Plantin by Compeer Typographic Services Ltd.

MACMILLAN OF CANADA
A Division of Canada Publishing Corporation
Toronto, Ontario, Canada

For Alexander

Acknowledgements

Some of these stories have been previously published:

"The Man of My Dreams" in *The Macmillan Anthology 1*, eds., John Metcalf and Leon Rooke, Macmillan of Canada, Toronto, 1988.

"What We Want" in *Coming Attractions 2*, eds., David Helwig and Sandra Martin, Oberon Press, 1984; in *Hockey Night in Canada*, Quarry Press, 1987; excerpts on CBC Radio, Alberta Anthology, Edmonton, 1983; and in *Women and Words: The Anthology*, Harbour Publishing, 1984.

"His People" in *Prism International*, Vancouver, Vol. 26, No. 4, Summer 1988.

"Tickets to Spain" in *The Fiddlehead*, Fredericton, No. 146; in *87 Best Canadian Stories*, eds., David Helwig and Maggie Helwig, Oberon Press, 1987; and in *Hockey Night in Canada*, Quarry Press, 1987.

"How Myrna Survives" in *The New Quarterly*, Waterloo, Ontario, January 1989.

"The Gate" in *Canadian Author & Bookman*, Volume 58, Number 2, Winter 1983, and in *Pure Fiction: The Okanagan Short Story Award Winners*, ed., Geoff Hancock, Fitzhenry & Whiteside, Markham, Ontario, 1986.

"Losing Ground" in *Event*, Volume 10, Number 2, December 1981.

"Stranger Than Fiction" in *The Malahat Review*, December 1989.

Excerpt from "Railroading Or: Twelve Small Stories with the Word 'Train' in the Title" in *Books in Canada*, Volume 18, Number 7, October 1989.

For information on dreams, astronomy, painting, among other things, I would like to acknowledge the following references:

The Dictionary of Dreams: 10,000 Dreams Interpreted by Gustavus Hindman Miller, Prentice-Hall Press, New York, 1986.

The Dreamer's Dictionary: A Complete Guide to Interpreting Your Dreams by Stearn Robinson and Tom Corbett, Taplinger Publishing Company, New York, 1974.

Painting: A Complete Guide by Kenneth Jameson, Thomas Nelson and Sons Ltd., London, 1975.

Exploring the Night Sky: The Equinox Astronomy Guide for Beginners by Terence Dickinson, Camden House, Camden East, Ontario, 1987.

Exploring the Sky by Day by Terence Dickinson, Camden House, Camden East, Ontario, 1988.

The Prentice-Hall Concise Book of Astronomy by Jacqueline and Simon Mitton, Prentice-Hall of Canada, Scarborough, Ontario, 1978.

The Sun, The National Enquirer, Consumers' Distributing Catalogue and *"Your Horoscope"* by Jeane Dixon, 1988.

The poem "The Issues" by Sharon Olds, which appears in "His People", is used by permission (from *The Dead and The Living*, by Sharon Olds, Alfred A. Knopf, Inc., New York, 1986).

I would also like to thank the Ontario Arts Council and the Canada Council for their generous support of this project. I would especially like to thank John Metcalf for his editorial work in selecting these stories for publication.

Table of Contents

THE MAN OF MY DREAMS

*I dreamed of myself in a dream, and told the dream,
which was mine, as if it were another person's of
whom I dreamed. Indeed, what is life when thinking
of the past, but dreaming of a dream dreamt by
another who seems sometimes to be oneself?*

Stopford Brooke, Diary, June 8, 1899

1

In the stories I read, the female characters dream in great detail of daring escapes from prisons, kitchens, and burning shopping malls; of reproduction, reincarnation, and masked terrorists tracking them through quicksand just when they are about to give birth. In these fictional dreams, the ex-husbands or lovers are delightfully drowned in vats of warm beer or are pelted to death with wormy apples thrown by throngs of scorned women in their white negligees. These lucid dreamers wield axes, swords, scythes, and the occasional chainsaw which lops off those unfaithful legs like sugar cane. The male characters in these clever stories dream muscularly about cars, hockey, boxing, and taking their mistresses and/or their mothers out for chateaubriand and escargots.

All of this seems significant and makes good sense to me. I nod while I'm reading and often underline.

2

In the stories I write, the female characters dream about black stallions which burst into flames, carrying their young daughters to certain death in lakes a hundred feet deep; about alcoholic surgeons who keep taking them apart and putting them back together again like jigsaw puzzles, sometimes missing a piece; about bullfights at which they're wearing their wedding gowns and the matador rides the bull before he kills it and then a team of mules drags the dead bull away on its back like a giant insect and the crowd throws red roses, hysterical; about trains, catching them, missing them, chasing them; about babies, having them, losing them, selling them; about tunnels and eggs.

When they wake up in the morning, these women are gratified to remember every little detail of these dreams and tell them to their sleepy husbands or lovers who are not really interested but pretend to be as they slurp up their coffee and scratch. The women say, "Last night I dreamed you were dead," and the men say, "That's nice, honey. Where the hell are my socks?" And the women just hand those socks over without even having to think: they know where everything is, they just *know*, and they're talking about going into dream therapy and the men say, "Sure, that sounds like fun, honey. Go for it."

These male characters dream sturdily, if at all, about wrestling, drinking, baseball, sky-diving, and pouring vinegar on their fish and chips when they were happy little kids. More often, though, they wake up in the morning with a simple erection and say, "Boy, I was dead the minute my head hit the pillow. I slept like a baby."

In the stories I write, I take it for granted that these men snore and roll over forty-seven times a night while these women beside them wander and moan, commit adultery, murder, and magic. This is along the lines of my mother always saying, "When men get upset, they drink. We women, we cry."

Of course, I write fiction.

3

In real life, I dream about telephone bills, frying pans, oranges.

The dream telephone bill is ten pages long, an astronomical amount, past due, which has me calling all over town trying to track down who owes me how much for which calls. Nobody can remember phoning anybody long-distance on my phone ever in their entire lives. They tell me you have moved to a country where they don't speak English.

To dream of a telephone foretells meeting strangers who will harass and bewilder you. For a woman to dream of using one warns that she will have much jealous rivalry, but will overcome all evil influences. If she cannot hear well on the telephone, she is threatened with evil gossip and the loss of a lover. If the telephone is out of order, it portends sad news.

The dream frying pan, red, Teflon-coated, is being returned to me by the man next door and it is three times as big as the one I loaned him in the first place, which was the one my mother gave me for Christmas three weeks before she died. He grins foolishly out from under a white baseball cap as I try to make him understand that this is not the right pan, this is not *my* frying pan. I give up eventually and get busy scrambling a dozen farm-fresh eggs for brunch.

To dream of pots and pans foretells that trivial events will cause you much vexation. To see a broken or rusty one implies that you will experience keen disappointment.

Oranges, twice I have dreamed about oranges.

The first orange dream, which I had when I was pregnant with Ben, is set in Atwater, the eastern town where I grew up. I am by the water around the docks and grain elevators. My friend Bonnie and someone named Lynn are there too, all bundled up in big coats and plastic hats because it is cold and raining. You are at work or in the bar drinking with the boys. We three women discuss this, shaking our heads and smoking in the rain. I go walking down to the water alone and then along the shoreline, which is icy and treacherous. I am thinking about a football star I knew in high school who got a summer job on the railroad and fell from a boxcar his first day out and got both his legs cut off at the knee. I am cutting up an orange with my Swiss Army knife and throwing the slices to the sea-gulls. I walk back along the shoreline, being extra careful not to slip on the ice because suddenly I am pregnant. I pick my way back to where Bonnie and Lynn are still huddled together on an iron bench.

I awoke then, suddenly and fully, as if at a noise in the night: breaking glass or footsteps, but there was nothing.

The second orange dream, which didn't amount to much, is set in Hazelwood, the western town where you and I lived together. I am squeezing a whole bag of oranges to make juice for our breakfast. There are mountains out the window. You are at the kitchen table in your longjohns looking at the newspaper. I smell my orange-dipped fingers and you read me my horoscope.

To dream of eating oranges is signally bad, foretelling pervasive discontentment and the sickness of friends or relatives. A young woman is likely to lose her lover if she dreams of eating oranges. But if she dreams of seeing a fine one tossed up high, she will be discreet in choosing a husband from among her many lovers. To slip on an orange peel foretells the death of a relative.

4

In real life, I dream about my dead mother, young again in the garden there beside the peonies. Or I dream that it is my father who is dead instead.

5

In real life, I dream about grocery-shopping.

My parents, both of them alive in this dream, are here to visit Ben and me in this eastern city where we have come to live. I am at the A&P buying six ears of corn despite the fact that both my parents have false teeth and will have to scrape the kernels off the cobs with a fork, which is harder than it looks. I go over to the 24-Hour Deli Counter which features fresh peaches, three-bean salad, and pickled eggs. A woman slicing meat explains that everything on her counter is twenty-four hours old or less. "This beef, for instance," she tells me, waving a knife, "this cow has been dead for less than twenty-four hours."

I go around the store picking up the ingredients for Chinese Pork: pork tenderloin, three green peppers, mushrooms. I decide I will use fresh mushrooms. My mother, who gave me the recipe, always used canned, but now I will show her how much better it is with fresh. But all the mushrooms they have are brown and shrivelling, more stems than caps. Frozen lemonade, limeade, and orange juice cans go rolling down the aisles with messages on them.

To dream of pork predicts continued prosperity whether you eat the meat, cook it, serve it, or buy it.

In the morning I dug out the recipe, one you always loved. It was written on a small blue-lined white card in my mother's neat, strong hand:

CHINESE PORK

½ lb. pork tenderloin
2½ tsp. soya sauce
2 tbsp. flour
1 tbsp. butter
1 chicken bouillon cube
½ cup boiling water
1 green pepper, cut in strips
1 (10 oz.) can sliced mushrooms, drained

Cut tenderloin in narrow strips. Brush strips with soya sauce, roll in flour. Melt butter in fry pan, add meat, and brown. Dissolve bouillon cube in ½ cup boiling water, add to fry pan with other ingredients. Cover and simmer about 15 minutes. Serve with rice. (Serves 2.)

The recipe told me nothing about either you or her. It was just something she sent me once when she was dieting, a low-calorie one-dish meal that looked good on the table, good enough to photograph, good enough to eat. We traded recipes, she and I, just as I imagine other women do, but when I went back to Atwater for the funeral, I found the ones I'd sent (Sour Cream Meatloaf, Quick Spaghetti Sauce with Clams, Chunky Chili) not even filed into the box. She had never even tried them, so I made the meatloaf for my father, who liked it very much. Of course, he would.

This was the day before the funeral. My father and I had been out all morning making the arrangements and Sonja, the woman next door, was minding Ben. When I went over to pick him up, Sonja sat me down with warm spice cake and coffee. I remembered her as cooking, always cooking, bringing over cast-iron pots and crockery bowls covered with tinfoil, still steaming.

That day she was making sauerkraut soup, which I said I had never heard of but it sure did smell good. So she told me the recipe, and also one for perogies, which she'd been making twelve dozen of once a week for thirty years. These were family recipes, passed on to her by *her* mother, who was still alive but laid up these days with a bad back. Sonja had never written them down herself but performed them magically from memory, like playing the piano without sheet music. I tried to follow her directions, scribbling them on the back of an envelope: a little bit of this, a little bit of that, simmer till it looks done.

Ben hopped happily around the fragrant kitchen, eating peanut-butter sandwiches and singing the *Sesame Street* theme song. Sonja and I smoked and drank coffee and talked about people I hadn't thought of for years, until finally she just wondered why my mother had never told her about Ben until he was nearly two years old.

6

In the dream about the bacon (this was years ago), you say, "I hate pork, you know I hate pork, why are you feeding me pork?"

I say, "You're lying, you asshole. You men are all alike," you being the one in real life who, every single time I made roast pork on Sunday, would say, "Oh goody, pork sandwiches for my midnight snack. They always give me the best dreams."

It makes sense to me that women should dream about food.

To dream of eating bacon is good if someone is eating with you and your hands are clean. Rancid bacon is a suggestion to see a doctor. Cooking bacon augurs a surprise or gift, which will please you very much.

The next morning I was still mad but could hardly explain myself, not sanely anyway, as I slammed around the kitchen, making lousy coffee and slapping together a cheese-and-tomato sandwich for your lunch, knowing full well that you hated how the bread would be soggy and pink by noon.

Either you were ignoring my mood or you were just getting used to me.

Your best dreams, your pork-induced visions, were all about work: the backhoe, the Cat, the scraper, the grader, you were operating all of them at once: knocking down trees, digging up boulders and whole mountainsides, grading steep slopes perfectly within an inch of your life so help me, loading twenty trucks a shift, unloading them all again at the other end, waking me up with your twitching as the dump truck bucked beneath you, box up, shrugging out the last of its load.

To dream of machinery foretells undertaking a project which will give great anxiety, but will finally result in good for you. If the machinery is idle or derelict, it indicates approaching family or employment problems.

I handed you your lunch and cursed you out for taking my last cigarette.

All you said was, "I'm so tired. I've been working all night."

I said nothing and glared at your hands, nicotine-stained and speckled with scabs and fresh scrapes which you liked to enumerate each evening over supper. Particularly purple and ugly were the two flat knuckles on your left hand, squashed one afternoon between a boulder and the tailgate, a story you loved to tell repeatedly in the bar, wrapping it up with, "Well, I guess that's what they mean by 'Caught between a rock and a hard place', eh?", not mentioning how you threw up at the sound of your own bones grinding.

You were gabbing on about how in the dream you nearly rolled the truck and then the other guy just missed you with the bucket of the backhoe, until I said, gritting my teeth and spacing my words, "Can't you just be quiet for once?"

I always told you I hated to talk in the morning because, after sleeping for the last eight hours, I had nothing to talk about but my dreams and who wants to hear all that crap?

People change.

7

My best talking time was after we went to bed. We weren't having sex much any more by then, so maybe my babbling was just a way of filling in the time. One night I remember we were talking about Italians, their industriousness, how they would come over from the old country with nothing and build up successful companies in concrete or construction. Then I told you about all the Italian women I'd worked with that one summer at the bank in Atwater. This covered lasagna (Angelina), Italian weddings (Loretta), arranged marriages (Teresa), and how some Italian women get so fat and sloppy after the first baby (Rosina) and how some Italian men fancy themselves such Romeos and like to let their chest hair show (Rosina's husband, Guido). Then I discovered you had lint in your belly button, which put me in mind of that girl I knew at the Atwater United Church who had no belly button and how we used to serve at church teas together.

And you said, "Sleep, sleep, woman, I'm begging you to let me sleep."

That night all of my dreams were accompanied by organ music.

Pleasant organ music heard in a dream is an omen of satisfying sexual prowess. To hear doleful singing with organ accompaniment denotes you are approaching a tiresome task and probable loss of friends or status. To see an organ in church warns of despairing separation of family members and death, perhaps, for some of them.

8

I dreamed I was trying to steal another woman's baby from a furniture store. Then my mother offered me $3,000 and a fancy orange sports car if only I would leave you and go live with her in a mobile home in Florida. She said, "If he really loved you, he'd marry you." We were in Sonja's kitchen, eating cabbage rolls and borscht, and the car was parked right across the street, running.

9

The reasons for our leaving each other are not especially clear. I wish you had left me for another woman. Such triangular situations are so common, so understandable. By way of compulsive comparison — myself to her, my hair to hers, my hips to hers, my cooking, my cleanliness, my clothes, my big eyes to hers — the pain would become so much more accessible, acceptable.

I wish you had left me for another woman or I wish I had left you for another man because then either or both of us could dream of revenge.

To dream of taking revenge is a sign of a weak and uncharitable nature, which will bring you trouble and loss of friends. Such a dream is a reminder that you must give consideration if you expect to get it.

10

I went to a dinner party at the home of another writer. We had a chicken, tender and meaty enough to have been a turkey, which she'd bought from the Hutterites. The other guests were writers too and one or two film-makers. They talked about people I didn't know, movies I hadn't seen, books I hadn't read. I couldn't blame them: they all knew each other, I was new in town and not about to admit that no, I wasn't especially fond of Henry James and hadn't got around to reading Chekhov yet. Over dessert (fresh strawberries in heavy cream), they began to trade their dreams around the table like a deck of cards. They had earnest, intelligent dreams, intricate like lace or the way a prism in the window will cast colours on the backs of your hands.

"I was sitting with a group of Cossacks drinking black tea from a silver samovar. Then one of them turned into Dostoyevsky and we were debating crime and punishment until he wanted to know about Australian Rules Football and what does this word 'nuclear' mean? The windows were white with frost and a wolf howled."

"Oh, I've had that one too!"

"I was preparing Boeuf Bourguignon, sipping a good Chablis. Gurdjieff was coming for dinner. Afterwards we would play croquet and the sunset would be perfect."

"Marvellous!"

"I was having my first haircut, a child of two. Vidal Sassoon was the barber and I was reading to him from Sartre's *Being and Nothingness*."

"Wonderful!"

"I was a peacock, preening."

"Oh-oh, we all know what that means!"

I felt inadequate and pushed the strawberries around in my bowl the way Ben does when he doesn't want to eat. But there was no escaping them.

So I told my recurring dream, the one where I am in bed, sweating and scared, trying to call for my father but the sound won't come out. Everything in this dream is detailed and true; it has recast itself into every bedroom I have ever lived in. Finally, after years of this, I woke myself up one night screaming, "Dad! Dad!" and you held me and I never had the dream again.

This was so obvious as to seem shallow.

11

The puppy, I assume, dreams about cats and other dogs, raw steak maybe on a good night. She twitches and whimpers, thumps her stubby tail on the floor.

The cat, I assume, dreams about birds, mice, and other cats, a nice fresh can of tuna. She sighs.

What does Ben dream about? I like to think that he is dreaming about running, flying, cuddling, sailboats, ice cream with sprinkles, Big Bird, and lambs. I do not like to think he is dreaming about the time when he, at two months, cried all night and I whispered, hysterical at four in the morning, "Shut your fucking mouth, you little bastard!" and then laid my wet cheek against his monkey face and rocked him and watched till the streetlights went out, smelling his perfect skin.

He is too young, he will not dream about you. Oh, he may dream about your photographs, your guitar, your bald head, as I sometimes do.

To see a bald-headed man in a dream warns to guard against being cheated by someone you trust. For a young woman to dream of a bald-headed man means she must use her intelligence against listening to her next marriage offer. Bald-headed babies signify a happy home, a loving companion, and obedient children.

He is too young, he will not remember his grandmother either. For the rest of his life, he will suspect that all of the strangers in his dreams are either her or you.

12

Often I dream that I am dreaming. But still, such knowledge does not keep me from the fear.

13

When I dream about you now, you are always wearing that red shirt.

14

Two months after my mother died, my father came here to visit
Ben and me. The night before he was scheduled to arrive, I
dreamed that when he did, my mother was with him, wearing
her pink shortie nightie and a scarf. In the dream, I thought very
clearly, *Well, of course, I should have known this would happen.*

I went to pick him up at the airport, the little old-fashioned
kind where the passengers still have to walk down the steps
and across the tarmac in the dark windy night. I stood behind
the chain-link fence and watched for him, my tall father, thinking he would be wearing that stupid hat he always wears when
he has to do something official like go to the doctor or fly. But
there he was, coming at me bare-headed — and alone, of course.

An East Indian family got off the plane behind him. The
man, in jeans and a plaid shirt, held a sleeping child against
each shoulder. The woman behind took tiny steps in her purple
sari, cuddling a wide-awake fat baby whose soother fell out of
its mouth and rolled across the parking lot as she passed me. I
was feeling too cruel or isolated to point this out to her and the
taxi they got into backed right over it.

I had two dreams about planes while my father was here. In
the first, a small red-and-white plane had crashed in my backyard, sending up fireworks instead of flames, and we were only
surprised, not hurt or frightened. In the second, I was driving
my father back out to the airport to go home but it ended up
that Ben and I boarded and he stayed behind, waving. I knew
it was all a mistake but there could be no turning back now.

I told my father this one at breakfast as he held Ben on his
lap and fed him toast with strawberry jam, but I never told
him about the fireworks.

15

During my father's visit, I had one of those dreams where you
keep coming almost awake but you don't want to, so, mirac-

ulously, you are able to swim back down and pick up where you left off.

In the dream, you and my father are in the kitchen, talking about fishing. Your father, you are telling him, tied his own flies. I am making hamburgers and salad, bringing you both another beer. My dead mother, I discover, has been laid out in my new queen-size bed. I try to walk into the bedroom but see her folded hands and think I am going to throw up. I back away, then force myself forward again and then again, gagging. I never do get into the room before I wake up.

There was something in this dream about lettuce, about peeling away all those pale-green leaves. Or was there? Maybe I just made it up, searching for a symbol, trying to get surreal.

16

Four months after my mother died, Ben and I went back to Atwater to visit my father. Each day he said, "Maybe we should go out to the cemetery this afternoon," until finally one day we went. I took pictures of her headstone with the lilies in the rain, something which did not strike me as an odd thing to do until after I got the prints back and could not think where to put them.

When we got back to my father's house, Ben fell asleep and I lay down too, on my parents' bed. There was thunder and lightning all afternoon. I am still afraid of storms, not the lightning so much, which is swift and can kill you instantly, but the thunder, which is unpredictable and makes you hold your breath waiting for it.

In the long dream we are driving in from the country, my mother, father, me, in a taxicab at night. I am obsessively worrying that I will have to drive in the dark, will wreck the car and kill us all. But no. It turns out that the cab driver will take us all the way to wherever we are going.

We stop at a supper club on the highway, eat steak, treat the cab driver too because he's such a nice guy. He holds my hand on the way back to the car. Then we are just travelling for a long time.

When daylight comes, I am alone in the seedy downtown section of a strange city. I walk along many slummy streets, looking for a bookstore. I even climb over a chicken-wire fence. I pass a little old lady in a green dress who says, "It's hard to get around these days," so I help her over the fence.

I go below street level into a narrow room and find it filled with colourfully dressed people and bikers. I meet a young blond man wearing an Indian shirt, the embroidered kind with mirrors.

He says, "My name is Chris. I've fried my brain. I used to be a Hare Krishna and they killed my brain. Look into my eyes, they are dead, empty, insane."

We make love and I say, "No, your eyes are beautiful, neither dead, empty, nor insane."

A short blonde woman with a shirt just like his, dirty little hands and feet, comes over and watches us. She is his girlfriend, Kathy. She leaves.

Making love again, he says, "I'm dead, I can't feel anything."

I say, "I'll make you feel it."

He is on top, I climax, he doesn't, but says, "Still, you made me feel something, more than Kathy can."

We make love once more, I'm on top, I come twice, calling his name. He comes too and cries on me, with love and relief.

Back on the street, I'm waiting for a bus at a huge complex intersection where eight streets converge. Behind me is a Safeway store, an A&P, and an IT&T. My watch reads 10:17 a.m. I am being blown around in the hot wind and, hanging onto a parking meter, I tell the man beside me that I wish I had a pen so I could write down the street names to find this place again.

But I've lost my purse and I panic, until I look in the pockets of the green army parka I've acquired. There I find my wallet, cigarettes, address book, and two library books: *Disturbances in the Field* by Lynne Sharon Schwartz and *Technique in Fiction*.

The bus comes and I am riding to my parents' house, thinking of how mad they're going to be that I stayed out all night. So I decide to let my mother help me choose a dress for the dance tomorrow night. This is bound to make her happy again.

It was the kind of dream that you think takes hours, the kind of dream that makes perfect sense when you first wake up and then proceeds to mystify you all day long.

17

I have never dreamed about the lilies.

To dream of a lily denotes coming chastisement through illness and death. For a young woman to dream of admiring or gathering lilies denotes much suffering coupled with joy. If she sees them withering, the sadness is nearer than she suspects. To dream of breathing the fragrance of lilies denotes that sorrow will purify and enhance your mental qualities.

18

From my mother's closet, I chose a green linen suit and a white blouse, and put them in a brown paper bag. I did not know beforehand that I would also have to give them her underwear: a slip, bra and panties, pantyhose. Shoes, they said, were optional. I didn't put them in because I couldn't bear to think of anyone putting them on her feet. My father at the last minute put in the emerald earrings and pendant he'd given her for Christmas three weeks earlier.

As we shuffled past the coffin, he moaned and held his arms out, leaning forward as if to kiss her. I pulled him back and led him away because I was afraid.

After the service, everyone went to Sonja's for sandwiches and dainties, dark rum and beer. Sonja gave me a huge pot of spaghetti sauce which I served with salad for supper that night to the relatives gathered in my father's house. You called long-distance with your sympathy.

That night I slept in the bed of my childhood and my feet kept bumping the borrowed crib where Ben slept at the end. He sighed and said, "Sorry." I counted the books on the shelves like sheep.

That night I dreamed of your lips, which I was always fond of.

Sweet lips in a dream signify a successful sex life and happiness in love. Thick, overly sensual, or ugly lips forecast failure in love but success in business. Sore or swollen lips denote deprivation and unhealthy desires.

At breakfast, my father said, "I had a kooky dream last night. I dreamed that your mother had left me and they said she was living with some guy on Market Street. But I said, 'No, she's dead, it can't be true, she can't be over there with him.' "

I kept on scrambling farm-fresh eggs for Ben.

19

The only childhood dream I can still remember is the one about the giant camel. I am in the school basement, wearing my black patent-leather shoes and my new tartan skirt with the gold pin. I am hiding in the bathroom, where all the toilets are short and the concrete blocks are painted pink. The camel is upstairs in the kindergarten room. His hooves come through the ceiling like shovels. I am washing my hands and there is hair on the soap. There is never any doubt that the camel will get me.

To dream of a camel means you will have to work hard to overcome your obstacles. If the camel bore a burden, unexpected wealth, possibly in the form of an inheritance, will come your way. If you rode the camel, your future is bright indeed.

20

I often dream about Lake Street in the east end of Atwater. In this dream nothing happens and I'm not in it. In this dream it is always five o'clock in the morning and raining. Cars with their headlights on pass each other all up and down the wet street, swishing and splashing to a halt, idling and waiting for the light to change. The tavern has its windows bricked up. The Chinese grocery and the pawnshop are bankrupt, vacant, the apartments upstairs condemned by the health department. Winos lounge and sleep or die in the doorways of warehouses filled with washers, dryers, fridges, stoves, dishwashers, and stereos. Bats cling and swoop. The rain stops, the sun comes up hot, and the sidewalks steam.

There is in this dream a persistent and clammy sense of danger which does not materialize and is never explained.

21

I dreamed about buying a refrigerator in the chocolate-brown colour no longer popular among major appliance purchasers (so the salesman informs me while eating a peanut-butter and banana sandwich) but I just have to have the brown anyway. Then I call Annie Churchill, who I graduated from high school with and haven't seen since, although I seem to know that she is married to a dentist now and happy about it. I tell them what I've just bought, how much I love it, how much I've changed. "You're getting so domestic in your old age," he says or she says.

After a grainy digression that has to do with a party and changing my clothes, there is a slow-motion section about an enormous mound of cocaine being kneaded into a pound of raw hamburger and stashed in the fridge door behind the eggs because the cops are coming, I can hear the sirens.

To see a refrigerator in your dreams warns that your selfishness will injure someone trying to gain an honest livelihood. To place food in one brings the dreamer into disfavour.

22

I thought I was coming down with something, so I lay on the couch all afternoon, aching and feverish.

I dreamed that my friend Bonnie was running a home for retarded deformed children.

I dreamed that I went to see a lady who had advertised for someone to walk her two white sheepdogs.

I dreamed that you went to Texas and shaved off your beard for the first time in fourteen years.

I dreamed that my mother was finally teaching me how to iron a shirt properly.

Just before I woke up, I dreamed about Janet, who is married to your friend Roger now. She was always wearing blue jeans, bow-legged, flat-chested, a real tomboy, always playing in mixed softball tournaments. They had such a good relationship that she could stay out all night drinking with the girls and Roger didn't mind. In the dream I am at the ballpark with hundreds of other fans waiting for the game to start. I am alone and searching for someone to sit with. Janet is the only person I know. As I make my way towards her, she says to someone else, "I've gotta go to my feminist class. 'Bye now." I am carrying my new puppy in my arms and suddenly baseballs are being thrown at us. I am running away, shoulders hunched to protect the puppy, who has turned into a rabbit. The baseballs bounce off my back like ping-pong balls.

23

I have been, among other things, giving Ben his bath before bed, watching a made-for-TV movie about a compulsive gam-

bler (female), pushing Ben's stroller up a steep street in the
heat and feeling profoundly sorry for myself, when a certain
sneaky word has come to me without warning:

Chimera.

It is one of those words which, for years, I've had to look
up every time I come across it because I keep thinking it has
something to do with water or light, shimmering.

> **chimera** *n.*   1. (Gk Myth.) A fire-breathing monster
> with the head of a lion, the body of a goat, and the tail
> of a serpent.   2. An impossible or foolish fancy. (Gk
> *khimaira*, chimera, "she-goat")

The image which invariably follows is of a gorilla straddling a
silver airplane wing, beating its hairy chest and roaring in at the
innocent bug-eyed passengers. The airplane is flying low at night
through fraying cloud cover and the eyes of this gorilla are red.

This doesn't shake me up nearly as much as it used to and
I am able now to wonder maturely how this gorilla got into my
head in the first place. Was it a movie or a dream? Who can I
ask?

*To dream of a gorilla portends a painful misunderstanding, unless
the animal was very docile or definitely friendly, in which case the
dream forecasts an unusual new friend.*

This is like thinking of that November night in the Hazelwood Hotel, you and I drinking draft beer because we were
broke, and some guy came in and said there was a dog frozen
dead out front, said it was Bonnie's dog, Blitz. The entire bar
emptied and outside we found that someone had let Blitz off
her chain and put in her place a dead Doberman, frozen, its
throat slit. So then we all got talking about that crazy guy in
town for a month or two last summer, the one who always
carried an empty pizza box under his arm and who chased his
Doberman down Main Street with an axe that one time when
the dog wouldn't mind.

So then it was last call and you and me and our friend Mike bought a case of off-sales and went over to his place for a sauna. I think of the three of us running naked in the backyard, rolling around in the snow like puppies, having heard that's how they do it in Finland. And in my drunkenness, Mike with his bulging eyes and acne-ravaged skin was starting to look pretty good to me. And I was ranting on about Remembrance Day, which had just passed, and how I was so proud of my father for what he had done in the war, fairly weeping with the intensity of my unexamined admiration, and Mike said, "I don't believe in war," and tried to talk me out of it, but I said, "I don't either but still . . ." and would not be swayed. So then Mike went and called his mother long-distance in Ontario at three in the morning and told her how much he loved her.

You said, "It's time to go home, I'm seeing triple and I might call my mother too, she's been dead for years," and when you tried to stand up, you knocked over the lamp, spilling kerosene all over our clothes, and I was screaming, "How stupid can one person be!"

The next morning we soaked our clothes for a while in the bathtub, then gave up and threw them away.

I don't think this was a dream but it should have been. That time I called you to check, you said you didn't remember any of it. Sometimes you're no help at all.

What I really want to know is: how did we get home without our clothes?

24

I got my hair cut. That night I dreamed of going back to the beauty parlour, wanting to show the nice lady how good the new style looks. My mother is with me. This lady has light-red hair, long red fingernails, and freckles all over her hands, what my mother called "age spots". She is talking on the phone and smoking when we go into the shop. All the chairs and dryers have been removed — all that remains is the reception desk and this French Provincial telephone.

The hairdresser recognizes me immediately, puts her hand over the mouthpiece, and asks, "Did you ever figure out how John died?"

What on earth is she talking about? Then I remember that while she cut my hair we talked about *Another World*, her favourite soap opera.

I say, excitedly, "No, no, I didn't, but here's my mother." She is standing near the glass door in a red pantsuit. "She's been watching *Another World* since before I was born, she'll know." I turn to my mother and ask her how John died. She's looking right at me but can't hear me. I am yelling but still she can't hear me.

When my mother was here for Christmas three weeks before she died, I was always angry because she couldn't hear the doorbell or the telephone and the TV was turned up too loud. She might get a hearing aid, she said, someday.

When my mother went into the hospital the first time, she got my father to tape *Another World* on the VCR every day so she could catch up on the action when she got home. This last time, when the doctors were still trying to figure out how to tell her she was dying, she told my father not to bother. He told me this when he came to visit Ben and me, he told me this was how he knew that she knew. "Remember how mad she used to get when they put the ball game on instead of her show?" he asked.

Remember how when the U.S. bombed Libya and I called home to say I was watching the news all day and I was scared and she said, "Well, if you don't like it, change the channel." And the next morning I went down to the A&P and bought a case each of baby formula and cat food, praying, *Please God, let Ben live to be old.*

If you were here with me now, would I tell you all this in the morning over breakfast, fresh-ground coffee and brown toast, soft-boiled eggs?

You were always trying to figure out how to get the eggs just right at the high altitude of Hazelwood. "It's perfect, it's perfect!" you'd say before you tasted it and then you'd say, sadly, "No, no, thirty seconds more, just thirty seconds more, and it would have been perfect."

Until finally one winter morning you were satisfied, so I got out the Polaroid and snapped a shot of it: The Perfect Six-Minute Egg. We kept this picture on our bulletin board for years. I study it now: egg in the egg-cup, a half-eaten piece of toast on the Blue River plate on the wicker placemat on the blue tabletop, a coffee mug with a bottle of Baileys Irish Cream beside it, also dental floss, dirty ashtray, and a pink pepper shaker which is one my mother gave me when I first left home, called carnival glass, which used to come in boxes of detergent.

25

The dreams I hate the most are those in which every person, place, and thing keeps changing into some other person, place, or thing and then back again. Even the ground seems to shift and bubble beneath my dreamy feet and occasionally it disappears altogether.

26

You become my father watching the ball game and drinking frosty beer, he becomes my mother melting, she becomes Ben eating ice cream with his fingers.

27

The coffee cup in my left hand becomes a piano and the cigarette in my right a spatula.

28

The front step of my father's house becomes a conveyor belt and then the house itself a restaurant.

29

Ben becomes a kitten even as I hold him in my arms which are turning into saxophones.

30

Waking, I open my eyes and cannot imagine for a minute where in the world you or I might be.

31

I used to dream that Ben was crying in the night. I would wake up, get out of bed, go to the kitchen, take the bottle out of the fridge, heat it to exactly the right temperature by instinct, and when I got to his room, there he was fast asleep. He'd never moved, never cried, never made a single sound.

32

Sometimes now I am pregnant in my dreams, but the pregnancy is never what the dream is about, is merely the condition I happen to be in as I board buses, go to parties, make pizza, or fly.

33

When Ben was three weeks old and I could almost sit down normally again, I had an erotic dream about Dr. Long, the one who delivered him, the handsome one who interrupted his Sunday-afternoon golf game three times to come to me in the delivery room and listen to me hollering, "Do something, do something, can't you do something? What kind of doctor are you anyway? I don't want to do this any more, I want to go home now." The one who said, "Wow, look at that, the blood squirted right across the room!" The one who handed Ben to me softly and said, "He's perfect like a flower," even though when the nurse said, "Look, look, it's a boy!" I wailed, "I don't want to look!" because after eleven hours on that table and everything going wrong — monitors, oxygen, Demerol, forceps — I thought he was going to have a big purple birthmark all over his face.

In the dream, Dr. Long was caressing me in his surgical greens, spreading me open gently on that table and burying his face in my milk-filled breasts. I awoke embarrassed and disgusted with myself.

Sometime later, in a confessional fit, I told this dream to Bonnie, who is my best friend and so I can tell her anything, disgusting or not, and she will still like me. Dr. Long had delivered her baby too. And she laughed and said, yes, yes, she'd dreamed of making love to him too. We snickered and compared details.

Sometime later still, here in this city, I was having lunch and white-wine spritzers with two other women I hardly knew. I was making fun of my former self by telling them this dream and they marvelled and said, yes, yes, they'd had it too about their obstetricians and never told a single soul till now. One of these women had had four children, grown now, all delivered by the same fat, fatherly man who had also taken out her tonsils when she was six. She had dreamed of making love to him in the laundry room. We were so relieved, the three of us, to find ourselves feeling normal for a change that we laughed and laughed, hugged each other round the table, and sat there drinking all afternoon.

34

I have not slept with a man in over ten months. Every night for a week I dream of sex. I have perfunctory sex with everyone but you, including Roger who married Janet, Mike who had the sauna, David Coleman who was in my grade ten Health class, and the man in front of me in the checkout line at the A&P on Wednesday, buying Kraft Dinner, Oreo ice cream, and a comb. I have elaborate and extended dream sex with the man next door who borrows my frying pan and lifts weights in his front yard in his small red shorts. When I see him in the bank the next day, I blush furiously and fidget. But he does not seem to recognize me from either the street or the dream.

35

There are whole days when nothing goes through my mind but you. Then I lie down and dream all night of shopping with my mother, buying a bag of potatoes and a pair of blue high heels. What does this say about me? I wonder, I worry. Am I missing something serious in my psychological makeup? Am I missing the point? What's wrong with me anyway?

36

The night you left I dreamed about washing the kitchen floor.

WHAT WE WANT

We could be anything.
We could be wives.
We could be terrorists.
We could be artists.
We could be wizards.
We could be women but we're still dressing like boys.

What we want is a change in style.

★ ★ ★

Penny and Pat are secretaries. There's nothing wrong with that. All week long they're typing and talking on the phone for hours, mostly to other secretaries, sometimes to each other. Evenings they're watching the sit-coms, rinsing out their pantyhose, ironing a skirt for tomorrow. Penny and Pat have been friends for years.

One wants kids, the other one doesn't.
One's been married, the other one hasn't.
One wants to get married, the other one doesn't.
Guess which one?

They both live in the mobile-home park. They're paying for their trailers, adding on a spare bedroom, a sundeck, what about a greenhouse, trying to make them look like real houses instead of like trains.

Saturday afternoons they get together for pots of drip coffee and a piece of pie at one trailer or the other. All morning they've been grocery-shopping, washing clothes, vacuuming, polishing, and dusting, and they're sure ready for a break. They deserve it.

They're over at Penny's admiring her new blue linoleum and figuring out how much it'll cost to repaint yellow in the spring. Then they're talking about the summertime, next year, last year, they'll be having barbecues, playing baseball, working on a tan. Winter is no fun. They might take a night course: Chinese cooking, volleyball, or beginners photography. They're tired of rug-hooking. But some of the things that get planned will just never get done. They're like dreams that way, plans, potent at the time but quickly shed.

The men that Penny and Pat live with are truck drivers. They've gone downtown in the 4×4 for a beer with the boys. They'll be talking about gravel and unions by now, smelling like diesel fuel. Men.

It's cold and the trailer cracks. White smoke streams straight up from all the other trailers, drawn in together like covered wagons. Penny and Pat assume they're filled too with warm women in clean kitchens, drinking black coffee and spilling their guts, saying, How true, how true, it's all true.

They make perfect sense to each other.

Last week I was ready to throw him out.

Me too.

But things are better now. We have our ups and downs.

Us too. Ups and downs, well yes, how true.

You won't believe what he did.

Never mind, listen to this.

Well, he came home drunk again last night.

Him too?

I've never seen him so drunk.

Me neither.

He passed out at the supper table. Put his head right down on his plate. Chicken pot pie all over his face.

Do they ever laugh. Some things are bearable only because you know you've got someone to tell them to later and laugh.

More coffee and the conversation goes like booster cables between them. Sometimes they're saying the same things over and over again, three times, four, just to be sure they're getting through.

He's a good man though.

Yes.

A good man, yes.

Yes.

He's so good to me.

Yes.

He treats me like a queen.

A good man, yes.

When the boys come home with a pizza, the girls are still sitting there putting a little rum in their coffee and laughing their fool heads off. The cat goes smugly from lap to lap.

* * *

Sometimes we want what they tell us to want.

We want a gas barbecue and a patio to put it on.

We want younger-looking hairless skin and a mystery man to rub it against.

We want a Hawaiian holiday, sun-drenched, and a terrific tan that lasts all year round.

We want fur and a dishwasher too but we don't expect to ever really get them. This gives us something to dream about, something harmless to hope for.

Promise us anything but give us an American Express card.

We're not as bad as you think.

What we want is original as sin.

* * *

Evelyn is a photographer. She's also divorced. So which came first, the chicken or the egg? She wants to be famous and fairly rich. She may be already famous, already rich (fairly), but artists are just never satisfied. She wants to be all the rage in Paris. After dabbling desultorily in landscapes, living rooms, and freaks, Evelyn does mostly portraits now, self-portraits, vegetable portraits, some fruit too.

She's living alone in an elegant studio apartment over some old warehouse down by the docks, of course. It's an unsavoury neighbourhood, yes, but the apartment inside is perfect. One big room, high ceiling, green walls all covered with her own work. She's meeting herself every time she turns around, first thing in the morning, last thing at night. Evelyn thinks it may well be the best place in the whole world.

Her first piece in this vein hangs now over the king-size bed. It's called: *The only thing worth caring about is food.*

There's Evelyn in bed in a cheap motel room nursing a cracked WATERMELON which has leaked red sticky juice all over her belly. Arranged in piles on the lumpy sheets are PARSNIPS, CELERY, ZUCCHINI, and ten copies of *The Joy of Cooking*. Her stretch marks are like slugs. Some people have said this piece is too obvious. What do they know?

Evelyn's best-known piece is called: *I spy with my little eye something that is edible.*

It is a series shot in Safeways downtown and it stars Evelyn and six of her friends, life-size. There they are, each curled up in a shopping cart holding up flash cards that say:

> BROCCOLI
> BRUSSELS SPROUTS
> CANTALOUPE
> LEAF LETTUCE
> CALIFORNIA GRAPEFRUIT
> STRING BEANS.

Evelyn's flash card says:

> BUY ME.
> I'M A NUTRITIOUS
> AND DELICIOUS
> LITTLE PEACH.

The critics usually admire Evelyn's courage, her sense of humour, her technical ability, and her vast and brutal talent, quote, unquote. Evelyn has been alone for years and she figures it's probably just as well, saves having to defend herself and decamp. She cuts out the rave reviews and sends them to her ex-husband, Gerry, who is still writing a bad novel in Michigan and never replies. He has stopped sending her money and Christmas cards. She could care less.

This afternoon Evelyn's working on something wonderful called: *Portrait of a woman wearing metal*.

She sets up the camera in the kitchen, takes off all her clothes, and climbs into the stainless steel sink, which has been polished like a mirror in preparation. She puts the colander on like a helmet, one CARROT sticking straight out the top. She poses patiently in the hysterical heat, sweat trickling down her sides, back, nose, and into her mouth.

Later in the darkroom she will decide that her baggy SWEET POTATO breasts are far more expressive than her face, which is too pale, too bland, an ordinary old POTATO.

Evelyn knows that she's not getting any younger, she's closer to forty than thirty now. She could care less; in fact, she's kind of relieved. Youth, it seems in retrospect, was nothing more than a damp guilty invasion of privacy. And marriage was like when she worked in that bank one year — a misguided attempt at being, if not exactly normal, at least ordinary.

Now she's well-seasoned with furious secrets.

She wants to be admired from afar by those heavenly young curious men who come to her shows and want to buy her a drink or a vegetarian pizza afterwards. They never have enough money to buy her any of the things she really wants. And so sometimes they're all falling in love with her just when she's walking away.

★ ★ ★

When we can have whatever we want, we want Beaujolais in crystal, good to the very last drop. It makes us feel silky and smart.

*When we can have whatever we want, we want rich red food,
the kind that's hard to come by:*
   lobsters with claws
   succulent berries and cherries out of season
   steak tartare dripping.
It makes us feel bloody and wet.
   *When we can have whatever we want, we want a crystal chandelier for the dining room. It makes us feel vicious and spoiled and
it will cut you when it falls.*
   Some people say we're already vicious, already spoiled.
   Not spoiled enough.
   Not vicious enough.
   When we can be whatever we want, we want to be exquisite.

What we want is deluxe.

★ ★ ★

Sandi goes out shopping almost every afternoon. Her man
Stan's on midnights at the mine, he's working, always working,
bringing home the pay cheque, bringing home the boring old
bacon. He's sleeping all day and Sandi's just got to get away.
I don't want to disturb you, sweetie. And besides, his humid
snoring bulk in the bedroom drives her up the wall. She can't
sing, she can't dance, she can't even vacuum.

She puts on some more makeup and runs for the bus that'll
take her way across town to the mall.

Once there she walks up and down for a while, just looking
in the store windows, admiring the shoes, the anorexic double-
jointed mannequins, and her own reflection in the glass. She
sits down for a while and has a smoke which she butts in some
potted plant. She recognizes some of these young punks who
are just hanging out, they're here every day too. Why aren't
they in school? Why isn't she? They're always eating buttered
popcorn and footlongs, slouching around the record store,
stealing the odd little thing. That girl with the pink hair must
be some kind of freak.

Sandi tried stealing once too, a pair of fake gold earrings shaped like zipper heads. But it was no big deal. Buying things is more fun.

She has a toasted bacon-and-tomato sandwich and a hot fudge sundae (which gives her pimples and courage too) at the lunch counter in Zellers.

She likes to look at everything. I'm in no hurry, just passing the time. Just looking thanks, this stuff is junk. She likes to buy barrettes, mascara, pantyhose, shampoo, and a zodiac key ring, Cancer.

She's looking half-heartedly at wee frilly baby clothes. She knows she's too young yet for a baby. Some people said she was too young to get married too, just seventeen. But that's different. You can always get rid of a husband if you have to, but you can't divorce a kid if you decide you don't like it after a year or two. The two people in the world she would like to talk to most right now are her mother (who's gone to Hawaii for the winter with her new husband, Bert, who's better than the first two anyway, richer) and Linda Ronstadt.

She's trying on ten pairs of shoes because the salesman has nice big eyes behind those silly glasses and he's rubbing her arch, well sort of, and admiring her ankles, well maybe. This is something like Cinderella but sexier.

She's trying on a purple sweater shot with gold threads through and through. She's trying on that new brand of jeans that everyone's wearing, they're all the rage, they're the ones you see on the side of the bus. They look better on the bus. She's trying on five purple T-shirts with different sayings on the front. Purple is the greatest because it means something. Purple is like orchids and eggplant, exotic.

Sandi's standing in her old blue ski jacket in the pink dressing room thinking that she's naked, bony, and nippleless like those bald-headed mannequins and the shoe salesman stands there staring. He's never seen anything like it. She just wants him to see her, she's not sure what will happen after that. After that, it doesn't really matter.

She just wants him to stop thinking she's dumb and half-dead just because she's so young, so married. That's only the way she looks, not the way she feels.

She wants him to know what she's really like.

She wants him to know every single thing about her that there is to know.

She's going to get one of those black velvet paintings, either the one with the bullfighter or the one with the big eyes crying one tear, for over the couch, and good old Stan, he'll just have a fit.

So let him.

★ ★ ★

Picture this:
Our eyes are like bruises.
Our legs are like milk.
Our breasts are like magnets.
Our hips are like instincts.
Our teeth are very cultured pearls.
But our hearts, our hearts are sweet, sweethearts.

What we want is a new disguise.

★ ★ ★

Lillian dreams about surgeons. She used to be a nurse.
She's on the table in the operating room
blinking in the bright light
waiting for the cocktail party to end.
Everybody she knows is there
sipping dry martinis
eating little crackers
sucking their thumbs.
Her daughters are drinking tequila and swinging.
Somebody plays a piano poorly.
The surgeons come at her from all directions

like bees
kissing through their surgical masks
tickling her with feathers or forks
mental as anything. They take her apart like a puzzle
painless bloodless
pass her thighs around on a plate
bite-size delectable lox.
There's nothing to fear.
There's nothing to fear, dear.
She knows there's nothing to fear.
When they put her back together again
she's a new improved model
deluxe lovable wise and her breasts are perfect.
Only trouble is sometimes they get too drunk
forget how the puzzle fits
leave her spread out all over like that
one arm dangling from the door knob
smelling fishy.

Lillian's husband Hank is a half-crooked new- and used-car salesman. Lillian's twin daughters are half-crazed teenagers but she's not sure how crazy because they're never home anyway. They might be out getting pregnant, addicted, or arrested right now. You never can tell. What the twins say they're doing is visiting the museum, studying at the library, or attending an afternoon of chamber music. Do they really expect her to believe that? They do it on purpose, they want to be unnatural, they want to annoy her, they think they want to be writers or something.

This family lives in a happy beige house with a view, a verandah, three bedrooms, and a two-car garage. Lillian's in the kitchen right now whipping up hundreds of cookies for Christmas, rolling them in finely chopped walnuts, topping each one with a clot of raspberry jam when they're cool. The whole house smells like a TV commercial.

Hank's out in the garage changing the oil or something. Lillian's waiting for the last batch to bake, licking her fingers, and flipping through last month's *Vogue* or the numbers on the television dial. Outside, the wind is coming up grey, bringing snow at last.

Oh good, it'll be a white Christmas after all.

What's wrong with this picture?

They sniff at her all day like dogs, the dreams. She wants them, doesn't, wants them, doesn't, wants them, doesn't, does. It does not seem possible or necessary to tell anyone or do anything about the surgeons. What you don't know won't hurt you.

★ ★ ★

We want.
We sing.
We like.
We scream.
We see.
We say.
We can say it without saying a word.
We can be cunning.
We can be brave.
We can be lazy.
We can be maidens all in a row, singing the postpartum premenstrual brand-name blues.
We can be dragons too.
We've got personalities we haven't even used yet.

What we want is a fight.

★ ★ ★

Mitzi May is a tricky kind of gal. She keeps a room in some run-down hotel, the kind you see from the bus, with steamy little windows lined with ketchup, milk, and beer bottles. There was some woman died down the hall one time. It was the smell finally brought them around. The room when they broke down the door was filled with bird cages. Worse than the death was the sadness. But Mitzi isn't sad, Mitzi doesn't worry, Mitzi's just rolling along.

One time she met this funny old boy in the alley and he's telling her, You've never seen life. He's trying to catch some broad who's crawling away from him, puking. And Mitzi just smiles up one side of her face and takes off after the guitar player from The Deadbeats who's taking her to a big party tonight. But she never forgot either.

She comes out at night like a dew-worm. The city this summer is stuck on hot, new wave, heat wave, swollen. The highrises radiate silver sluggishly. She's not afraid of anything, this one, no one can hurt her, no one can touch her now. She's getting on her best dress, all silver like armour. Her breasts are like badges or the poke of a gun in your ribs.

She cruises the all-night donut shops, checking out the fifty-eight varieties, baked every day, fresh coffee too, one free refill only. Everything's fresh here, country style.

Mitzi wears black lipstick just for a laugh and talks all night about her new tattoo.

Baby you're not listening.

The guy at the next table slumps deeper down into his fresh cup of that fresh coffee.

Honey what you want?

He's looking around for the waitress who's supposed to come and save him. The guy's a simple insomniac, innocent, listening to country music on a portable tape player. Help me make it through the night. This is just too corny to pass up.

Sweetheart let me help you. I could make your dreams come true how true.

Sugar I could do things do some things for you make your blood boil over make it run ice-cold.

When the cops come in on their nightly rounds, the first one says, Hey Mitzi, what's a girl like you doing in a nice place like this? Ha ha ha.

They're both smirking at her, wiping their foreheads with the backs of their hands like bus drivers. But even they're afraid to touch her, she's so excitable, this one, she's a real lizard, this one.

She's really something, that one, the other one says as sulky Mitzi sashays away, packing a purse like a suitcase, and singing The Rolling Stones.

She's pretty snappy-looking tonight, this one. She thinks she's going to some pizza palace where the coffee's better and they've got wild music on the jukebox. She thinks she's going dancing.

★ ★ ★

We want to be dangerous.
We want to be wicked.
We want to be enormous.
We want to run rampant.
We want to get savage and leave the whole sad world behind us,
hanging by a thread.
Boom.
Boom.
Boom.

What we want is a getaway car.

★ ★ ★

We could be anything.
We could be wives.
We could be terrorists.
We could be artists.
We could be wizards.
We could be legends in our own time.

What we want is a change in style.

HIS PEOPLE

Holly met Nick for the first time in the shared driveway between their two houses. She was backing out the door Monday morning with the car keys in her mouth and a wicker basket full of dirty clothes in her arms, heading for the laundromat. She was also talking to herself: "And don't forget to put out the garbage, dummy."

Nick was coming down the driveway. "Morning," he said.

"Oh hi, and here I am talking to myself," Holly said, blushing. It was a hot day already and Nick was undeniably attractive in his little white shorts.

"Taking him to day care," he said. His small son kicked up the gravel behind him. "Stop that, Nicky. Right now. Three last month."

"Laundry," Holly said, gesturing at her dirty underwear with her chin, which was narrow and rather pointy, a part of herself she'd never really liked.

"Hear you're from Alberta." Nick motioned towards her red-and-white licence plates which had expired two months ago, but you had to pass the safety check in Ontario before they'd give you new plates and Holly was still getting around to taking the car in. "I was there once, went to pick him up. Cost a fortune to fly there, what a place. You're lucky to be out of there. His mother was no good. Cherie."

Holly already knew that Nick was divorced, lived with his grandmother, and was just out of jail. He was looking for work. He spent whole weekends sitting on the front porch with his feet up on the iron railing, watching Nicky play in the driveway. Holly admired his patience with the boy, who cried a lot and seldom did what he was told.

Throughout the month of July, Holly noticed, the whole humid city seemed to spend the evening on the porch. Up and down the block, her neighbours hauled out the straight-back kitchen chairs, drank lite beer and wine coolers, fanned themselves, and swatted mosquitoes with the newspaper. Cars passed occasionally, ferrying children or dogs with their heads hung out the windows, or teenagers playing their car stereos full blast so everyone would notice them and know they were cool. In the park at the end of the block, the children were calling back and forth, pushing each other around in the wading pool, or swinging violently, trying to work up a breeze.

Next door, Gran fanned up her skirt and Nick took off his T-shirt and wiped his face with it. His hairless chest shone and he was studying the oiled torsos in a weight-lifting magazine. The day before, Sears had delivered a whole set of barbells which Nick set up in the garage. Then he spent two hours with his cousin, Frank, on the punching ball he'd rigged up in the backyard. The sound was like slapping or tom-toms.

"Worst summer in twenty years," Gran called across to Holly on her porch, having another beer, and reading *The Dead and the Living*, poems by Sharon Olds. She'd be taking classes at the college in the fall. "It's not the heat it's the humidity'll kill you," Gran said in her gravelly voice. "Hard on them." She nodded towards little Nicky, who was riding his tricycle madly up and down the driveway, whining. "Quit that. Hear me? Hyper. I never seen a kid can't sit still for a minute. Heat's hard on them."

Nick ignored her and the boy both.

"Nick you make him stop that. Leg's bad today." Gran propped her foot up on the railing, patting a deep circular scar around one kneecap, which protruded like a burl.

Nick yanked the tricycle away and put it in the backyard while Nicky screamed.

"What a kid," Gran said, massaging her knee. "Hyper. And he's even worse since *he* come back and now he's even worse since she come back, Viv." Nick's mother, Vivian, and her new husband, Walter, who was in the armed forces, had just returned from Germany, where he had been stationed for three years. Nick's father, Lloyd, was Gran's son. "But we weren't having none of ours brought up by the likes of her," Gran said. "So him and Lloyd went out west and brung him home. She got three other kids anyway, who knows where *they* come from."

When the daylight faded, Holly put down her book and went inside for another drink. She turned up the radio in the living room so she could hear it outside.

Nick appeared on her porch with a bug light. "She's gone in to put him to bed, she wants to watch *Mike Hammer*." He hooked the bug light to the iron railing and plugged it in. "Been trying to get up my courage to come over here. Thought you might be needing this." The bug light glowed a humming blue-violet, snapping when the mosquitoes hit. He pointed to the green mosquito coils Holly had arranged around her front steps. "Those are no damn good." He sat down on the bottom step, leaned against the stucco wall, and slapped himself vigorously. "Allergic. See this." He twisted around to show her a large red welt on his lower back. "Swell up like a grapefruit, scratch for days." He stood up and sprayed himself front and back with a can of Off. "Here, let me spray you."

"They don't seem to bother me much," Holly said, but stood up anyway and pirouetted slowly while he sprayed her all up and down. "Would you like a chair?" she asked.

"I'm fine."

"Would you like a beer?"

"Don't drink. You're always reading, what're you reading?"

She handed him the book and, by the bug light, he studied the cover photograph: a man and a woman nude, her front, his back, *Adam and Eve* by Frank Eugene.

"Never heard of it," he said.

"This one," Holly said, opening the book and leaning into the mauve snapping light to read:

The Issues

(Rhodesia, 1978)

Just don't tell me about the issues.
I can see the pale spider-belly head of the
newborn who lies on the lawn, the web of
veins at the surface of her scalp, her skin
grey and gleaming, the clean line of the
bayonet down the center of her chest.
I see the mother's face, beaten and
beaten into the shape of a plant,
a cactus with grey spines and broad
dark maroon blooms.
I see her arm stretched out across her baby,
wrist resting, heavily, still, across the
tiny ribs.
             Don't speak to me about
politics. I've got eyes, man.

"I only read the facts," said Nick.

"What?"

"You know, *National Geographic* and Matthew, Mark, Luke, and John."

"What?"

"You know, the Bible. I'm studying it every day. The priest come to see me, he give me the books. Do you know the world?"

"I don't think so."

"I think you do. The Lord He says if you know the world, it'll hate you."

"Well, yes, sometimes I think the world does hate me," Holly admitted. "And I wonder why."

"All you gotta do is give yourself over to the Lord and He'll show you the Way."

"Oh, I just love this song," Holly cried, jumping up and running inside to turn up the radio. She sat back down, casually closer to Nick, and sang along with Fleetwood Mac: *If I live to see the Seven Wonders/I'll make a path to the rainbow's end/ I'll never live to match the beauty again*, thinking of the man she'd left behind in Alberta but it never would have worked out anyway, she knew that. She was lonely and wondering if Nick would kiss her goodnight.

There came the sound of sirens close by.

"Fire," Holly said.

"Cops," Nick said. "Once they found a dead body in a house around the corner, you know."

Just then his father, Lloyd, with his new wife, Freda, pulled up front in his immaculate maroon Pontiac Parisienne. "He's taking me over to the mall tomorrow buy some clothes so I can go to church from now on. Nice clothes and a fishing rod, going to do some fishing too," Nick said as he was leaving.

"Gimme a ride to the mall?" Nick called from his open kitchen window. Holly was out in the driveway washing her car. "She wants to rent a steam cleaner do the rugs. Might as well do yours too while I'm at it. Missed a spot there."

He hopped in. "You're up early. Some days I'm just crawling out of bed at noon and there you are in the kitchen window all dressed and everything already and I think, Wow."

Walking from the car to the mall entrance, he said, "Sometimes I just hate coming to this mall."

"Why?" Holly asked, thinking with a thrill that there was someone inside he didn't want to see, someone from his criminal life, or maybe he'd broken into one of the stores (which one? Radio Shack, Big Steel, Birks) or shoplifted something (what? pearl necklace, suede coat, a gun) and got caught.

" 'Cause this is where the fat people shop. You know, from Willow Ridge, the suburbs."

And the two women coming out of The Bay as they went in were bulging and jiggling in their terry-cloth shorts sets, laughing and licking on chocolate ice cream.

When they got the steam cleaner, Nick discovered he'd forgotten his wallet, so Holly showed her I.D. and counted out the twenty-five dollars.

"Are you two together?" the clerk asked suspiciously.

"I guess so yeah," said Nick.

"What were you in for?" Holly finally asked him. They were watching fireflies in the grass. There was heat lightning in the west but the rain never came.

"You know?"

Holly nodded but of course he couldn't see her in the dark and looking away like that to the park where some kids were drinking beer around a picnic table, a case of twenty-four stashed behind the wading pool.

"Suppose *she* told you."

"Frank."

"None of his damn business. Watch him he'll steal you blind get the chance. Just no good even if he is my cousin. She'll be sorry letting him come around here. Going to get some smokes."

Holly watched him striding across the park, past the mound of rocks in the middle which he'd told her was an Indian burial place. "They're talking to me sometimes, the skeletons, the spirits," he'd said. "You don't believe me do you?"

He stopped to talk to the kids drinking beer in the park.

In ten minutes he was back. "Those kids, this one kid," he was laughing, "says he just got out this morning, they're celebrating. So I says, You're stupid kid, you got no sense. Here, I got you a popsicle."

The next morning Holly saw that the picnic table had been left balanced carefully on top of the Indian rocks.

Nick thought he had a job cooking down at Mr. Pizza Patio but then when he showed up for his first shift, they said forget it because they had found out he'd done time. "The boss the jerk," Nick told Holly, "he goes, When did you get out, so I go, Yeah and when'd you get off the boat, buddy?" Holly swore she'd never order pizza from that place again.

Then he did get a job, pumping gas at the 24-Hour Texaco out by the 401. His mother, Vivian, bought him a 650 Yamaha to get back and forth to work. "He's got money to burn," Nick said, meaning Walter, his mother's new husband. "Got a state-of-the-art German stereo and a $8,000 wall unit. Porsche. Gonna get Nicky a real jungle gym."

Nick and his cousin, Frank, who only had a ten-speed, tinkered with the motorcycle endlessly. When they weren't taking it apart or putting it back together, they were washing it.

"Lend me some money?" Nick asked Holly one night on her porch.

"How much? What for?"

"Insurance. $150. Can't drive it till I get it."

Holly hesitated. She didn't like lending money to men because it seemed only to create complications.

"Well?"

"I don't know."

"Pay you half in two weeks when I get my cheque. Other half next cheque. I'll mow your grass change the oil in your car and who's gonna shovel your snow this winter?"

"All right, yes," she said. Yes, she wanted him to know she had faith in him, never mind his past. Yes, she wanted to help him make something of himself after all. "I suppose you'll never be home now," she teased.

Nick just laughed and walked her to the bank, where she couldn't help wondering if the teller counting out the cash might think they were married or something. She handed Nick the bills. "And don't you go killing yourself on that thing." She hated the way she sounded. "They'll all blame me."

"They don't need to know," Nick said, "and don't you be telling them neither."

Walking through the park on her way home from downtown, Holly stopped at the wading pool to shift her shopping bags around. She'd bought some groceries and three summer dresses on sale, red, blue, yellow, like long T-shirts, which she planned to wear with her elastic black belt tight at the waist to show off her legs which she'd always liked, their pretty bony kneecaps and their slim smooth calves.

From the pool, she could see Gran stationed on her porch and wished for a way to sneak home without having to walk past her and hear her say yet again, "Worst summer in twenty years it's not the heat it's the humidity hard on them." Being a congenitally polite person, Holly could only nod and agree enthusiastically.

She and Nick had said little more than hello in over a week. He was working, he said, extra shifts at the gas station, going to his father's for dinner with Nicky, going to his mother's to watch movies on the new VCR, going to see his parole officer once a week. Holly could hear him racing in and out of the driveway on the motorcycle at all hours. Sometimes she was lying in bed reading and then she would tiptoe into her dark kitchen to watch him riding away. Sometimes it woke her up. Once she complained, just kidding, about the noise and from then on he wheeled the bike down the driveway and halfway to the corner before he started it. Or he'd coast in with the light off. So she never knew any more when he was coming or going, at home or away.

He rode up behind her in the park on Frank's ten-speed, the spokes clicking. He said, "Well I don't have to worry about him, she took him for all weekend." Holly felt cosy being able to decipher this code, which meant Nicky was staying with Vivian and Walter, as he often did lately. He practically lived there. Gran was insulted by this and complained about how spoiled he got there, staying up late, eating Smarties all day and ice cream. "I raised him for a year and a half," she told Holly. "Up all night and toilet-training too. He flushed a toy car one time had to get a whole new toilet. I done all the work, now she comes home thinks she can just take over."

Nick grunted as a police car cruised the perimeter of the park. "Hey you, I'm over here," he called, holding his arms out in front of him, hands back to back, miming being hand-cuffed. "They're always watching me now. Anything goes wrong around here you watch they'll be on my doorstep."

"Where'd you go Saturday?" he asked.

"Just out." Holly had gone to the show with a friend, female, from the college, and then bar-hopping.

"Heard you come home three in the morning for godsake."

"I saw your lights on, yes."

His cousin, Frank, came over one night with his ghetto-blaster and a large tumbler of 100-proof Jack Daniels. Nick was at work. Frank was wearing his black Jack Daniels T-shirt with the sleeves ripped out to show off his tattoos: a prancing blue unicorn on the right biceps and *Frank loves Penny* in script on the left, but he was going to see about getting this one covered up or removed.

"Got any apple juice?" he asked Holly. "I like it with apple juice. Divvy it up, you have some too. She got it in the States." Gran had spent the previous weekend visiting her brother, Ted, in Michigan where, she told Holly the night she returned, everything was better and cheaper than here. " 'Cause they know how to stand up for themselves those people," she said. "Not like here we just take it all lying down whatever they tell us. Price of coffee I'll never drink it again. You watch."

Holly went into her kitchen and mixed up the juice. Frank fiddled with his tapes and cranked up Whitesnake: *Here I go again on my own/Down the only road I've ever known/Like a drifter/I was born to walk alone.* His girlfriend, Penny, who waited tables down at Subway Submarine, had recently left him for a drummer. So now Frank was renting two rooms with a kitchenette in Gran's basement and listening to love songs, loud.

They sipped their drinks, which were gruesome, and tapped their feet to the music, singing along. They could relate to the lyrics, the loneliness, both of them.

"He'll be jealous he catches me sitting over here," Frank said.

Holly giggled.

"He thinks a lot of you, no really," he said.

"You'd never know it half the time."

"Oh that's him. She says he changed since he got out this time, got God and all that. I don't see no change. He's always been the golden boy around here. Can't do no wrong far as she's concerned. He's mean to that kid, you know. Nicky loves me more than him. He don't do a thing around here. Won't even take out the garbage and her with her leg."

"I've noticed that," Holly agreed, cosy with conspiracy against Nick, who hadn't been over for nearly a week.

"It won't last long. He don't like me I make him look bad. Here he is."

Nick on his motorcycle roared past them up the driveway and slammed the back door on his way into the house. They heard his helmet hit the floor. The screen door slammed again and they could hear him pounding on the punching ball out back. Holly, half drunk on the overproof whiskey, found this rather amusing and flirted harmlessly in her short blue sundress with Frank all evening long till he went home to pass out.

Towards the end of August, Holly quit drinking and sat on the step angelically sipping her ginger ale right out of the can, so Nick would notice and know it wasn't spiked.

"I quit drinking," she tells him.

"Yeah sure," he snorts. "Till the next time."

"If you can do it, so can I."

"Maybe. My parole I got no choice. Get caught drinking back in for six months."

A woman in a pink sweat suit jogs past with her breasts bouncing and her Walkman turned up so loud they can hear it like an insect.

"She'll get cancer," Nick says.

"What?"

"Jogging without a training bra'll cause cancer, you know."

"That's crazy!"

"Cherie said."

"She was kidding you."

"No way. It's true. She read it in a book."

When Holly goes inside for two more cans of pop, Nick nods. She can tell that he is pleased with her.

"The Lord He don't hold with drinking," he says. "Once me and my buddies sat down in that field over by the Pen all day and we were drinking a case of two-four just so those poor buggers in the yard they'd know what they were missing. Was when she lived up on Concession Street. Them guys always coming around the house looking for a party drinking her rye stealing her stuff. Then I did some time and she got hit by that car, drunk driver. In the hospital she was throwing bedpans at the doctors, you just ask her, till they let her out. That was my first time in, break and enter that's all I ever done wrong. Got in with that bad crowd, don't see them no more. This guy I ratted on be out in three years says he's coming to get me but I'm not worried, got God, my weights. Look at that."

Holly is surprised to see a raccoon ambling across the close end of the park, right here in the middle of the city. And sometimes in the morning there is the stink of skunk in the air.

Once she asked Nick why the squirrels here are black, when out west they were brown. And she still marvels at the sound of the cicadas, which she never heard in the west, a vibration like a plucked high wire, a sign of hot weather.

"Well that's Alberta for you," Nick said, satisfied.

"Groundhogs last year," he says now.

Steve Winwood on the stereo is singing: *All the doors I closed one time/Will open up again/I'll be back in the high life again.*

"I been in three times now but the Lord He forgives me."

Nick puts an arm around her with unusually obvious affection. "And He understands about a man needing a woman now and again too."

Holly has been waiting for just the right moment, this moment, to give him the card she is fingering fondly inside her sweater pocket. The size of a credit card, it is covered with tiny white printing on a shiny silver background, which reflects Nick's face as he leans close to the bug light to read.

The blue title in italics says *Footprints*:

One night a man had a dream. He dreamed he was walking along the beach with the Lord and across the sky there flashed scenes from his life. In each scene there were two sets of footprints in the sand: one belonging to him and the other to the Lord.

Looking back at the scenes, the man saw that many times along the path of his life there was only one set of footprints. This bothered the man so he questioned the Lord.

"Lord, You said that once I decided to follow You, You'd walk with me all the way. But during the lowest and saddest times of my life, there is only one set of footprints. Why did You leave me when I needed You most?"

The Lord replied, "My son, I love you and would never leave you. In your times of trouble when you see only one set of footprints, it was then that I carried you."

Nick was telling Holly the story from jail about this guy who tried to cut off his thing, you know, his *thing*, with a plastic spoon, then a comb, and then finally he slammed it in a steel door. "It was those doors," he said, "those steel doors slamming all night long. It was those doors made me feel like I was being tortured. Never slept the whole time for the sound of those doors slamming. It's those doors I dream about, slamming."

Holly, horrified, asks, "Did he die? What happened to him?"

But Nick doesn't know. He can't remember and seems never to have wondered. This is not the point of the story.

They are camped out on the sofa bed in Holly's living room, which is the only room in the house cool enough (not very) to sleep in, for though the quickening evening darkness of September has moved the whole neighbourhood back inside most nights, the humidity still hangs and the air will not move.

They are watching a TV documentary called *In Search of Dracula* in which the narrator says, "Story-telling wards off vampires."

Nick says, "Garlic." He does not talk much about the Lord any more.

Talking this night before they fall asleep in each other's arms, they discover that they both always wear pyjamas for fear of having to get up in the middle of the night and run (Holly) or fight (Nick).

During this night they both dream, at different times, that someone is standing at the front door looking in at them. Close to morning, Holly gets up and pulls down the blind.

When Nick sneaks home across the driveway at 6 a.m., Holly can hear Gran hollering, "Where the hell have you been?" She goes into her bedroom and shuts the door so she cannot hear the details of the lengthy argument. All day long she wonders what he said.

Holly and Nick are lying on Gran's couch watching rock videos and she has her head in his lap. There is so much big furniture jammed into the little room that there is hardly space to walk around. On the wall facing Holly's house, there is a large velvet painting which, in the flickering television light, might be of horses rearing or of women dancing, but Holly keeps thinking it's a window and she catches herself looking over every few minutes, trying to see out. Nick is telling her about the new bunk beds Gran has ordered so he and Nicky won't be so crowded in their little bedroom. They are whispering for fear of waking Gran or the boy. None of his people, it appears, are to know about their relationship yet.

Nick says, "Don't get me wrong sometimes."

"What?" His thought processes are often hard to follow.

"Sometimes when I don't see you, don't get me wrong. I just don't want to get serious. After Cherie I know all about love, just don't want no part of it no more. It aches my mind."

Holly reaches up and strokes his face, which she loves, consoling him and not believing a word of it.

"Just gonna live here forever," Nick says, stretching. "Never pay no rent again."

"But how can you stand it? A grown man still sleeping in bunk beds. I could never live with my family now."

"But my people they're different, let me do what I like. They're always trying to give me things. The bike. Now she wants to buy me a car. Camaro, I want a blue Camaro."

Holly is reading in bed when she hears Nick ride up. Over the sound of the bike there comes a delighted wild whooping.

Holly goes into her kitchen to peek out at him. He is already inside Gran's house where the kitchen light comes on. He leans against the sink with his back to the window, his helmet still on him like a huge insect head. He takes it off, bending forward so she can see his mouth moving but she can't hear the words: the screen is closed now against the cool night. The other person puts a small hand up on each of his shoulders and he kisses her.

They come back outside, the girl drunk and staggering around in the driveway until Nick steadies her tenderly. She is wearing blue jeans, a white T-shirt under a baggy black cardigan with a can of beer in each pocket. She is pointing at something in Holly's backyard and laughing her dizzy head off. Holly can see her clothesline reflected by moonlight in Gran's kitchen window. She has hung from it this morning her new summer dresses all in a row. In the window in the wind now, they flap and collide like decapitated bodies, headless chickens, hopeless. They will hang there for two days before they dry in this humidity and then they will be spotted with mildew which will never wash out.

Nick and the girl drink the beer. Then he wheels the bike down the driveway with her on the back clutching him, saying, "Are you sure about this?"

Holly goes back to bed saying out loud, "So what? Who cares? I don't care what you do or who you do it with," goes back to reading her poetry books because classes have started.

A few minutes later she can hear sirens. They would be, she estimates, just to the far corner of the park by now, somewhere between the black cannon that points down Clergy Street and the monument to that dead minister who founded the church on the corner in 1893. She imagines them crumpled together on the cool grass, his head like an egg now inside the helmet and hers just flattened and still, like a plate.

He could end up back in jail, the fool, when they arrest him for violating his parole.

Or he could be dying even now, repenting as the scenes of his life flash like sheet lightning, promises out of the southern sky.

TICKETS TO SPAIN

"In the dream there was always a sound like bees, faint and far away, but then not really a sound at all, more like having water in your ears. It was the sound of thousands of people all in one place, all at once waiting."

I was telling Howard this dream this morning while he shaved. Leaning naked against the sink to get closer to the mirror, he pulled his face all out of shape and sighed. I was sitting on the edge of the tub in my housecoat, talking to his reflection, damp and steamy-looking from the shower.

"At first we weren't there and then we were, but we didn't know for sure *where* we were until they brought out the bull and everyone was cheering and jumping around in a fever. They were all strangers, men mostly, doe-eyed and handsome with oily skin."

I am always having dreams about strangers, dreams that I'm not in yet or have just left. I handed Howard a towel, one of the red ones Robin gave us for our anniversary. We've been living together for three years. The towels were mostly a joke. We'd been arguing amongst ourselves for days — do bulls really charge when they see red? Robin said no, I said yes. Robin said, "How would you know?"

"They were all speaking Spanish, things that aren't in the phrase book, and eating, these men. They kept passing food over to me — ice-cream cones, olives, half-eaten oranges, hot dogs dripping mustard. They do have hot dogs there, don't they?''

''I think so, Miriam,'' Howard said, around a mouthful of toothbrush and mint-flavoured paste. I watched him solemnly spit, wipe his mouth, put on his glasses, and start fixing his hair. Howard has always been particular (vain) about his hair. This is one of the things I would never have suspected about him when we first met because he had a convertible then.

''It was so real — the bull shaking its head, twisting and lunging, forward and away; the picador up on his horse, tormenting and stabbing. You were making notes on a paper napkin and I was saying stupid things like: 'Oh the poor thing! Does it know it's going to die? I want to go home.' The sky was so hot it looked white.''

''It won't be like that, Miriam. Don't worry — you'll love it. Everyone does — the drama,'' Howard said, patting my knees and heading for the bedroom to get dressed.

Howard and I have been going to Spain for a year and a half. It all started, I suppose, at that foreign film festival at The Plaza. The Spanish entry, *A Night Sky*, was melancholy and turbulent, dense with subtitles and classical guitar music. Juanita, the voluptuous over-heated heroine, was falling in love all the time with swarthy political men who were everywhere in the unyielding countryside. They were all so intelligent and intense, with stomach muscles like rock.

Then my sister, Robin, went to Spain for the summer and came back brown and spiritual, with intricate symbolic stories of revolution, renaissance, and throbbing hotel rooms. This was all the proof I needed. Spain was another world, the one I should have been in all along.

It was more my dream than Howard's to begin with. But then he swallowed it whole. In the way of young couples seriously in love, we are always assimilating. Sometimes it gets confusing, this Siamese-twin trading of tokens, blue jeans, and dreams.

''At first I was sweating but then it was rain on my face.'' The rain in Spain falls mainly on the plain.

This summer we are really going. After so much anticipation we are determined not to be disappointed. I have been buying travel guides and studying the phrase book, *Spanish in Three Months*. We practise and practise until we can have whole conversations like:

"I am very fond of apples. *Me gustan mucho las manzanas.*"

"I prefer pears. *Prefiero las peras.*"

"We like oranges best. *Nos gustan más las naranjas.*"

We are always collecting mementoes of Spain: castanets, rough clay pots, a stuffed bull with a spear where its heart should be, posters of flamenco dancers and the young men running the bulls through the streets of Pamplona. In this picture there are eleven bulls altogether, two white ones, and the boys are running barefoot in a pack, all in white with red scarves wound around their waists. One boy is leaping, he could be dancing. Another is doing a somersault or he could be falling and breaking his neck. It is all so dreamy and daring. Boys will be boys.

Sometimes we buy bottles of good Spanish wine to drink with our friends. We put on the classical guitar tapes and show them our souvenirs, as if we've already been there. Sometimes I wish we had.

"For a while in the dream I was wearing a white wedding gown with a rose in my teeth, a red one, of course, which means blood. You were wearing a black tuxedo with a white carnation and smoking a fat cigar. For a while it was like a rock-and-roll video and I thought we were going to dance. But then we were just normal again and no one was singing."

We used to talk about getting married. Sometimes now I think we did and I just can't remember. Just as I can't remember how, according to my mother, when I was five, my sister Robin, who was ten, tried to drown me in the bathtub. Something like that you'd think would leave a permanent mark on you, distinguishing, if not disfiguring. But it didn't, and I'm not afraid of water or my sister either.

"The matador was like a ballet dancer, or a scrap of paper blown around by the wind, and then he was riding the bull instead of killing it."

The matador knows that his chance of meeting death in the ring is one out of ten, and the odds are one to four that he will be seriously wounded. His suit is called the *traje de luces*, the suit of lights.

I was talking and passing over underwear, socks, clean shirt, suit pants to Howard in precise order, as if we were in surgery. Our bedroom is small and crowded with a matching pair of antique dressers with mirrors and, stuck in the middle like a raft, a king-size bed that seems to be spreading. The trees outside the window shed into it a greenish wavering light like that inside an aquarium. This is our morning ritual: I tell him my dreams and make the bed; he gets dressed up as a shoe salesman.

"In the end, a team of mules dragged the dead bull out of the ring on its back like a giant insect."

I handed Howard the lint brush. We imagine that shoe salesmen are notoriously neat. Would you let them fiddle with your feet if they weren't?

We went into the kitchen to have coffee. I worked hard on that room, hanging plants in the window, wicker baskets on the wall, and pots and pans from the ceiling. Shiny bottles of spices and fragrant herb teas sit on open shelves above the stove, and the cupboard doors are yellow to match the floppy old roses on the linoleum.

"The matador was a hero heaped with roses. The crowd went wild, smearing hysterical wet kisses all over each other and us."

It was one of those dreams that you think you've been having all night long and nothing will stand still and you wake up feeling scared of everything.

"Do you see?"

* * *

After Howard left for the store, I poured myself another coffee, turned on the TV, and curled up on the couch. I half-watched *The 20-Minute Workout*, where all those pliable nubile women get up early to contort themselves in their skin-tight leotards, sweating just enough to make their hair curl prettily. Three more, two more, one more. Synchronize crotches.

This morning I mostly ignored them, feeling little compulsion to join them and almost no guilt. What's the point? They have no breasts and do not eat French fries. Instead I studied the phrase book. I am learning to say, among other things:

"I should like to see a bullfight. *Me gustaría ir a una corrida de toros.*"

There are other practical conversational sentences which I've memorized just in case.

"It is a beautiful day. *Hace un día hermoso.*"

"I am ashamed. *Me da vergüenza.*"

"Do it again. *Vuelva usted a hacerlo.*"

"My friend used to wear her clothes too tight. *Mi amiga usaba sus vestidos demasiado estrechos.*"

"I just want to sit in the sun and doze. *No quiero más que sentarme al sol ly dormitar.*"

From my spot on the couch, I could see right into the living room of the house across the street. An ordinary family lives there, husband, wife, half-grown twin daughters with braids who came bouncing over the day we moved in to tell us, happily, that our house was haunted. When I run into the wife at the grocery store, we chat about the neighbourhood cats digging up her flower beds and peek curiously into each other's shopping carts, as if reading tea leaves or palms.

This morning, as usual, the fat husband in his red housecoat was riding his exercise bike and looking out the window. I suppose that he could see me too, wandering around in my housecoat (blue), watering the plants and straightening the pictures, talking to myself with explosive Iberian gestures.

I was just deciding to get dressed when the phone rang. It was the travel agent. "I'm calling about the two tickets to Spain. They're ready. When can you pick them up?"

I called Howard at the store and he said we'd go tonight after work. On the phone he was friendly but careful, swallowing several times as if someone was listening or his tie was too tight. Shoe salesmen, we hypothesize, are circumspect about their private lives. On the odd occasion, at a movie or a bar, when we run into someone Howard works with, he always introduces me as his wife. Sometimes this irritates me but I smile fetchingly and try not to guzzle the sugary little cocktails they buy me. The store is an exclusive downtown boutique where summer sandals start at a hundred dollars. We can't afford to shop there.

The Spanish are a very shoe-conscious people. A high polish on the shoes is a tradition passed down from the *caballero*, whose shiny boots served notice that he rode his own horse and did not walk along dusty roads with lesser men. Madrid has one street — Fuencarral — lined with shoe shops from one end to the other.

In real life, Howard is a playwright. He has been working on the same play for nearly two years. It's even been finished a few times. We've gone out for expensive dinners to celebrate, congratulating ourselves with champagne in silver buckets. But then Howard changes his mind or the characters change their minds and they are all dissatisfied all of a sudden and Howard happily starts the rewrite. Afraid to cut the cord, babies leaving the nest, all of that. We assume that playwrights, like all artists, are supposed to struggle and squirm.

Howard's play has had various endings and titles over time — in this incarnation it is called *Tickets to Spain* and they all live almost happily ever after.

The set consists of two rooms in a small old house on a tree-lined city street.

The kitchen, stage left, is spacious and bright, very warm and wifely. Plants in the window, wicker baskets on the wall, pots and pans hang from the ceiling. Yellow cupboards, old-fashioned well-worn linoleum, round wooden table in the centre.

The bedroom, stage right, is smaller and darker. Seen through the window is a huge elm tree which casts the room in a watery greenish light. Two old-style dressers with mirrors, a king-size bed

*in the centre covered with a colourful hand-made quilt in the Log
Cabin pattern.*

At first the bed was covered with a Guatemalan blanket but
then my mother sent us the Log Cabin quilt which has been
making its way around my family for decades, and the Guatemalan blanket got rewritten.

*It is mid-May, about four in the afternoon. The kitchen is rich
with sunlight and cigarette smoke hung in layers like veils.*
DAVID BARNES *is seated at the kitchen table, staring out the
window, smoking and drinking coffee. He is wearing dark dress
pants and a rumpled brown cardigan.* DAVID *is about thirty-five,
slim, and dark-complexioned.*

Sometimes DAVID is drinking beer out of a can, dressed in
jeans and a sleeveless white undershirt. He is always handsome.
Sometimes he has his head in his hands. He is depressed, not
drunk, although at times it can be hard to tell the difference.

DENISE BARNES *enters stage left. She is an attractive woman,
about thirty, very tanned and healthy-looking, dressed in a dainty
sundress, eyelet cotton, very white. She is carrying a bag of
groceries with a loaf of French bread sticking out the top.*

Sometimes a bunch of tulips sticks out of the bag. I like
DENISE best when she has blonde hair done in a perm, unruly
but angelic around her little face. When it is raining she wears
a baby-blue jacket and matching scarf.

DENISE *puts the bag on the table and looks at* DAVID *sadly.*

Angrily.
Lovingly.
Guiltily.

She puts her hand on his shoulder.

She ignores him altogether.

DAVID: Do you still love me? *(He lights another cigarette.)*
DENISE: I don't think so, no.
DAVID: Please don't leave me, Denise.
DENISE: I can't go on this way. *(She heads for the bedroom.)*
I'm going to live with my sister.

DAVID: Do you still love me? *(He lights another cigarette.)*
DENISE: I think so, yes.
DAVID: Please don't leave me, Denise.
DENISE: I'll never leave you, David. *(She heads for the
bedroom.)* We can work it out. *(The telephone rings. They know
it is the lover. Neither moves to answer it.)*

Sometimes DAVID and DENISE are married and sometimes
they're not. It doesn't seem to make much difference in the
long run. They have taken turns at being unfaithful and at
being fooled. But there is always a lover, somebody's lover,
male or female, with an unstable mind or a murderous bent,
phoning, following them, ruining their lives. They have exper-
imented with staying together, splitting up, group sex, suicide,
and murder.

They've even got their tickets to Spain. I'm glad when they
get to go, sorry when they don't, and depressed when the plane
crashes. Or I'm just as happy when they stay home, worried
when they go, and curious when they take the lover with them.
Sometimes the lover is Spanish. They are learning the
language:

"Do not go away until it stops raining. *No se vaya usted hasta
que cese de llover.*"

"See whether my umbrella is behind the door. *Mire usted a
ver si mi paraguas esta detras de la puerta.*"

"Nobody likes to be deceived. *A nadie le gusta que le
engañen.*"

"Lunch is ready. *El almuerzo est á servido.*"

I have grown rather fond of DAVID and DENISE and can always sympathize, no matter what happens to whom. They are nice people and I'm always relieved when Howard lets them live. I imagine how tired they must be by now of the paces he persists in putting them through.

This morning in the study, more commonly known as "Howard's room", I dusted, emptied the ashtray, gathered up coffee cups, crumb-covered plates, and a pair of socks. In Howard's room, according to law, I do not touch or remove anything else.

I also turned on the tape recorder which Howard uses when he is rewriting. This cannot, I think, strictly be considered snooping — the play, after all, is destined to become public property (someday). But I don't tell Howard I'm doing it either. It is like turning on the soap operas when you're ironing — something you do every day but wouldn't admit to just anyone. Like listening in on the people at the next table in a restaurant. Howard does this all the time but denies it.

One night at Giorgio's we took a table beside a handsome young couple who didn't talk much and played with their pasta. Then the woman said, "Before you know it, she'll be yelling at you in public, just like I used to." The man looked pained.

DAVID *is taking* DENISE *out for Italian food, trying to break it to her gently.*

DAVID: She is a quiet and gentle woman.

DENISE: Before you know it, she'll be yelling at you in public, just like I used to. *(She reaches for a roll.)*

DAVID: You still do. *(He takes a drink of wine.)*

This morning I sat down at Howard's desk to listen.

DENISE: In the dream there was always the sound of drums, faint and far away, but then not really a sound at all, more like having water in your ears.

DAVID: I'm tired of hearing your dreams, Denise. You've never asked for mine.

Bees, it was bees, there was always the sound of bees.

★ ★ ★

This afternoon I met my sister, Robin, and her lover for lunch at The Village Green. It was one of those days when every stranger you see on the bus looks like someone you know, someone you used to know, someone you're sure you know from somewhere but you can't quite put your finger on it. Who is it, who are you, who do you remind me of?

Dwight Maguire was my lover last year, before he fell in love with Robin. We are all very civilized and (try to) find this situation amusing. I don't have a lover these days, other than Howard I mean. I suspect sometimes that he has one or is in the process of getting one, but I have no proof, am not even looking for it yet.

The Village Green is an airy, healthy-looking place filled with little glass-topped tables and many unsteady little chairs. There are aggressively healthy plants hanging everywhere and also some large leafy ones in clay floor pots that make you feel as if there is another guest at your table. The white walls are covered with posters advertising art show openings that took place five years ago in large American cities that no one here has ever been to. There are also many large photographs of vegetables — bright green broccoli big as trees, plump tomatoes precisely sliced to show off their shapely seeds.

It is the kind of place that tries to convince you that you are really somewhere else, in some more serious-minded metropolis where everyone is self-employed and artistically inclined.

We all ordered Caesar salads, flaky croissants, and the house drink, champagne and orange juice on ice, called O. J. Bubbles.

"Miriam, Dwight, Robin, how nice to see you all," said the waitress. They all know us there. They probably gossip about us after we leave, speculating about our arrangements, sleeping and otherwise. We keep showing up for lunch in various combinations of two or three, sometimes all four of us, sometimes just Howard and Dwight together. DAVID and DENISE do the same. We are all so mature. Why do I wish sometimes that we could all just make a scene, throw lettuce and forks, hate each other and get it over with?

DAVID *is sitting at the kitchen table while* DENISE *paces furiously around him.*
DENISE: How could you?
DAVID: I lost my head.
DENISE: You're losing your mind.
DAVID: You're driving me crazy.
DENISE: I've never been so embarrassed in my life.
DAVID: You've still got lettuce in your hair. *(He laughs maniacally.)*

The restaurant filled up rapidly around us. It is a popular place, drawing businessmen and bank tellers on their lunch hour, university professors and their favourite students, new mothers gracefully breast-feeding. There is always some young man alone in the corner, reading or writing in his journal. I like the look of this and think that Howard should do the same, in a tweed suit jacket with leather elbow patches. But Howard says they're probably writing grocery lists and letters to Mom asking for money.

A naturally gregarious man who delights in the intricate art of conversation, the Spaniard spends much of his time in cafés and bars. He is probably a chain-smoker and rolls his own cigarettes from his favourite cheap tobacco. He is rarely a heavy drinker.

Seated at the next table was a well-dressed young couple politely putting away vast plates of lettuce. The woman put down her fork and slipped off one diamond earring, just the way my mother does when she's getting ready to talk on the phone. By proxy for Howard, I automatically eavesdropped.
"How could you?" said the man (husband).
"I didn't want to hurt you," the woman (wife) explained.
"But you did."

"I couldn't help it."

"I'll never forgive you."

"More coffee, folks?"

I wondered why everybody seems to be conducting their crises in restaurants these days. There is something about sharing a well-prepared generous meal which arouses, all at once, a false sense of security, the illusion of normalcy, and an abstract promise of intimacy. In addition to this emotional trickery, restaurants also ensure the relative safety of hurting someone you (are supposed to) love in a public place as opposed to your own inescapable living room.

Robin nudged me. "Stop staring at those people, Miriam. It's rude."

Robin and Dwight were still talking about some party they'd been to the night before, a birthday celebration for one of his friends.

"I was having a wonderful time," Dwight said, "until you started bitching."

"I wanted to go home. You were ignoring me."

"I was not."

"You were drunk."

"I was not."

"You were disgusting."

"Maybe a little."

Before you know it, she'll be yelling at you in public.

Today, as always, Robin wore a flowing cotton dress and sandals. She has a broad peasant face, permanently tanned, and with her flaxen hair wound up in braids, she was looking like a milkmaid. On first seeing Robin, you would expect her to be the warmest, most understanding woman you have ever met.

In reality she is phlegmatic and persistently narrow-minded. She is hard on everyone, does not allow them their weaknesses, be they alcohol, excess emotions, or love. She is no good with children or small animals. She is mightily offended by television and most jokes told to her by men. She seems always on the verge of ridiculing Dwight or discarding him altogether.

I have almost always adored her and would follow her around if she'd let me. I did hate her for a few years after I found out she'd tried to drown me, but then I had to forgive her. Just as they say, blood is thicker than water. But we have never really been a close family.

All Spanish families are alike. Rich or poor, large or small, they cling together and take a profound interest in each other's lives. Children seldom leave home until they marry. Family life centres around a large late lunch which Mother has spent most of the morning preparing.

I imagine Howard and me, poor white waifs, being hugged into the heart of a big Spanish family with clean singing children, fat aunts always cooking for jolly uncles who are always eating and tickling us. I am learning to say:

"We are very glad that our father has come home again. *Nos alegramos mucho de que nuestro padre haya vuelto a casa.*"

"I am very like my mother. *Me parezco mucho a mi madre.*"

"She is going to marry her cousin. *Ella se va casar con su primo.*"

Robin and Dwight sulked through their salads, Robin sternly, Dwight theatrically. But by the time the coffee arrived, they were cuddling and teasing again. I was foolishly feeling left out and had to bring up the time that Dwight, drunk, had proposed to me. "But what about Howard?" I'd asked. I had never seriously considered leaving Howard for Dwight. We are the kind of couple that everyone else thinks is perfect and will stay together forever. I suppose we will. "He can come too," Dwight had said.

Robin, whose only emotional fault is jealousy (retroactive as well as concurrent), tolerated this nostalgic reverie rather well and said nothing. Neither did Dwight.

It came as no great surprise to me when Dwight fell in love with Robin. I supposed that most men would eventually. I was not in a position to put up much of a fight anyway. Howard knew about the affair by then and was talking in sad whispers, smoking in the dark till four in the morning. He had always been critical of Robin but discovered that he liked her immensely once Dwight fell in love with her.

Dwight is a widower, his wife having died two years ago of a swift and savage cancer. When I loved him, I thought of him as soft and sore, slightly infirm, as if recovering from major surgery. I pampered and petted him constantly, thinking of how much he needed me to be strong. Robin, on the other hand, spares him nothing and gives him just enough, and it looks as though he'll never leave her.

"The travel agent called this morning. Our tickets are ready," I told them.

"The Spanish are an amazing people, so intense," Robin said. Everything that Robin likes lately, including movies (films), books, and women especially, is amazing and intense.

Taking my hand in an uncharacteristic gesture, she said, "Once you've been there, you'll *know*," as if the whole country were hers to give me. Dramatically, mystically, she said, "In the searing sunshine, there is nowhere to hide. Death is no longer dark. Spain is a landscape with figures. Houses bake in the sun. It will change your life."

There can be no turning back now.

Going home on the bus, I got out the phrase book, which, I find, I have taken to carrying with me everywhere, like a lucky rabbit's foot. The man beside me edged stiffly away as I began muttering to myself like a befuddled old woman in black, counting her rosary beads.

"However difficult it may seem, you must try to do it. *Por difícil que parezca, usted debe probar a hacerlo.*"

"The more I give him, the more he wants. *Cuanto más le doy, más quiere.*"

"It is no use saying that. *No sirve de nada decir eso.*"

* * *

I was expecting to spend an agreeable evening at home, Howard in his room writing, me curled up on the couch reading or watching TV. I was in the mood for a whole series of stupid situation comedies where everyone is immaculate, articulate, and can sort out their respective but interwoven problems in half an hour, not counting commercials. The ordinary family across the street watches TV every night. They never close their curtains, having nothing, I imagine, to hide. From my spot on the couch I can see their screen clearly, colours and faces, car and cat-food commercials, in their dark living room. I'm always pleased when I see that we're watching the same program.

When Howard writes in the evening, I can hear him doing the dialogue out loud, running through one speech over and over until he gets it right. DAVID and DENISE have lately shown a tendency towards interchangeable lines. It hardly seems to matter any more who says what. In the way of young couples seriously in love, they have embraced the theory of osmosis and turned themselves into a reversible jacket. They are, as Robin would say disparagingly, joined at the hip. And of course they will look alike when they are old. But, as always, there are difficulties.

DAVID: I never *really* loved you.
DAVID: I never really *loved* you.
DAVID: I never really loved *you*. (*He lights another cigarette.*)
DENISE: I never really loved you *either*.
DENISE: I never really loved you *anyway*. (*She heads for the bedroom.*)

But tonight when Howard got home, just after six, he had company. Which is not unusual. He has lately acquired the habit of bringing strangers home for supper, as if they were bag ladies in need of a hot meal. Howard has a way with people.

Just coming out of the kitchen, it took me a minute to realize that tonight's guests were the ordinary couple from across the street. Their names, it turns out, are Cindy and Mike. We had drinks and made neighbourhood small talk, Howard insisting the whole time that they must stay for supper. Finally Mike phoned over to tell the girls to order pizza.

From childhood on, the average Spaniard has been taught to share — and share he does, quite often putting himself out in order to help the friend or stranger who stands before him. Politeness demands offering a meal to a stranger, who answers, "May it be good for you. *Que aproveche.*"

Mike, looking even heavier up close, was wearing low-slung jeans and a greasy T-shirt which revealed a roll of hairy flesh that hypnotized me. In sandals, his stubby toes were hairy too. No wonder Howard is always washing his hands. Maybe he should have been a dentist.

Cindy, the wife, was dowdy but inoffensive in an ordinary summer dress pulled tight across the breasts. Every so often she would let her little hands flop down limply into her lap, exhausted or resigned to the inevitable. She admired everything in our living room, especially the fake fireplace decorated in a mosaic of black, red, and white tiles. I put violets where the fire should be. She also wished she had a couch just like mine, old and overstuffed, reupholstered in grey and maroon stripes. Wiggling around on the couch, nervously sipping their drinks, she and Mike talked more to each other than to either of us.

Mike experienced unpredictable moments of loquaciousness.

"We went to Europe once. It was a wonderful experience, wasn't it? So educational."

"That was before the twins, of course," Cindy explained.

Obviously Howard had already told them about the trip. Why is he always telling our secrets to strangers? (Since when was it a secret?) They are nice people, Cindy and Mike, so why do I hate them? I already know that no matter what happens, I will never like them.

I did not want them to know anything about me. I did not want them in my house, in my living room, in my bathroom snooping through my medicine chest looking for contraceptives and prescription drugs. I did not even want them living across the street from me. I was feeling vicious.

I waved the phrase book at them.

"Would you like anything to eat? *¿Quiere usted comer algo?*"

"No thanks; I am not hungry, but I should very much like a drink. *No, gracias; no tengo hambre, pero de buena gana bebería algo.*"

"Please pass me a clean plate. *Sírvase pasarme un plato limpio.*"

"I do not like stale bread. *No me gusta el pan duro.*"

They didn't laugh.

While I was in the kitchen trying to figure out what to feed these people, Howard put on a tape of Spanish guitar music. I danced briefly back into the living room, snapping my fingers and twitching my skirt, clenching a rose (wooden spoon) in between my teeth. This time they laughed. Howard was showing them our souvenirs from the trip.

When a Gypsy woman grows too old and fat to dance for a living, she can be found with the blind beggars, peddling castanets, charms, flowers, and photographs.

I went back to the kitchen and Cindy trailed in behind me. "Do you need some help?" There was not much to do with leftover lasagna and garlic toast.

Howard put on a tape of his play, a scene I hadn't heard before, one that shouldn't have been written yet. Howard was getting uncannily ahead of himself. Or playing tricks on me.

DAVID *and* DENISE *have had company for supper, some new people they've just met.* DENISE *is already in bed.* DAVID *enters. They are talking in the dark.*

DAVID: Are you awake?

DENISE: Just barely.

DAVID: Nice people, aren't they?

DENISE: Nice enough.

DAVID: Why are you being so difficult?

DENISE: I'm not sure. *(She rolls over onto her back and stares at the ceiling.)*

DAVID: What are you afraid of?

DENISE: Something. Sleep.

DAVID: I don't want to go to Spain any more.

DENISE: I don't want to go to Spain any more.

"What a beautiful kitchen. I love those little baskets on the wall," Cindy was saying. Another drink had loosened her up. "You remind me so much of my sister, she's a poet." I was tearing lettuce while she chopped celery savagely. I did not want to remind her of anyone.

"Oh? Where does your sister live?"

"She died two years ago. Drowned." I felt instantly guilty, as if I'd killed the poor woman by not wanting to be like her.

Encouraged somehow by my silence, Cindy continued, "I have dreams. In them she is going up the stairs for a long time and when she finally gets to the top, she turns and smiles down at me. But I can hardly see her, it is like opening your eyes underwater. And when she speaks, it is in some foreign language that I don't understand. I feel like I am swimming. Sometimes there are candles. Her hair was the colour of the water when they found her and I wanted to think the fish swimming into her mouth were coming out poems, but they told me it couldn't be true."

"Supper's ready!" I hollered hysterically. I am afraid of this woman.

We had just stopped exclaiming over the sudden change in the weather — a spring thunderstorm coming up quickly from the west, darkening the evening sky ominously — and started eating when the lights flickered and went out. I had been looking down at my lasagna, trying not to stare at Mike, who mashed everything on his plate together with a fork and then shaped it into a perfectly round pile before attacking it. Like a child, for a minute I thought I had been struck blind, punished for once and for all. In the darkness Mike chewed steadily.

Howard laughed and lit the two candles I'd set out on the table to excuse my earlier craziness and appease my guilt. But I hadn't gone so far as to light them. Wavering in an imperceptible breeze, they threw long jumping shadows around the twilit kitchen. Cindy gasped, stretched her arms out, and took first me and then Howard by the hand, as if we were holding a seance. I thought I would scream in the silence.

When the lights came back on a few minutes later, I thought there should be a noise but there was nothing, only the light, flooding.

They went home early, I went to bed, and Howard went into his room to make notes. I forgot to tell him about the tickets. Just before I fell asleep, I could hear him talking, into the tape recorder or into the telephone, to some dark woman over the ocean feeding the bulls, with a rose or a candle in her teeth.

There is never any doubt then that one has arrived in Spain.

HOW MYRNA
SURVIVES

They were all in their early thirties. An age at which
it is sometimes hard to admit that what you are living
is your life.

— Alice Munro, "Accident",
The Moons of Jupiter

1.   Myrna Lillian Waxman is thirty-two years old and lying
on the couch all the cool afternoon. The couch is a
cautious grey corduroy which wears well and doesn't show the
dirt. Myrna has covered herself with a green-and-yellow quilt
made by her distant cousin, Annette, before she was hit by a
freight train at the level crossing a quarter-mile from her house,
which she had travelled over twice a day for twenty years. On
the wall above the couch there is a silk-screen print of footprints
in the snow in which the bushes are black, the snow is blue,
and the footprints, white, are those of a small desperate animal
with only three legs.

There is a certain amount of guilt attached to sleeping in the
daytime but Myrna has managed to convince herself that she
needs or deserves it. She is letting her mind wander between
waking and sleep, willing herself to sustain this surreal state

for much longer than any normal person would, because this, she is convinced, is where her best ideas come from and where all of her problems are solved. (This may also happen, though less reliably, when she is having a bath or driving alone in the car.) In the end, though, she usually falls asleep anyway and dreams about sex or love or a staircase transformed into egg-shells beneath her bare feet, or maybe all three.

This habit of napping in the afternoon can be tricky for Myrna at this time of year, late autumn, because there is a certain quality of light at a certain advanced hour which she finds she must avoid waking up into. It is that time of day when, normally, you would be going through rooms turning on lights without thinking about it, your husband (if you had one) would be driving home from work, and you would be stirring something savoury on the stove. It is a cold light in the late afternoon, and grey, sinking, heartless. It is almost flu-orescent in the way it magnifies all of your flaws and failures till you barely recognize yourself. It is when you know for sure the day is over, you've had your chance and missed it, there is nothing to be done about it now, and so you go on into evening.

Before she lies down, Myrna puts her little travel alarm clock on the coffee table beside her and sets it so she can be safely up and doing something when the light, defeated, goes down and the day slops, or at least drains, out of her like blood. What she likes to be doing best is folding laundry.

She heaps her clean clothes on the couch, extracts each arti-cle (T-shirt, underwear, blue jeans, towels, that black-and-white flowered skirt with the elasticized waist which hangs so prettily and which she will wear out to dinner if anybody asks her) and smooths it out on the coffee table, taking the time to pick off the lint balls and appreciate the new-improved-fresh-scent of the detergent. She folds carefully and slowly, with calm concentration, depositing each item in its appropriate pile. While she folds, she thinks about her ex-room-mate, Rose. She is teaching herself to do things the way Rose did them. Rose, who could spend an hour folding and patting her sweat-ers, arranging them like woolly pillows in piles on the top shelf of her closet. Rose, who got up an hour early every morning to iron her clothes for work so that by the time Myrna came to, the kitchen was filled with the nurturing smells of coffee and hot cotton. Rose, who brought to every little thing she did such a serenity and single-mindedness that you just knew her mind was perfectly clear, healthy, and GOOD.

Rose has since married and moved to Vancouver. Myrna hasn't heard from her in nearly a year. She automatically assumes this unnatural lapse to be somehow her fault but, as of yet, has done nothing to make amends.

Emulating Rose now, arranging all her clean clothes in her clean closet, with every button buttoned and all the wrinkles shaken out, Myrna is filled with a distinct sense of accomplishment. She feels competent. She feels content. She feels like a good person for the time being and the dangerous hour has safely passed.

With the alarm clock set and the washing machine spinning sturdily in the basement, Myrna on the couch is thinking now, unaccountably, of when she was twenty-one, an undergraduate student in English Lit, engaged to marry Gordon Bates, a Business Admin major. Both she and Gord had a night class Thursdays from seven till ten. His was Advanced Accounting and hers was Creative Writing, her favourite. She was secretly in love with her professor, Dr. Diamond. Either good old Gord hadn't figured this out yet or, if he had, he wasn't letting it bother him.

Dr. Diamond (or Bernie, as he encouraged his students to call him — something which Myrna never could bring herself to do, this name being so colloquial or trivial, so unsuitable) was married to a dilettante sculptor named Jocelyn Bringhurst, who was always telling the story at university parties of how she'd once met Salvador Dali and Moon Dog at a coffeehouse in New York City in the sixties. Myrna cannot now remember who or what Moon Dog was anyway.

Dr. Diamond and Jocelyn Bringhurst had two small sons, Adrian and Damian, of whom Dr. Diamond often spoke at length, joyfully. One Thursday he brought them to the writing class when the baby-sitter unexpectedly broke her leg.

And where was Jocelyn? Never around when he needed her, Myrna supposed with satisfaction. And why had she kept her maiden name anyway?

The children played quietly in the corner of the classroom with their crayons and their little trucks, little angels. Myrna fantasized about how Dr. Diamond would finally come to his senses and leave Jocelyn, taking the children with him, of course, and she, Myrna, would bring them up beautifully.

After class each Thursday night, Gord would take Myrna down to Dino's Pizzeria for a couple of beer and a fifteen-inch double pepperoni with double cheese. The few nights they decided to be daring and order something different, Myrna went home feeling cheated, irritable, not even full yet. If they didn't go to Dino's, they went to the A&W for teenburgers or to Country Style Donuts for cinnamon crullers. These variations too left Myrna feeling unsatisfied and surly.

Over their food, Myrna and Gord talked about their respective classes: debits, credits, dialogue, description, and suspense. Dr. Diamond was a demanding teacher with impeccable literary standards and occasionally his sarcastic comments on her earnest efforts reduced the hopeful Myrna to tears over her pizza. Once he told her she was too normal to ever be a really good writer anyway, and she didn't drink enough either. Gord thought his Accounting prof was a bona fide idiot and so was always imbued with righteous anger after his class. So they had plenty to talk about while they ate, sucking back their beer and waving their hands around, energized but ineffectual. And then they would go home around midnight to their respective parents' houses, where they both still lived.

All of this was more or less unremarkable at the time and, Myrna realizes, probably still is. Being twenty-one was, in itself, unremarkable. And, if the truth were told, nothing had turned out the way Myrna thought it would. She'd gained twenty pounds but got an A in the course. The last night they had a party at Dr. Diamond's house instead of a regular class. They sat cross-legged in a circle on his green Persian rug, drinking dark rum and reading poetry tensely to each other.

Myrna surreptitiously studied his bookshelves and snooped in the medicine chest and two kitchen cupboards. Dr. Diamond drove her home last and kissed her once, sideways in the car. A year later he left Jocelyn and married Maureen, a mousy graduate student in Renaissance Lit. Jocelyn got Adrian and Damian but Dr. Diamond and Maureen soon produced two more offspring of their own, Chloe and Cassandra.

Myrna and Gordon Bates never did get married. She lost interest somewhere around the time she was supposed to be choosing her china pattern for the Bridal Registry at Birks. Gord soon after became a card-carrying member of the Progressive Conservative Party and married an ex-beauty queen whose father owned a furniture store.

But knowing all of this now does not cloud Myrna's sense of the state she had lived in then: that quality of twenty-oneness when absolutely everything was a promise, when her expectations were inchoate and unbounded, not yet unbearable, when there were just never enough hours in any given day, and sometimes she couldn't get to sleep at night for the sheer jumble of joy and the future working through her. This is a state of being which she is always trying now to get back, to get back TO.

An image comes to her of her twenty-one-year-old self strolling down the street (any street in any weather) and she is thinking and thinking, always thinking, carrying a book bag, tossing her high head, and her posture is loose-limbed but perfect. This picture is like one of those in a child's colouring book where every object, including the cumulus clouds, is outlined in black and those pure Crayola colours all stay neatly inside the lines, absolute. Except you always have to leave the hands and faces white because there is never a good flesh colour in the crayon box.

Now at thirty-two Myrna feels, by comparison, muddied. She has to admit that sometimes she gets tired of herself. She has come or is coming to understand that her life can no longer be seen as a temporary condition. She has to admit that maybe her old friend, Jane, was right when she said, "It's not true that it gets easier as you get older. No. It only gets harder. Too much water under the bridge.'' Jane has now vanished southward, to California or Arizona, Myrna forgets which, so maybe that makes a difference.

Now Myrna has a sense of herself as accumulating day by day layer upon layer of residue or something like silt: half-remembered conversations, arguments, heartbreaks, friendships which faded for no good reason but can never be resumed now, things she was supposed to do but never got around to, promises broken like dishes or the blood vessels in her left cheek, sins she has committed but forgotten or else convinced herself they weren't so bad, yes, sins. It is like the bathroom floor with those tiny grouted tiles that she never can get clean and then there is the mildew growing on the window-frame and the soap scum around the tub. But she is so tired and sometimes when she looks at that ground-in dirt, sometimes when she thinks of herself, she just wants to sob and gulp air. But even this seems like too much trouble — or too melodramatic anyway. Sometimes she just wants to scream and then sleep.

2.   This is how Myrna survives.

3.   Every morning Myrna wakes up early. She has a new PermaFoam mattress on her queen-size bed which is so comfortable that she hates to get out of it. But she gets too guilty if she sleeps too late.

Every morning it is like waking up in a strange hotel room with all your clothes on and the phone is ringing. Every morning it takes her a few minutes to get her bearings, to determine that yes, she really lives here: yes, there is her ceramic cat mobile hung by the window, her Olivia Parker orchids art poster on the closet door which is safely shut against nightmares, her new quilt in a mauve-and-blue pattern of leaves and vines which she got last week half-price at The Bay and she carried it out to the car in her arms like a child. Every morning it takes her a few minutes to decide or remember what mood she's in today. Sometimes she feels really good, but if she lies there long enough, comfy or not, all the reasons (or excuses) why she shouldn't will come whining around again.

So she gets up and throws her old grey cardigan over her flannelette nightie, pulls on her paisley kneesocks and her panda bear slippers. This crazy get-up makes her feel funky and self-assured, the kind of woman who can wear anything she damn well pleases and still look great, the kind of woman who thinks nothing of being twenty-five minutes late for everything, neither explaining nor apologizing, when she finally does show up, for her tardiness, her messy hair, or the cold sore on her upper lip. Myrna just wishes there was someone here to observe this disguise, but she also knows that she will die of embarrassment if anyone comes to the door, and she has never been late for anything in her life.

Over coffee and cigarettes at the kitchen table, Myrna reads and listens to the radio. She doesn't watch TV in the morning any more because there is always the carnage on the Detroit cable news. There is always some young black kid getting shot dead by mistake when the gunman was really aiming at his own mother, the neo-Nazi next door, the pizza delivery man, or the pimp in the Cadillac idling at the stoplight. And the game-show contestants always have names like Earl, Mabel, Flossie, and Melvin, and they don't have a care in the world. They want to say hi to all their friends watching back in Boca Raton, Muscle Shoals, and Memphis. They get to guess the prices of Trident Sugarless Gum, Uncle Ben's Converted Rice, and a set of Lee Stick-on Fingernails, glamour length. They win big: refrigerators, golf carts, three-piece bedroom suites, or A NEW CAR! They are jumpy, so noisy they make Myrna want to cry or throw things.

So Myrna makes her morning list which, like most things, is a double-edged device, producing great feelings of accomplishment and/or guilt according to how many items are/aren't crossed off at the end of any given day. Myrna optimistically means to:

1. Bath and wash hair
2. Change bed

3. Letter to Rose
4. Bank
5. A&P: bread   celery
            milk   onions
            cheese   green pepper
            eggs   mushrooms
            hamburger   sour cream
            kidney beans   toilet paper
            frozen quiche canned tomatoes
6. Work on story.

Against all odds, Myrna is a writer, and every morning, to
prime the pump, she likes to read a few chapters of some book
good enough to be inspiring but not SO good as to induce
paralysis with its shameless brilliance. Over her third and
fourth cups of coffee (a fresh-ground blend of Brazilian and
French Roast which she invented herself last week and is justly
proud of, though no one else has ever tasted it), she makes
notes of the ideas that have come to her lately from one place
or another. Things like:

1. While dressing herself up for the date, she couldn't help
    but think about chickens.

2. The man at the bar in the black cowboy hat ordered up
    another round for the house. He liked to play the big
    shot. Nobody else's money was good around him.

3. I was pushing the stroller up to the A&P to get the baby
    some prunes and there was this ambulance coming
    towards us. It turned left at the lights, heading over to
    Rideau Street, and there was me, pushing the baby in
    the heat and hoping it was for you.

4. At moments like this, Dorothy's husband, Sven, would
    always say, "Kooks, Dotty. This whole world is full of
    kooks. What's the world coming to? That's what I'd

like to know." And at moments like this, Dorothy would always wonder how she'd come to be living here in Houston, married to a man named Sven, of all things, and he's wearing a sombrero and never been anywhere near Sweden in his life.

Myrna fully intends to expand on these ideas later in the day. For now, she likes to get them down before she loses them. She likes the feel of her favourite pen in her hand first thing in the morning.

An odd phrase comes to mind and sticks, like a song or a name, knocking: it says, "All the length of . . ." Feeling playful and creatively eccentric, she writes:

1.　All the length of the dead garden
　　there were raspberry canes.

2.　All the length of the clothesline
　　there were pink baby clothes and beach towels.

3.　All the length of the roof
　　there were loose shingles slapping in the wind.

4.　All the length of the street
　　there were empty garbage cans, up-ended and rolling.

5.　All the length of the stadium
　　there were blonde cheerleaders waving red pom-poms.

6.　All the length of the forest
　　there were trees burnt black in the fire.

7.　All the length of her arm
　　there were bruises.

8.　All the length of her life
　　she was happy.

Myrna does not expect anything much to come of this exercise but it was fun, like flexing, and she calls it "Longing".

4.   Myrna smokes too much.

5.   Myrna drinks too much coffee.

6.   Myrna has often been told she thinks too much.

7.   Myrna waits for the mailman, who finally trudges up the driveway at 10:36 a.m., looking red in the face and grim. He leaves three bills, an envelope full of discount coupons for diapers and dog food, a flyer from Beaver Lumber where they have two-by-fours and padded toilet seats on special. Myrna is fed up.

8.   She drives downtown with the window open and the rock-and-roll radio up full blast so the handsome young construction workers at the corner of Princess and Division will notice her and know she isn't exactly what she appears to be in her dark-blue compact with her seat belt on. She sings along loudly and puts a look on her face she thinks of as saucy.

9.   She parks in the Marion Springer Memorial Lot on Queen Street which is out of the way but there is always a space. She walks the three blocks to her bank. It seems to be one of those days when every second person she passes has something wrong with them. There is a man with one arm, the empty sleeve of his white jacket pinned across his chest like a beauty queen's banner. There is a little girl with a bulging pocket of lumpy scar tissue on one side of her mouth and her left eye is three times as big as her right, protruding and watering, pointing right at Myrna. There is that smelly man she always sees, in greasy jeans and a lumberjack shirt, talking to himself and barking. There is a mongoloid woman riding in a shopping cart, wearing short white gloves and waving like the Queen, pushed along by a woman old enough to be her grand-

mother but who is probably her mother. Myrna knows that's
how these things can happen because her own mother, on ugly
occasions requiring excuses, apologies, or some vague kind of
justification, often reminded her, "I was nearly forty when I
had you. You're just lucky to be normal."

Standing in line in the bank, she tries to shake off the insid-
ious fear these poor people have put in her. She's hoping she
won't run into anyone she knows, someone who will corner
her, and then she will actually have to smile at them and make
some street small talk, as if she were happy to see them. She
concentrates on not catching anyone's eye. By the time she gets
up to the teller's wicket, she is able to make minor pleasantries
about the weather and the mechanic in Hamilton who won $2.2
million in the 649 draw Saturday night.

10.   In the A&P she gets out her list and loads up her cart,
immensely enjoying the way the purchase of yellow toilet paper,
whole-wheat bread, and a family-size can of kidney beans on
sale can give her such a sense of self-worth. Standing in the
check-out line, she feels confirmed in her pursuit (disguise) of
normalcy (domesticity) and would like to point this out to the
woman behind her, who is talking baby talk to her little girl in
the cart which is filled with jars of baby food and a jumbo pack
of ninety-six ultra-absorbent diapers.

Once Myrna was buying a fig tree along with her usual groceries and the woman behind her explained all about how it
would need lots of water and lots of sun and then half its leaves
would fall off anyway but this was nothing to worry about
because a fig tree will just do that sometimes, shedding. And
then it was such a beautiful plant, and only $14.99, that the
woman went back and got one for herself, even though the last
thing in the world she needed was another fig tree. Every time
Myrna waters her fig tree now, she thinks about that woman.

Myrna waits her turn and chuckles at the tabloid headlines:
CHOCOHOLIC MOTHER GIVES BIRTH TO SUGAR-COATED BABY
BRIDE'S STOMACH EXPLODES AT WEDDING RECEPTION
79-YEAR-OLD PRIEST MAKES 15-YEAR-OLD TRIPLETS PREGNANT.

The cashier seems pleased when Myrna fishes around in her wallet and quickly comes up with the exact change.

11.   Myrna likes to take herself out to lunch. But she doesn't go to the Pizza Hut any more because they always bring the food so fast that she thinks they feel sorry for her, having to eat lunch all alone. Either that or they want to get rid of her. She gets so nervous eating there, what with all the good cheer and rushing around, that she's afraid she'll choke and terminally disgrace herself, face-down in her food.

She doesn't go to Bonnie's Bistro any more either because the last time she did, there was an elastic band in her French fries.

She doesn't go, at least not very often, to The Waterworks Café, which is a popular place where all the local artists, writers, musicians, and aspirants like to congregate. She does go there once in a while because every time she walks by, she feels like she's missing something.

The Waterworks is tastefully decorated in trendy pastels, mint green and dusty rose, with original artwork on the walls, oil paintings and silk-screen prints with price tags in the corners. They play eclectic music. The menu features soups, salads, pâté, a selection of items which can be attractively served on a croissant, and twenty-seven varieties of mineral water, domestic and imported, sparkling and still. It is a small place, meant to be intimate, but there is not even a decent space between the tables, so you are always bumping the back of your chair into the back of the chair of the person at the table behind you. And they are always bumping your chair just as you are trying to get a spoon full of hot soup (home-made minestrone, or cream of broccoli) up to your mouth.

The other patrons wander from table to table, carrying their cappuccino or Perrier, congratulating or commiserating. Myrna must be feeling impervious and relatively intelligent in order to go into The Waterworks because, once inside, she feels like an impostor or an intruder. She secretly yearns to be part of this group but knows she will never pull it off.

Myrna likes to have lunch at Martin's Gourmet Burger Palace where the efficient waitress named Donna brings her a coffee and says, "The usual?" while Myrna is still taking her coat off, arranging it on the back of her chair. She sits so she can see out the window. She has bought a lottery ticket before coming in and sits for a while with it in her hand, trying to decide if, when she scratches and wins, she will jump up and down screaming her head off, "I won! I won!" or if she will just sit there smiling gently, sure of herself, her secrets, and the future.

She reads *The New Yorker*, especially the "Goings On About Town", though she's never been there and doubts she ever will because she is afraid of big cities.

She observes the people at the next table, a party of five, three men and two women, drinking pear cider and wearing quiet office outfits. One young man in a grey trench coat passes around a blue binder with the title "Focus on Dermatology" on the cover. Myrna cannot imagine what these people are going to do with the rest of their lives, once this lunch is over. No matter how often she comes here, she never sees the same people twice.

Sometimes, by the time Donna brings her food (a mushroom and bacon burger with Caesar salad instead of fries), Myrna has got to feeling guilty for being there, wasting time when she should be home washing the floor, doing the laundry, cleaning that mildew from the bathroom window-sill because sometimes she thinks she can SMELL it. She should be at home THINKING. Mostly, she should be at home WRITING. At the very least, she should be finishing up the rest of the things on her list because these are the parameters she has set for herself, these are the promises she must live up to
in order to feel justified
in order to wrest
      wring
      rake
      rescue
      resurrect order out of chaos
             value out of worthlessness
             or the tidal fear of it.

While in Martin's, she writes in a small hard-covered note-book which she carries in her purse at all times. She writes about how the sight of Canada geese travelling across the sky in their v spring and fall always gives her a lump in her throat which she has never been able to figure out. But suddenly, in the act of writing it down, she sees that this natural phenomenon is an affirmation that all is right with the world, that things indeed are unfolding as they should. And the lump in her throat comes from the precious duplicity of simultaneously believing this and knowing that it's not true.

Myrna likes the image of herself writing in restaurants and, for a few minutes, everything makes sense.

Myrna leaves a good tip and waves at the waitress on her way out. She has seen this Donna several times on the street but they do not acknowledge each other, as if they keep a shameful secret between them, as if Myrna keeps having lunch at Martin's with somebody else's husband instead of alone.

12.   Myrna doesn't have to eat lunch alone. There are always some women who try to befriend her and so she feels grateful, tries to encourage them, tries to be sociable, tries to be a good listener and tell them her troubles in return. But she finds as soon as she tells them one little thing — as soon as she tells them about the time she ran into her ex-lover, Peter, with a woman named Ingrid at The Calabash Bar when he'd said he was working and then she drank so many double Scotches while watching them slow-dance and laugh that she fell down on the corner of Barrie and Princess and there was a cop right there at the light and he picked her up, literally picked her up off the sidewalk, and took her home and she wanted him to put on the lights and the siren when they pulled into the driveway but he wouldn't — as soon as she tells these friendly women something like this, then they want to take over her whole life: they want her to tell them everything.

And then she feels guilty for not telling them about the time she got drunk on home-made red wine and smashed the telephone to smithereens with the empty bottle and then she threw up in the hallway and in the morning she couldn't remember doing either of these things but there was the phone in pieces, still plugged in, shards of green glass all over the kitchen, and there was the vomit on the hardwood floor. She just says how she doesn't drink alone any more because she's heard it's a bad sign, and self-destructive.

She feels guilty for not telling them about how this morning just before dawn she had an erotic dream of such beauty and power that she woke up having an orgasm and felt good all day, about how walking to the A&P yesterday she couldn't remember what she was going to buy so she turned back and went home crying, about how last night she thought of the words "dim sum" and liked the sound of it so much that she ordered Chinese food for supper, let the chicken she'd defrosted yesterday just sit there and rot, and in the back of her fridge there is a pot of spaghetti sauce that's been there since August.

She compensates by telling them that she talks to herself when driving the car, orders pizza so often that they know her name and address as soon as she says hello, how she likes to sleep in the afternoon, how sometimes she goes to bed at eight o'clock, even in the summer when it's still light out, just because she's had enough of THIS day.

She says all these things in such a charmingly self-deprecating manner that these generous women invariably want to reciprocate. They tell her how they do these and similar silly things, but Myrna knows they're lying to save her feelings, to save her from thinking she's crazy.

13.   The true art of telling stories on yourself, Myrna suspects, involves being able to rearrange, exaggerate, or denigrate the facts enough to make yourself look good or, failing that, blameless. This is called fiction.

When relating, for instance, the story of her visit to her parents out west last summer, she says how on the Friday night she thought she'd just walk down to The Cecil Hotel, which was close, and have a quick beer just because she hadn't been there for ten years nearly and was feeling nostalgic. She doesn't say how really she was climbing the walls of her parents' hot little bungalow, her mother was already repeating herself after only two days, her father was planted in the swivel chair, drinking a forty-ouncer of rum, staring out the bay window at nothing, and Myrna went storming out in an inexplicable rage which was never mentioned again.

At The Cecil (which hadn't changed much, was still a dive, overcrowded and vaguely criminal), she stood drinking beer at the bar until she caught the eye of a handsome black-bearded biker by the pool table who motioned her over, bought her a drink, said his name was Leonard but they called him "The Drake", pleasta meetcha. It turned out that the slim French woman playing pool like a shark was his girlfriend, Jacinte. Resting her heavy breasts on the table for the long shots, Jacinte was cleaning up at a buck a cue and proudly handing him her winnings after each game.

But Jacinte went home early because she had to work in the morning. Then Myrna was buying and The Drake was pumping her quarters into the juke-box and pulling up his black Harley-Davidson T-shirt to show her his tattoos. There was a lion, a wolf, a dragon, a cobra, and the omnipotent eagle. Myrna said, "I like a tattoo," and touched them.

The next thing she knew they were kissing at the table. The Drake was putting his whole tongue in her mouth and she was feeling invisible the way she always did when she was drunk: as if nobody could see what she was doing so she thought she could do anything. The Drake said how much he'd like to take her for a ride but he'd lost his licence for five years, vehicular manslaughter, and so now they had a car, which he called a cage, and Jacinte did the driving. He walked Myrna back to her parents' house, kissing and pleading, and when she tells this story, Myrna doesn't say how she just wanted to get rid of him. His tongue was too big, and rough like a cat's. She'd already got what she wanted, which had little to do with him in the first place.

Four days later she flew home and Brian, her lover at the time, met her at the airport with flowers and a bottle of pink champagne, which was romantic but not like him at all. At three in the morning her phone rang. It was The Drake calling to say he'd bought a bus ticket, he'd be there Sunday at eight. Then Jacinte grabbed the phone away from him, yelling, "Who the hell are you talking to? I'll kill you, I'll kill you!" Myrna hung up, unplugged the phone, put a butcher knife and the empty champagne bottle on the top shelf of her bedroom closet, not sure yet who she should be frightened of. Brian from the bed asked, "Didn't you tell him about me?"

Telling this story, Myrna says how she felt terrorized for weeks afterwards but that was the end of it, thank God. Except (she doesn't say this part) she told Brian that the biker had called her again, not once, but twice, when Brian wasn't there, was sleeping, Myrna suspected (and correctly), with another woman.

She doesn't say how she kept expecting to be punished but nothing ever happened, nothing changed, and she could still look herself in the eye in the bathroom mirror in the morning without flinching or cringing. This consummate failure of justice, poetic or otherwise, this failure of a call or a need for atonement to appear gave her a licence, she felt, to do whatever she wanted, because nothing made any real difference after all and you really could get away with things without being caught, damaged, or disfigured.

But of course this new lease on life was fleeting, and when considering whether to write a story about this story, she eventually abandoned the idea because whatever promises it contained (of violence, retribution, or morality) could be neither broken nor fulfilled in the end, not convincingly anyway.

14.   Myrna doesn't pick up strange men in bars any more. There is the fear of disease, of course, and the problem of breakfast: what to make without appearing too domestic or grateful, or whether to just stay in bed with her head covered up, waiting for him to comb his hair and leave.

There is the perennial problem with the ones you wish would stick around because you would like to spend the rest of your life (or at least the rest of the weekend) with them, so you offer coffee, an omelette, grapefruit, buttermilk pancakes, but he is shrugging on his jean jacket, edging towards the door at 6 a.m. because he has to go fishing, has to go rip the engine out of his truck, play baseball, move a piano, feed the dog, and you know you will never get him back into your bed again.

But the ones you never want to see ever again, not even in the grocery store by accident, the ones you will cross the street to avoid, are always calling and driving by your house and falling like feathers in love with you.

They have no sense of humour, none of them. There is the way the bedroom begins to fill up with their long faces and the only thing left to do is redecorate or move.

15.   Myrna is walking back to her car on Queen Street. At the busy corner of Queen and Clergy, a man with no legs is trying to manoeuvre his wheelchair over the curb up onto the sidewalk. His head lolls alarmingly to the left and the stumps of his thighs are wrapped in white bandages.

Myrna turns and walks in the other direction.

Her heart is beating so hard that the blood seems to be escaping the ventricles, filling up her whole chest cavity, hot and shameful, bubbling like soup all down to her knees.

She is swallowing and swallowing, like the time she was driving through a trailer park at night (she didn't know anyone who lived there, she was just cruising) and a cat ran out in front of her, green eyes like marbles in her headlights, and after she hit it she just kept driving until she was home.

16.   Myrna checks her answering machine as soon as she gets home. She is disappointed when there have been no messages but, on the other hand, she often doesn't feel up to returning the calls she does get, even when they're long-distance from people she hasn't talked to in years. Their phone numbers get accidentally erased.

Sometimes, feeling anti-social, frightened, or smug, she leaves the machine on even when she's home. In the instruction manual, this impersonation of absence is politely referred to as "Screening Your Calls". Eating supper, soaking in the bathtub, lying on the couch reading *The Unbearable Lightness of Being* by Milan Kundera, or watching *Family Ties* on TV, Myrna looks up and listens to disembodied voices speaking with false bravado into the machine: "Hi Myrna! It's just me! Haven't heard from you in ages! Just called to say hi! Call me back when you can!"

What she hates most are the hang-up calls when the machine faithfully records a click and then the dial tone or a maddening silence. Myrna plays back these calls over and over, trying to detect breathing, background music, or a sigh. Frustrating as they are, these mystery calls also fill her with exhilaration, with a premonition that someday soon somebody special is going to get through to her.

17.   Myrna is sitting at the kitchen table just around suppertime. She is working on the crossword puzzle in the evening paper, discovering that she knows:
1. a 4-letter word for ACIDITY (1-Across)
2. an 8-letter word for IN AN ADULT FASHION (10-Down)
3. a 4-letter word for GR. CHEESE (68-Down).
But she has to look up in her crossword-puzzle dictionary:
1. a 4-letter word for AVATAR OF VISHNU (94-Across)
2. a 4-letter word for CHIN. GELATIN (64-Across)
3. a 4-letter word for ONCE, ONCE (13-Across).

She is trying to decide if she should heat up the leftover chili from last night or should she just give in to temptation and order another pizza?

She is looking periodically over at the well-kept brick house across the street. She doesn't know these neighbours, still hasn't figured out who all lives there or what the connections are between them. One of them is a mailman who looks very handsome in his postal uniform, there is an older heavy-set couple who drive a blue Lincoln, a woman in a fur coat who comes over every day with or without a small child in a red snowsuit, there is a very old woman with long white hair who sits at the upstairs window in her nightgown (for a long time Myrna thought the old lady was watching her in *her* window but now she thinks she's watching TV). These neighbours are always juggling their cars around in the long driveway, backing out, pulling in, waving, honking, just driving away.

They have one of those pretty Tiffany lamps hung over the dining-room table (at least Myrna thinks it's the dining room). The multicoloured light which it casts makes the whole house look safe and inviting. Inside, Myrna imagines, there would be a cosy warmth, good smells of supper, the sound of the television news coming quietly from another room, laughter. The older man sits at the table with his back to the window, reading the paper, sometimes shirtless even in the winter so that his broad white back looks like a pillow.

One day at The Bay Myrna bought herself a Tiffany lamp too, also a tablecloth printed with flat-faced purple pansies and long-necked pink gladioli, also one of those new wooden dish-racks which looks like a book- or music-stand. She put these purchases on her charge card and hurried home with them. She ironed the tablecloth, laid it out, set up the dishrack, and hung the lamp above the table.

But later that evening, sitting under it doing another puzzle, she had to admit that she didn't FEEL any different. She supposed her house must LOOK different from the outside, to someone walking by, walking the dog or taking the air, or having just had a fight with their husband/wife over who was supposed to take out the garbage and needing to get away for half an hour, trying to figure out why nothing ever went right in their lives — to someone just walking by like that, Myrna supposed the house might look now like a home for happy well-adjusted folks with children, pets, and dreams.

This gives her some small satisfaction but, sitting under the lamp, which sheds its colours, she imagines, down upon her lustrous black hair like rainbows or leaves, Myrna has to admit that she doesn't FEEL any different: she still doesn't feel like the people across the street.

18.   After supper, Myrna does the dishes promptly, sweeps the floor, reads and watches TV at the same time, thinks about all the writing she will definitely do tomorrow, goes to bed early, and reads some more. She prefers a good fat hardcover, the weight of it expensive and significant in her hands. She does not like library books because they smell funny, the plastic jackets crinkle, and the pages feel coated and damp.

After she turns out the light, she curls up on her left side till she feels all warm and relaxed. Then she rolls over onto her right and falls asleep.

Sometimes she thinks about Rose, when they were roommates, announcing puffy-faced at breakfast, "I cried myself to sleep last night."

Myrna has never managed to cry herself to sleep. She has tried it the odd time when, at some suitably melancholy juncture, the idea seemed attractive enough in theory: the tragedy, the loneliness, the balled-up Kleenex all over the bed. But in practice she finds it impossible to sustain. For one thing, crying keeps her awake. And once she starts, she wants only to stop, to get up, eat, wash, smoke, something, anything to save herself at the brink. Because once she starts, she is afraid she will never be able to stop. She can only imagine poor Rose drifting off in mid-sob, waking up before the alarm with her fingers still in her mouth.

19.   Myrna has never doubted that she will survive. Oh, there was that one time years ago when some man had dumped her and she was drunk and thinking she'd drive her car into the river. It was February, the ice was rotten, and she would sink down slowly like a horse to its knees, nose first and the windows open. But then she realized how drunk she was and, with her luck, she'd probably get picked up for impaired on her way to the river and it would be just too embarrassing, losing her licence like that. So she threw the clock, several heavy books, and her cowboy boots across the room and stayed where she was: in bed fully dressed, listening to his favourite song, and pounding her pillow and her thighs.

By the next morning, she was already laughing at herself, writing "A Fate Worse Than Death" in her notebook — which is what she would have called the story she might have written about the story someday.

But Myrna never thinks about that time any more, she doesn't write or tell the story, and she does not remember the name of the man, the song, or the river.

20.   This is just some of how Myrna survives.

NONE OF THE ABOVE

The city is a conglomerate of oil-rainbowed bubbles, all of its unknown neighbourhoods dissolving one by one behind David and Belinda Boyce as they pass obliviously through on their way home in the five o'clock Friday rush-hour dark of early December. In other parts of the city,

(A)   a lonely woman may be eating Kraft Dinner right out of the pot, standing there in her housecoat, watching *The Young and the Restless*, trying not to cry in her condo on Elm Street.

(B)   an old woman may be lying dead in her bed-sitting room on Sixteenth Avenue, having been there four days, the newspapers piling up outside her door: maybe tomorrow someone will miss her or smell her.

(C)   a desperate young woman may be holding up a liquor store at the corner of Centre and Tenth, making off with all the cash and two magnums of French champagne.

(D)   a scorned woman may be slashing up the waterbed in a highrise on Dalhousie Drive, stabbing her unfaithful husband twenty-six times in the back, letting his lover go naked and screaming and free through the puddles already leaking through to the apartment below.

(E)   all of the above.

David Boyce is driving the old blue Pontiac, having stopped
to pick up Belinda at the plant store where she works on his
way from the pet store where he works. In the plant store
Belinda sells
(A)   African violets.
(B)   Wandering Jews.
(C)   geraniums.
(D)   rubber trees.
(E)   cacti and succulents.

In the pet store David sells
(A)   guppies.
(B)   parakeets.
(C)   lizards.
(D)   guinea pigs.
(E)   pit-bull puppies.

Belinda is
(A)   beautiful.
(B)   short.
(C)   tired.
(D)   young.
(E)   too young to be so tired.

David is
(A)   handsome.
(B)   tall.
(C)   smug.
(D)   young.
(E)   too young to be so smug.

Belinda is
(A)   innocent.
(B)   carefree.
(C)   contented.
(D)   lovable.
(E)   only occasionally depressed.

David is
(A) responsible.
(B) hard-working.
(C) ambitious.
(D) lovable.
(E) only occasionally insensitive.

Tonight, December 8, it is
(A) windy.
(B) snowy.
(C) icy.
(D) twenty below.
(E) pretty miserable for this time of year.

David drives with extra care because Belinda beside him holds in her lap
(A) a baby.
(B) an aquarium.
(C) an angel-food cake.
(D) a bouquet of rare orchids.
(E) a snowball melting all down her thighs.

David and Belinda (née Johnson), high school sweethearts, were married the summer after graduation at 3 p.m. on Saturday, August 8, three years ago. At the time, they expected their linked lives to play out happy and long. So far, they are
(A) correct.
(B) mistaken.
(C) convinced.
(D) surprised.
(E) still waiting.

In their early twenties now, they are still living in the same city where they were both born. Their city, it seems to them, will always be
(A) solid.
(B) snug.

(C) friendly.
(D) comfortable.
(E) home.

They have never had, either one of them, the slightest desire
to move to
(A) Toronto.
(B) Los Angeles.
(C) Indian Head, Saskatchewan.
(D) Amsterdam.
(E) Argentina.

With the generous help of their parents and the Bank of Mon-
treal, they have been able to purchase and furnish a semi-
detached home on Edelweiss Crescent in the new subdivision of
(A) Canyon Meadows.
(B) Silver Springs.
(C) Tuxedo Park.
(D) Greenview Estates.
(E) Briar Hill Heights.

In their new home there is
(A) a 12-cup Philips Coffee Maker. Dial-a-brew system with
     showerhead design water spreader. Pause control for one-
     cup convenience. "On" light and dust cover. Two-hour
     automatic shut-off if you forget! Drip reservoir in basket.
(B) a 20″ Colour Television. Quick-view feature means a clear
     picture seconds after you turn the television on! Off-timer
     automatically turns off television at a predetermined time.
     Charcoal-grey styling adds the perfect modern touch to
     your home!
(C) a Proctor-Silex Broiler Oven. Will bake, broil, toast, and
     keep warm! Continuous-clean interior, large window, all-
     purpose bake pan, dual-weight oven rack, easy-clean
     crumb tray.
(D) a Sunbeam Electronic Blanket with BodySensor feature.
     Personal Monitoring System monitors your entire body

while you sleep, compensating for any temperature changes it senses! 80% polyester, 20% acrylic.
(E) a Water Pik Home Dental System. The Command Control Pik allows you to control the water flow! Includes oral irrigator, electric toothbrush, 4 colour-coded jet tips and 4 brushes.

They are also saving their money for
(A) wall-to-wall carpeting.
(B) a microwave oven.
(C) a compact disc player.
(D) a new car in the spring, maybe a Volvo or a Ford Mustang Cobra GT Convertible.
(E) a trip to Hawaii next winter or maybe the West Edmonton Mall.

Having discussed the future at length, David and Belinda would like to have
(A) 12 children.
(B) 2 children.
(C) 0 children.
(D) a cat.
(E) a dog.

If they have a cat, she is sleeping like a sweater in the middle of the kitchen table when they get home. If they have a cat, her name is
(A) Puff.
(B) Tiger.
(C) Muffin.
(D) Bubbles.
(E) Bert.

If they have a dog named Rex, he is
(A) a cocker spaniel.
(B) a Doberman pinscher.
(C) a poodle.

(D)   a chihuahua.

(E)   not house-trained yet.

If they have a Doberman named Rex, he is watching for them loyally from his mat by the door. He greets them with exuberance and his jaws come shut with the sound of a wet handclap. While David has a beer and wrestles around with Rex, Belinda makes for their supper

(A)   Stuffed Herbed Chicken Breasts With Vinegar Sauce.

(B)   Steamed Broccoli Nouvelle.

(C)   Baked Parmesan Rice With Mushrooms and Sautéed Almonds.

(D)   Eggplant-Zucchini Salad.

(E)   Perfect Apple Pie.

Over their meal, they talk amiably about

(A)   how tender the chicken is, just delicious, done this way, also the broccoli.

(B)   how glad they are it's finally Friday and they can just relax.

(C)   how Belinda would really like to get her hair permed.

(D)   how David has a nasty corn on his left baby toe.

(E)   what they will do tomorrow.

Tomorrow being Saturday they will

(A)   stay in bed all day.

(B)   defrost the fridge.

(C)   wallpaper the bathroom.

(D)   watch football and drink beer.

(E)   go shopping at the mall.

At the mall they will buy

(A)   a cookie jar shaped like a duck.

(B)   a shower curtain with dolphins on it.

(C)   mauve sheets.

(D)   a shovel.

(E)   a hand grenade.

Over their meal they do not discuss
(A) the fact that David's younger sister, Andrea, has been arrested for shoplifting after stealing a blow dryer and a Rolling Stones record from Woolworth's when she had $100 in her purse and had just come from her weekly session with the shrink.
(B) the fact that Ginny Andrews who works with Belinda at the plant store is having an abortion, her third, in the morning.
(C) how yesterday there was fighting all night next door, Al and Suzanne screaming, glass breaking, and something round and solid, but soft too, like a head or a cabbage, hitting the wall.
(D) Belinda's recurring nightmare in which she is chasing David around Edelweiss Crescent with an axe until he stops dead in his tracks, turns around and shoots her, with a face on him like Bruce Springsteen.
(E) the threat of nuclear war which has permeated their whole young lives.

David and Belinda Boyce think of themselves as
(A) a lucky couple.
(B) an unlucky couple.
(C) a happy couple.
(D) an unhappy couple.
(E) they do not think of themselves.

After the dishes are done, Belinda puts on her terry-cloth bathrobe which she bought last weekend at Woolworth's for $70. The bathrobe, which she loves, is the colour of
(A) peaches.
(B) peppermints.
(C) lilacs.
(D) her eyes.
(E) broken glass.

Curled up in the corner of the sectional, Belinda is
(A) watching *Miami Vice*.
(B) knitting a green sweater for David for Christmas.
(C) painting her toenails that great new colour called Red Alert.
(D) playing solitaire.
(E) reading her horoscope in the evening paper.

Belinda is
(A) a Virgo.
(B) a Cancer.
(C) a Libra.
(D) a Pisces.
(E) an Aquarius.

David is
(A) an Aries.
(B) a Taurus.
(C) a Leo.
(D) a Scorpio.
(E) a Sagittarius.

If Belinda is reading her horoscope, it says
(A) Influential people are less likely to support your ideas. Postpone entertaining a new alliance. Relaxing at home appeals more than a night on the town.
(B) You finally see the light at the end of the tunnel! Have faith in your talents and let other people handle their own problems.
(C) Your optimism is contagious today. You will be happiest with your family and pets.
(D) Anything can happen this weekend and probably will. You love surprises! Stay in touch with friends overseas. You may want to take a trip.
(E) You get a second chance and make the most of it! Your popularity continues to grow. Use wit but not sarcasm to make a point.

If Belinda is reading David's horoscope, it says

(A) Career demands begin to get to you. Take a long weekend and recoup. Someone may be trying to deceive you by withholding facts.

(B) Be careful not to pledge something you cannot afford to give. Real estate transactions look good. Speculative ventures, romance, and meetings with siblings are favoured.

(C) Partner is more sensitive to your ideas and needs. Long-term financial security should be a top priority now.

(D) You may have more than your usual work to cope with. Your ability to produce when under pressure will impress an influential person. A family member's problems are not as serious as they seem.

(E) The world could be at your feet if you play your cards right. Get some exercise instead of a large lunch at noon.

This is like in high school when they played the Top Ten on the radio every night at 10 p.m. and, if Belinda could guess all ten songs right and in order, then the next day would be a good day. The next day

(A) they would not have to play basketball.

(B) Mrs. Sanderson, the biology teacher, would be away and they would not have to learn any more about those stupid fungi.

(C) they would have tacos for lunch in the cafeteria.

(D) her hair would look just right.

(E) David would walk her home from school, carrying her books and holding her hand.

This is like Belinda playing solitaire to pass the time when David isn't around and, if she beats the devil on the first try, tomorrow

(A) she will not have to make a funeral wreath.

(B) Mr. MacKay, her boss, will be in a good mood all day.

(C) the other girls from the plant store will invite her to lunch at Red Lobster.

(D) her hair will look just right.

(E) David will tell her he still loves her, without her having to say it first.

David does not appear to be around right now. He has

(A) gone to the basement to play with his model train set.

(B) gone next door to watch the hockey game with Al.

(C) gone out to walk the dog.

(D) gone to bed.

(E) gone.

Just before The National news comes on at ten o'clock, there is a knock at the back door. Not sure whether to answer it or not, Belinda turns on the outside light, temporarily blinding a man who has come to

(A) read the meter in the basement.

(B) demonstrate a new improved Electrolux vacuum cleaner.

(C) sell her a lifetime subscription to *Better Homes and Gardens*.

(D) mystify her with magic tricks, pulling parakeets out of a hat, plucking gold coins from her eyelids, turning purple orchids into flying fish.

(E) let her in on the meaning of life.

In the immaculate kitchen, the man says

(A) Thou shalt have no other gods before me.

(B) Thou shalt not make unto thee any graven image, or any likeness of any thing that is in heaven above, or that is in the earth beneath, or that is in the water under the earth: Thou shalt not bow down thyself to them, nor serve them: for I the Lord thy God am a jealous God, visiting the iniquity of the fathers upon the children unto the third and fourth generation of them that hate me: And shewing mercy unto thousands of them that love me, and keep my commandments.

(C) Thou shalt not take the name of the Lord thy God in vain; for the Lord will not hold him guiltless that taketh His name in vain.

(D) Remember the sabbath day, to keep it holy. Six days shalt thou labour, and do all thy work: But the seventh day is the sabbath of the Lord thy God: in it thou shalt not do any work, thou, nor thy son, nor thy daughter, thy manservant, nor thy maidservant, nor thy cattle, nor thy stranger that is within thy gates: For in six days the Lord made heaven and earth, the sea, and all that in them is, and rested the seventh day: wherefore the Lord blessed the sabbath day, and hallowed it.

(E) Honour thy father and thy mother: that thy days may be long upon the land which the Lord thy God giveth thee.

Belinda asks
(A) Who are you?
(B) Where have you come from?
(C) Why are you here?
(D) Am I guilty?
(E) What am I guilty of?

In the cosy living room, the man says
(A) Thou shalt not kill.
(B) Thou shalt not commit adultery.
(C) Thou shalt not steal.
(D) Thou shalt not bear false witness against thy neighbour.
(E) Thou shalt not covet thy neighbour's house, thou shalt not covet thy neighbour's wife, nor his manservant, nor his maidservant, nor his ox, nor his ass, nor anything that is thy neighbour's.

Belinda says
(A) I believe you.
(B) I believe you.
(C) I believe you.
(D) Yes, I believe you.
(E) Yes, yes, I see what you mean.

The man leaves
(A)   suddenly.
(B)   silently.
(C)   very carefully, stepping over the dog.
(D)   satisfied.
(E)   sanctified.

When David reappears about an hour later, Belinda is
(A)   still sitting on the sectional still painting her toes.
(B)   lying in bed with her head covered up.
(C)   laughing.
(D)   crying.
(E)   levitating somewhere over the kitchen sink.

Belinda
(A)   tells him.
(B)   doesn't.
(C)   tells him.
(D)   doesn't.
(E)   does.

If Belinda tells him, David says she must be
(A)   crazy.
(B)   drunk.
(C)   dreaming.
(D)   premenstrual.
(E)   truly blessed.

Because of this night, the lives of David and Belinda Boyce are forever
(A)   changed.
(B)   unchanged.
(C)   fulfilled.
(D)   unfulfilled.
(E)   forever finished for better or worse.

In her later life, Belinda Boyce will
(A) become manager of the plant store and proceed incon-
       spicuously over the years to stock the shelves exclusively
       with thousands of Prayer Plants and Venus Fly Traps,
       until the place finally goes bankrupt and is replaced by a
       massage parlour.
(B) give birth to a charming cherubic child named Joshua,
       who will give true meaning to her heretofore shallow life.
(C) write a bestselling book about her blessing and go on *Phil
       Donahue* talking in tongues.
(D) do twenty-five years in the Prison for Women for hijack-
       ing a jumbo jet to Jerusalem on which the in-flight movie
       was *Oh God II*.
(E) die peacefully at the age of eighty-seven, sleeping between
       the mauve sheets in the master bedroom of the house on
       Edelweiss Crescent, never knowing what hit her.

In his later life, David Boyce will
(A) buy a Cadillac Fleetwood, GM Executive, V8 loaded, air
       conditioning, power windows, power steering, power
       brakes, cruise control, gold, and die in a twenty-seven-
       car pile-up on the 401.
(B) join the Hell's Angels and die in a gang war.
(C) buy a Kentucky Fried Chicken franchise and die in a
       grease fire.
(D) take up windsurfing and die in a tidal wave.
(E) suffer eternal unenlightened life.

In his later life, the man who came to the back door will become
(A) a television evangelist.
(B) a Rosicrucian.
(C) a family man.
(D) a mass murderer.
(E) the burning bush.

No matter what happens in the rest of their lives, tonight, in
other parts of the city,

(A)   a contented woman may be tucking in her babies in a
      bungalow on Amethyst Crescent, kissing their smooth
      fair foreheads, singing them a lullaby sweetly, the one
      about how when the bough breaks, the cradle will fall,
      and down will come baby, cradle and all.

(B)   a carefree, only occasionally depressed, woman may be
      getting ready for bed on Baker Street, taking her face off
      with cool gobs of Noxzema, doing an Apricot Facial
      Scrub, brushing and flossing her pretty straight teeth,
      studying them closely in the mirror, so happy to see she
      hasn't changed a bit.

(C)   an innocent woman may be down on her knees beside the
      brass four-poster waterbed on Francis Street, praying fer-
      vently for forgiveness.

(D)   a tired, only occasionally peculiar, woman may be sitting
      at her typewriter in her study on Dunlop Street (the only
      room on the block with the lights still on, like a beacon
      in the night or, less obviously, an anchor), writing a story
      in which she tries, for no apparent reason, to make a
      connection between Christianity, astrology, and the Con-
      sumers Distributing catalogue.

(E)   none of the above.

THE GATE

We're on our way to Mapleside.

Our new station wagon — my father calls it "the suburban" — is black and my mother, fanning her face with a magazine, says for the fourth time, "I don't see why you had to have a black car, Roy. Black just absorbs the heat. I can't stand it!"

My mother's name is Natalie and she's a hairdresser. Her short dark hair, coated with hairspray, is perfect. She never touches it. I'm not supposed to tell anyone that she dyes it. As if I would.

The inside of the suburban rises around me in white folds: front seat, dashboard, doors. My father is driving too fast but I'm not worried. I'm reading all the road signs to him as they pass. The prairie unfolds around us and we're all sweating.

Up ahead, the broad-shouldered asphalt is liquefied by the sunlight. I'm expecting the car to fall off when it reaches that point where the highway seems to spill into the sky. I know it won't really — it doesn't — and I try not to be disappointed. I am twelve and I don't want to go to Mapleside today anyway.

We've already been driving for two hours and the windshield is covered with bug guts. I think I can smell them. My father swerves onto the shoulder to miss a dead skunk lying in the middle of the road. The smell makes my eyes water. My mother says, "Tomato juice. You have to use tomato juice to get the smell out." I try to imagine washing the whole car with tomato juice.

Around the next corner, there are red flashing lights and a policeman stops the traffic with a flag. We have to wait five minutes while another policeman directs a tow truck backing up to a transport truck which lies upside-down in the ditch like a giant silver beetle stuck on its back, legs waving, helpless. My mother says, "Look the other way, Sylvia. Just in case." Is that blood on the road?

Further on up the highway, my father guides the car left across the oncoming lane and pulls in past two green gas pumps.

"What are we stopping here for?" I ask.

"This gas station's the last before Mapleside," my father says. "Thought you might have to — "

" — freshen up a bit," my mother finishes. Her voice is sudden in the car — I'd thought she was asleep. "I think we could all stand to get out and stretch our legs a bit, don't you?" she continues gaily, feeling for the door handle with one hand, smoothing her dress down over nylon knees with the other, and looking back over her shoulder meaningfully at me.

I think briefly of refusing to get out of the car but realize it would be futile.

I clamber out of the back seat, my bare legs peeling off the hot upholstery like a Band-Aid. My father, lifting the legs of his suit pants and shaking them, stands beside the car and admires it.

"Do you want a pop, Syl?"

I wish he wouldn't call me that.

"No thanks, I'm not thirsty."

I am too.

My father strides purposefully away and my mother says, "Come on, Sylvia. The ladies' is over here, around the side."

I step carefully over the black tube which runs from the gas pumps to the building like a leash. I follow my mother around the side where we find a green door marked LADIES. Below the word is a painted figure, armless, with a white triangular skirt and one thick leg. This is much the way I feel in my new pink dress. My mother made it.

Inside, she runs the tap till the water comes out clear and cold, smelling of must and metal. The porcelain sink is stained brown around the drain. Holding me by the chin, she dabs at my greasy forehead with a wet lace handkerchief.

She says, "I want you to look presentable this afternoon."

I stand there obediently, concentrating on the wall over her shoulder. A hard-backed beetle inches up the tile and disappears through a hole under the wire-covered window. Lucky.

My mother keeps on talking. "Now Sylvia, this is your first funeral." As if I didn't already know that. "Your father and I have discussed it and since you'll have to go to one sooner or later, we figured it would be just that much easier on you if it was someone you weren't really close to — I know how sensitive you can be. You've only met Old Isaac once or twice and he's just a distant relative — the perfect choice, we decided." Her explanation makes me feel resentful and grateful both at once.

She lets go of me, rinses out her handkerchief, and leans close to the spotted mirror, inspecting her own face, which, of course, isn't nearly as dirty as mine.

I wait near the door, watching her draw new red lips on her mouth. The film of water on my forehead evaporates, leaving my skin feeling cooler but tight across the eyebrows. I can feel my white socks sagging around my ankles.

"There we go, we're all set," my mother announces, smacking her lips. She turns to me, smiling, and her front teeth are pink.

"You've got lipstick on your teeth," I say.

She walks past me, opens the door, and says, without looking at me, "Your socks."

As I climb back into the car, my father holds out a bottle of Orange Crush. When my mother isn't looking, I press the cold rippled glass against both cheeks.

A few minutes later, we turn right off the highway onto a gravel road. I am studying the back of my father's bald head, tracing the line between his sunburn and the smooth white dome of his skull. Being an important businessman at home in the city, he almost always wears a hat. But now, in the prairie heat, it's perched on the seat between him and my mother, white straw with a navy band. I keep thinking it will collapse like an angel-food cake. I don't really know what my father's job is, but he's always making appointments and long-distance phone calls.

My mother pulls a magazine out from under the hat and starts reading. But from the way she turns the pages so fast, licking her thumb every time, I can tell she's only looking at the pictures, which all seem to be of well-polished women and cars. Her fingers leave damp rings on the glossy pages. I try to look over her shoulder but she slaps the magazine shut and puts it back, face-down, under the hat.

My father is still driving too fast and we're leaving a cloud of dust behind us. I roll down the window and stick one arm out into the warm wind. I imagine that my skin will be instantly coated with colourless dust just like the brown weeds straggling all down both sides of the road. The wind rushes into the car.

''What're you doing back there?'' my mother says, turning in her seat. By now I've got my head halfway out the window, holding my mouth open to the wind.

''Sylvia! You close that window this minute! I don't want all that dust getting in here. Don't you forget we're going to a funeral — this isn't a picnic, you know.'' We never go on picnics anyway.

I close the window, look at my father, and roll my eyes. Watching the road ahead, his face is sweaty and blank. But I know that once we're alone, he'll shove my shoulder and snicker, saying, ''You sure know how to get your mother riled up, little girl.''

I turn my back to her and look out the rear window. She probably thinks I'm sulking. Let her. She fiddles with the radio but, impatient, gives up easily and the radio snaps back into silence like a rubber band.

I read the sign: MAPLESIDE – ONE MILE. My mother was born in Mapleside and my parents often go back for weddings, funerals, christenings, and sometimes just to visit. I seem to be related to half the town. The residents of Mapleside, all 816 of them (that's what the next sign says), have always seemed old to me, sand-coloured and dull. I can't imagine them ever living anywhere else. Even their babies look used.

The last time I was in Mapleside was two years ago when we came for the wedding of one of the cousins whose name I can never remember. My father got drunk so we stayed overnight with some more cousins — Ed and Betty Overing and their only daughter, Colleen, who live on a farm west of town.

My cousin Betty Overing is the fattest person I have ever seen. She is the daughter of this Old Isaac whose funeral we're going to this time. But he was still alive then and lived with them on the farm.

Betty's husband, Ed, was still alive then too, for a few more months anyway. Ed was a dairy farmer and always wore a dirty red bandana around his neck. I think he slept in it.

Colleen Overing was ten then, the same age as me. I had to sleep in her room. She kept putting her hands in my hair and whispering, "Pretty, pretty, you're such a pretty." She was always scratching herself and there were little round scabs all over her legs, some still bleeding. For weeks afterwards, I was sure she'd given me lice and I would wake up one morning bald like my father, with all my pretty hair just lying there on the pillow beside me.

That night, when Colleen and I were getting ready for bed, she pushed a chair in front of the door and said, "I have to show you my collection." Which turned out to be a lot of old black-and-white snapshots in a shoebox. She went through them all, one by one.

"This is my dad in the war." A much-younger Ed was standing with four other soldiers in front of a big sign that said:

DANGER: DO NOT GO BEYOND THIS POINT: VENEREAL DISEASE. They all had their arms around each other and around a black-haired woman laughing with no shoes on.

"Funny, eh?" Colleen said, poking me in the ribs. I laughed and had no idea whether it was funny or not.

"This is my grandpa killing a pig." Old Isaac had one arm stuck halfway up the pig's rear end. What?

"This is my mom chasing a chicken for supper. That's before I was born. See that bulge there? Well, that turned out to be me. Funny, eh?" Hilarious.

Before we left the next morning to go back to the city, Colleen took me out behind the chicken coop to show me the slough where her father drowned the barn cat's kittens.

This time, before we ever left home, I decided I wasn't going to let her scare me.

My father parks the suburban in front of the Mapleside Anglican Church, my mother puts on her little white gloves, and we go single-file through the churchyard gate. The church had been redone that spring in bright white clapboard and the townspeople had planted red peonies around it like a wreath.

Inside, the sunlight streams milk-coloured through new opaque windows and there are ranks of new blond pews, each with a small brass plaque nailed to the aisle end. We're ushered into a pew near the back by a bony young man whose pants are too short. His forehead is peeling with sunburn or acne. I smile at him just in case he's related but he doesn't smile back. He's no one after all.

The church is packed and people are still coming in, standing three-deep along the back wall. The whole town is here, rustling, sweating, and clearing their throats. My mother leans across me and whispers to my father, "Isn't it lovely so many people turned out?" My father's bald head nods amiably.

The congregation falls silent when the minister steps up to the pulpit. His bushy white eyebrows twitch and he's sweating too. Cocking his head like a dog, he looks out over everyone's head and seems to be talking mostly to the clock on the back wall. I can't hear him for the hum of an electric fan mounted on the wall at the end of our pew. Under the fan is a bouquet of red snapdragons and blue forget-me-nots wilting in an old jam jar of yellow water.

The woman sitting next to my mother keeps shifting around, adjusting a baby in her lap. I can't tell if the baby's a boy or a girl because its face is all scrunched up. We're all waiting for the baby to cry but it falls asleep suddenly and the mother relaxes, smiling gratefully at my mother.

A strange animal howling begins near the front of the church. The minister's mouth just keeps on opening and closing, so I decide this must be part of the funeral, something that happens all the time, one of those things my mother was trying to protect me from.

"That's Betty," my mother whispers behind her gloved hand. "You remember poor Betty." Betty has been "poor Betty" for a year and a half now, ever since her husband, Ed, went out behind the chicken coop one morning after milking and shot himself in the head.

I squirm forward, trying to get a look at her. She's still fat, maybe even fatter, and the rolls at the base of her neck wobble when she cries. I'd expected that grief would somehow make you hollow. Her shiny black dress is pulled tight across her shoulders and her bluish flesh bulges out around her sleeves. My mother pushes me back into my seat.

A faint smell of cow dung drifts back to me from the man in front. His head is nodding and I can't tell if he's sleeping or agreeing. A blue fly lands on his neck and just sits there.

Then everybody stands up and sings clumsily, picking their way through an unfamiliar hymn. My mother is singing too, her throat tight and muscular like a fist. My father stands up but doesn't sing. I've never heard him sing. At the front, all the women in the choir look bloated in their royal-blue robes. One warbling voice stands out above the other average singers. They're all singing with their eyes closed. The congregation slurs along behind them like boys in hip-waders.

From where I'm standing, I can just see one corner of the coffin. It takes me a minute to figure out that's what it is. Cool grey like seagull wings, its sides are studded with silver scrolls. It's closed and I'm disappointed because I thought I'd finally get a chance to see a real live corpse. Then again, my mother probably wouldn't have let me look anyway.

At some clandestine signal I seem to have missed, everyone starts to leave. Betty is still crying into a red bandana squashed up under her nose. Her other hand flutters at her black lace collar. Colleen is walking right behind her.

Outside, the congregation stands around in loose bunches. They're all shifting from one bunch to another or from one foot to the other in the heat. The women are talking and the men are batting at flies. Some are already making their way to their cars for the mile-long procession to the cemetery west of town. A knot of black-suited boys is moving towards the back of the church. Betty stands on the steps with Colleen and the minister, who is patting both of them alternately. Colleen stands sway-backed, watching the boys go through the back gate and out behind the church. They're all patting their pockets, looking for matches. Betty is managing a smile for the minister. I'm trailing my mother all over the yard.

"Come on, Sylvia," she says, steering me towards a circle of women who are all wearing loose flowered shifts and sensible shoes. "We have to be sociable at least. Your father's already gone to the car." I can tell she feels slighted by this.

As we approach, one of the women backs away from the group and exclaims, "Why, Natalie, I didn't see you in church. And is this your little Sylvia? My goodness, how she's grown! Dorothy, come and look at little Sylvia," she calls to one of the other women, as if I'm not really there or can't hear what she's saying. The other women draw more closely around my mother, delighted with her blue city suit and dyed-to-match peau de soie pumps. I feel proud of her.

I can see Betty and Colleen alone on the steps now, the minister circulating through the yard. Betty is gazing around vacantly while Colleen peers up at the bleached sky as if watching for rain or geese. Her black sateen dress is gathered in tight at the waist under a glossy red sash and a white paper rose. Her yellow hair is piled in uneven bunches at the back of her head. My own dark hair is curly and short because my mother doesn't believe in long hair on children. I feel clean and neat.

Colleen sees me watching her as they come single-file down the steps.

My mother moves away from the women and says, "There's poor Betty. We must go and give our condolences, Sylvia." Betty and Colleen stop, as if they're waiting for us.

"Oh, poor Betty dear, I'm so sorry," my mother croons, pressing one cheek up against Betty's. I wonder how long it will be before she dares take out her handkerchief and wipe the dirt away. "Your father was such a good man, Betty, so kind, we all loved him. His death is a blow to us all." No matter what happens, my mother always knows what to say.

"But Betty dear, we really must be going now," my mother says cheerfully. "Roy's waiting in the car. We'll drop by the farm before we head home. Will that be all right? I've brought you some things, a carrot cake and some bread-and-butter pickles. I'll see you then, dear." Betty sniffs and nods vaguely. Colleen ignores us both.

Before my mother can get to the gate, another group of women — younger relatives this time, some holding prune-faced babies and all of them smiling — have surrounded her.

"Natalie, how are you?"

"Natalie, what a lovely suit!"

"Natalie, your hair, I love the colour! I wish George would let me . . ."

I start back to the car alone.

"Hi, Sylvia." It's Colleen, and her voice is an unmistakable challenge. She never did like me. I just knew it.

She stands on the gravel walkway and puts both hands on her hips. Her hair is coming loose, hanging down her back in loops.

I am very polite. "Hello, Colleen. How are you?" My mother would have been proud of me.

"How's yourself?"

"Fine, thank you."

"What are *you* doing here?"

"Well, I'm here for the funeral — just like everybody else." But I know that's not quite what she means.

"He was my grandfather, you know," she says, jutting out her chin. This is some kind of accusation or dare.

Before I can think of an answer, she tells me, "He lived with us for years and years, you know, all my life. Every morning he sat across the table from me, eating porridge 'cause he had no teeth, just gums. They were always bleeding. He said he didn't need teeth. I have pictures of him when he was young — lots — in my collection. I always knew he would die."

Frightened by her outburst, I have no idea why she's telling me all this — she doesn't even like me. I suddenly hate my pink dress. It should have been black. Why didn't my mother tell me funerals only come in black?

"Did you cry in there?"

I shake my head. No, I didn't cry. I wasn't even listening.

My mother calls to me from the car. "Come on, Sylvia. Hurry up or we'll lose our place in line."

I start towards her but then I stop to dig for a nickel I think I see half-buried in the sand below the gate. I sift my fingers through dust, dead grass, and little stones. My mother calls again and I reach up to brush off the dirt. There was no nickel anyway. In circles I rub the sand in. The dust drifts brown down the front of my dress.

When I get to the car, I can see Colleen behind me, swinging on the gate.

LOSING GROUND

The photograph is black-and-white, printed on heavy cardboard. Two corners are chipped off like pieces of old paint. It is a picture of my grandfather sitting on a wagon in a field of grey grain. The wagon is pulled by two horses with hair like muffs around their ankles. One of the horses has its head down, one hoof extended. Its tail is caught flicking away flies, a small bird, the camera, and my ancestral eyes. The wind, which refuses to be photographed, is hung up in my grandfather's hair. This makes him look young and careless.

He was already in his eighties by the time I was born. Everyone called him Grandpa Blake and I never thought of him as having a first name.

The photograph was taken on the family farm near Balder, Manitoba. Around the time I was born, the farm was sold to a group of Mennonites. This was when my grandfather moved into Aunt Clara's house in Balder.

In all the farm stories that my mother told me, my grandfather figured as the patriarch, undisputed and self-proclaimed, a solid and sensible man. His father, my great-grandfather, was killed by the Indians when my grandfather was six days old. They threw his body in the creek and stole all the horses. I thought this was remarkable. My grandfather stayed on the farm for another eighty years and he never stopped working. At first my mother said she respected him.

When I got older and he was dead, she told me that she'd hated him.

He fathered twelve children, my mother was one of the younger ones. They all worked on the farm. The girls wore ankle-length dresses because my grandfather said showing your ankles was shameful. I imagine their skirts bunching up between their legs, the sweat trickling down their thighs, soaking through their cotton stockings. Hot prairie summer. Kerchiefs sliding down their wet foreheads, hair curling up in the sweat. Everybody wore work boots, brown lumberjack feet laced up with twine. Everybody knew what they were supposed to do. My mother figures she was born knowing how to milk the cows, bale the hay, and slop the pigs. She says, "It's taken me fifty years to forget. Finally." Sometimes now she speaks scornfully of people who are still farmers, working the land. She thinks they're doing things the hard way.

When the mares were bred with the stallion from the farm down the road, all the girls were kept inside the farmhouse. The blinds were drawn and the curtains were closed. They were also kept inside when the sow was giving birth and when Dolly, the old horse, had to be shot. All of these things, sex and birth and death, kept mixing up together. My mother thought they must be either extremely embarrassing or dangerous, something we must all be protected from. She and Aunt Clara can laugh about it now.

★ ★ ★

I never lived in Balder. My parents and I lived in Carlisle, Ontario, but every summer we went west for three weeks.

In Ontario, I was an only child and often lonely. We had no other relatives in Carlisle. But in Balder I became part of a huge dangling tribe, there were dozens of them. Like my grandfather, the rest of the Blakes (except my mother, who'd married late in life) all seemed to be exceptionally fertile, their respectives families like elongated arms stretching off in all directions. Those who didn't live in Balder were always coming out to visit, or planning to, writing long letters to Aunt Clara which she read out loud to my mother and me when I brought them home from the post office. These other relatives were the main topic of conversation among the Balder relatives and so it seemed that we were all there together at once. The bunch of them were constantly engaged in a variety of emotional activities, all of them tangled up together, waving their arms, getting married, getting into trouble (for the males this meant Jail, for the females, Unwed Pregnancy) or heading for it, having babies, moving around the country, growing older, suffering mysterious, painful, and lingering illnesses. Back home in Ontario afterwards, I tried to keep hold of them but they always faded away. They were all much more believable in the summer.

* * *

It took us one full day of driving to get from Carlisle to Balder. My father drove the whole way as my mother had never learned how. Her jobs were to light and put out his cigarettes, to pass him unwrapped sticks of Wrigley's Spearmint gum, and to keep talking so he wouldn't fall asleep. My job was to keep quiet and busy in the back seat. In aid of this end, my mother, for weeks before we left, bought a number of small items which I was not allowed to look at yet because they were *for the trip*. I thought this suspense was spectacular. The morning we left, these things appeared on the back seat in a brown paper bag which I was at last allowed to open once we were in the car, out of the driveway, and on our way. In the bag, there might be books, games you could play by yourself, sugary pink cologne in tiny bottles shaped like bells, cars, or birds, coloured pencils, notepads printed with kittens, my name, or pansies. The contents of the surprise bag kept changing as I grew older and then, I'm not sure when, it disappeared altogether.

In Balder we always stayed at Aunt Clara's house because she was my mother's favourite sister and my mother hers. This was something they had discovered only after growing up, because Aunt Clara was fourteen years older and had left the farm to get married when my mother was only six years old. Aunt Clara was a widow now.

There were about 800 people living in Balder then and the favourite joke around town was that half of them were widows. The men kept dying off and the women kept living on and on. There were old women everywhere you went. Very few of them remarried — there was nothing much left to choose from.

In Balder everybody knew me. When I walked downtown to collect Aunt Clara's mail at the post office, as I did every morning except Sunday every summer, people who passed me on the sidewalk smiled and said hello. Sometimes they called me by name and sometimes they said, "You must be Clara's little niece from Ontario." Some people drove by in their cars and waved. I waved back airily with Aunt Clara's keys (the one to her post office box held apart so I wouldn't get mixed up and embarrassed when I got there) as though I'd lived in Balder all my life.

When I was walking with my mother, some woman would always stop and say to her, "Now which sister are you?" Everybody said you could tell a Blake girl a mile off and none of them ever got any older.

More often, though, I walked with my father. Sometimes we went out in the evening. We were closer then than we ever would be again. We had discovered how much alike we were and so didn't talk much while we walked, just pointed out odd things to each other with no explanation. Occasionally someone would recognize him and say, "You must be Iris's husband and is this her little girl?" We were both hazily annoyed by this but we kept walking and never mentioned it. There was almost always heat lightning in the sky as it grew dark.

* * *

Aunt Clara looked after my grandfather for ten years. No one ever questioned this arrangement. Aunt Clara was his oldest child: it was as though she had inherited him. When she decided to put him in the home in Winnipeg, half the family was upset and the other half said it was about time. Aunt Clara paid no particular attention to either faction. After ten years, it seemed, he was all hers: she could do whatever she wanted with him. She took care of all the necessary arrangements, packed up his few clothes in a brand-new suitcase, put the suitcase in the trunk of her new Dodge, and drove him into the city herself. The black suit he was to be buried in was in the suitcase too.

In a letter to my mother, she wrote, *He'll never come out of there alive.* I took this to mean that there was little else he could be expected to do now except die. It was an unemotional issue. Most of his children were pragmatists.

That Christmas my mother sent Aunt Clara the money to buy a new pair of drapes for the living room. Inside the card, which featured a fat red Santa Claus in pince-nez reading his list and checking it twice, she wrote, *You'll never get the tobacco smell out of those old ones.* Putting the stamp on the front and two Christmas seals on the back, she turned to me and said fiercely, "When I'm too old to look after myself, I want to die. But if I don't, you just put me in a home right off the bat. You don't owe me anything!" For a few years, I thought this was both possible and true.

When we went to visit him in the home, it was a special trip to the city. My mother, my father, Aunt Clara, myself, some-times assorted cousins came too, we all went together, safety in numbers. I think they were still afraid of him. I neither dreaded nor looked forward to these trips. We usually went twice during the three weeks we spent in Balder. We drove the fifty miles to Winnipeg over easy-angled prairie backroads, watching the windshield sprout dust and dead bugs on the way. When I was younger, I counted Volkswagens and held my nose noisily whenever we passed a pig farm or a slough of dead water, curdling and thick round the edges like sour cream. When I got older, I drank warm Coke and read, sulky with impotent prepubescent anger at my mother because she had taken so long to get ready, saying, "I just have to put on my face before we go," dressing up for him, checking out her colour co-ordination and her lipstick. As though going to a lot of trouble to do something you really didn't want to do somehow made up for your reluctance.

While all these preparations went on, I waited and pouted in the garden, stealing peas and poking around in the potato hills. This brought out the garter snakes, which looked greasy but felt dry when they brushed across my bare feet. I was afraid of them but pretended not to be because I knew it annoyed my mother.

Sometimes, when I was feeling more generous, I waited on the front step, listening to the caragana seed pods bursting in the heat. The Mennonite boys drove by the house in their green pick-up truck, right fender gone. There were five or six of them, they seemed to go everywhere as a group, spitting sunflower seed shells and laughing. They waved and hollered hello as they passed, which produced in me that minor secret hysteria young girls are prone to.

On the way out of town, we always stopped at Flint's Family Store to buy a bag of peppermints for my grandfather. Flint's was the sort of place that sold everything: food, clothes, shoes, jewellery, hand-tooled genuine made-in-Canada cowhide key cases, newsprint paper in bulky pads called GIANT, and salt licks. At first I thought these last were for people. They came in different colours: blue, green, an odd red that looked like half-cooked liver. I wanted to bend down and lick one, preferably a blue one, blue being my favourite colour, but once I knew they were for cows, I was afraid I would be poisoned on the spot and die a horrible death underneath the check-out counter.

I rode in the back seat, my mother and Aunt Clara were in the front, smiling and chatting and patting each other. They saw each other just this once a year and for three weeks they talked non-stop. After a week, they were saying the same things over and over again and nobody seemed to notice but me.

My father was silent, driving in the heat, sweating and sighing. The road ahead of us glowed. By the time we got there,
the car, which was black, was coated with white dust. My father
always fussed about this and bought cans of Turtle Wax before
we went home.

★ ★ ★

The nursing home, called Paradise Retreat, was a flat, ochre-
coloured building set down like a wafer in the middle of an
asphalt parking lot. Once inside, we smiled as a group past the
front-desk matron. Past the first-floor cleaning lady, who was
always smoking, never cleaning. She was leaning, rumpled and
damp-looking, against the wall. Her cigarette, which was stuck
to her lower lip, bobbed at us as we filed past. Her teeth were
yellow, stuck into orange gums. She seemed to be flexing them
when she smiled, which was frequently and unpredictably.
Once I saw her coming through a doorway with her teeth in
her hand and her fingers in her mouth, rooting around for stray
bits of lunch.

My grandfather's room was at the far end of a long green
hallway. Corner room, corner stone, I assume the family paid
more for his corner lot. He shared the room with a man named
Harold Clausen. In the room were two beds, identically tucked
and folded. This precision allowed us to believe that he was
being well taken care of. These people were professionals, no
need to worry, no need to worry at all. My grandfather's bed
was covered with a grey blanket. There were bits of lint stuck
to it and a zigzag line of blue stitching was coming unravelled
around the edge.

The window, there was only one, was over my grandfather's
bed. Once inside the room, I stood close to the door, too shy
to move further in. From the doorway, I couldn't see out the
window. I had no idea what you might or might not see through
the net curtains.

My grandfather was always there in the room when we
arrived. He wouldn't go down to the TV room with Harold

because he couldn't see well enough. But he wouldn't admit this and he wouldn't wear the bifocals they'd fitted him with. He and Harold were nearly always angry at each other for this or some other reason. Harold called my grandfather "the old man".

"Come to see the old man, did ya? Well, good luck," Harold said. "Stubborn old goat hasn't talked to me in a week. I put his glasses on him one night when he was asleep and he wore them all morning before he even noticed." Harold thought this was a good one.

My grandfather would be sitting on the side of his bed. His slippers were red plaid, sliced open across the toes to accommodate his bulging bunions. He wore a plaid flannel shirt and baggy green work-pants held up by striped suspenders. He sucked peppermints two at a time from the bag we'd left him last time. The nurses doled out the mints so they'd last from one visit to the next. He was always accusing Harold of stealing them when he was asleep.

Sometimes he figured out who we were and sometimes he didn't. When he did, he always criticized my mother. "Iris, such a skimpy dress, can't you afford to sew yourself a new one?"

When he confused her with one of his other daughters, he said, "Where's the boy with the curly blond hair? Why didn't you bring him along?"

Once, eyeing my father, he said, "Who's this you've got tagging along with you, Iris? Where's Dan?" Dan was some phantom figure my grandfather nearly always asked about, but no one could ever identify him. We told him Dan was fine, just fine, hadn't changed a bit.

He had little to say to Aunt Clara and he never spoke directly to me. I just stood there by the door, chewing my fingernails, picking the scab on my knee, dabbing at the welling blood with a dirty Kleenex. He kept asking questions and my mother kept yelling answers into his ear, imagining that she could make him understand.

The women's ward was at the other end of the hallway. One of the women was called Old Mary. Sometimes she was docile and dim like the rest of them. Other times she rushed down the hall in her backless blue nightgown, screaming at random, at the walls, into open rooms, at her own feet. Her slippers were made of yellow terry cloth, like bags sewn shut around her ankles. Her white hair was spurting out in chunks all over her head. She ignored the nurse trotting flat-footed down the hallway behind her.

This nurse, whose name was Angela Carl, usually stopped by my grandfather's room to say hello to us. She was short and pretty with pale-red hair and pastel skin. She managed to look well-dressed in her white nurse's uniform. Her calves were thick and muscular and I imagined this came from chasing old people around.

Angela Carl told me they'd taken Old Mary's clothes away because she kept tearing them up and throwing them out the window or trying to flush them down the toilet. I had no idea whether Angela Carl thought this horrible or hilarious and no idea why she told *me* about it.

The next summer Angela Carl told my mother that Old Mary had started wandering at night too, sometimes crawling into bed with one of the old men. The night she tried to get into bed with Harold he pushed her out onto the floor. Harold was very proud of this and told us about it several times that summer, and the next one too.

He said, "I can still take care of myself."

The other men were afraid of her and hollered for the night nurse to come and save them. Old Mary also stole bars of soap from everyone and hid them in the sheets at the foot of her bed.

Aunt Clara said, "She's gone mental, poor thing."

Going mental, I discovered, was something that could happen to anybody at any time. There was no cause and no cure. Some women went mental when they got pregnant too many times or too late in life. Some men went mental from drinking too much and then they tried to kill their wives with knives, axes, pitchforks, and other assorted implements. The wife was usually saved by some passing neighbour and then she was put under sedation and the husband was taken away after being successfully subdued by four burly men from the provincial hospital. Mental people were uncommonly strong.

Some people who went mental died in the hospital. No one could tell me if these people died from being mental or from some other, less interesting, disease.

There were other people in and around Balder who were not exactly mental but who were "not right" either. This group seemed quite large considering the size of the town. Most of the people who weren't right were middle-aged bachelors who looked in women's bedroom windows at night. They were persistent but inept and so were always getting caught in the act.

One of these was Charlie Connor. The Connor family was as indigenous to Balder as our own and Charlie had been looking in bedroom windows for years. No one was seriously afraid of Charlie but, as Aunt Clara said, it was best not to encourage him. So she had blinds and brocade drapes on both bedroom windows and we all undressed in the dark. It was also important to leave the bathroom light off if you had to get up in the night. The rest of the townspeople seemed to regard Charlie and the others who weren't right as unfortunate but unavoidable nuisances.

Younger people who weren't right were "slow". They were mostly girls. This was seen simply as a sadness for the family involved, unless one of the "slow" teenagers began talking about marriage and babies, and then it became a serious scandal, something that someone should put a stop to before it got out of hand.

Aunt Clara, who knew a lot about such matters and so was my main source of information, seemed to be sorry for and scared of Old Mary both at once. When Angela Carl caught up with Old Mary and got hold of her arm, she would lead her back down the hall to her room. Old Mary walked along passively beside her, holding her hand. They swung their arms between them.

My grandfather paid no attention to Old Mary. All the nurses told us he was a model patient. I gathered we were meant to be proud of him for this. Actually, I thought he was rather dull.

Harold, on the other hand, seemed disappointed if Old Mary didn't make it down to their end of the hall before Angela Carl caught her. He took great delight in tormenting her, bulging out his eyes and opening his mouth wide, imitating her screams without making a sound. If she came too close, he poked his fingers into her matted hair and pulled. Sometimes he rushed down the hall behind her, nodding his head and flailing his arms in time with hers. Aunt Clara thought this was shameful but she laughed at him too.

Harold spent as little time as possible in their room, preferring to pass the hours in the TV room, where he flirted gently with the caved-in old women who were always knitting and passing out cups of hot lemon tea. Sometimes they bickered over who Harold liked best. He was impartial and said, "The days are so long for the ladies if I don't go round and perk them up a bit."

Every night Harold deposited his boots and his socks in the hall by the door. Every time he said, "Stop a horse dead in its tracks, that smell would. We'd be suffocated by morning if I left them in here." We all laughed politely.

My grandfather kept his boots by the bed and he wouldn't let the nurses move them to the rack behind the door. He always needed to know they were there, right there. Maybe he was expecting a fire in the night, preparing for an emergency exit. My mother told me about the night the farmhouse caught fire and he wouldn't let the children out till they'd all put on their underwear. My mother said her hair was singed and his moustache too.

★ ★ ★

It was an antique moustache, dark-red and drooping. When I was a small child, I'd duck my head down whenever he tried to kiss me. Then my mother would poke me and push me towards him. He smelled like whiskey, tobacco, and porridge. He rubbed his moustache all over my chin and down my neck. I giggled because I thought I was supposed to, but it hurt and gave me a rash.

This was when he still lived with Aunt Clara in Balder. When we stayed there, I slept in the living room on the roll-away. I lay awake and listened to dry cricket calls and trains on the main line right across the street. Aunt Clara's house was on Railway Avenue. When the passenger train came through, it was all lit up, the people inside eating and reading and talking with just their heads showing. I had never been on a train then and I was so impressed by the size, the motion of them, forward, ever forward, headlong. I imagined then that the train must cross the whole country without ever stopping.

A bed creaked at the back of the house. Then fumbling feet. My grandfather did this every night. He sighed as he stood up. He banged his thigh on the bureau, found his balance, and headed for the bathroom. I could hear the palm of his hand pressed flat against the wall, sliding across one wooden door, around the loose glass knob, over a blank space of much-painted wall, stopping at the open door. Inside. Door shut. Muttering and the sound of irregular splashing into the toilet bowl. A few minutes more and he would come out, go back to bed, snuffling and readjusting himself.

The summer before he went to the home in Winnipeg he kept falling asleep in the bathroom. Aunt Clara would get up then and lead him back to bed. They didn't speak. I kept my eyes shut and was embarrassed to be listening — I thought they both must know.

In the daytime, he fixed himself in the straight-backed chair by the stove. He smoked his pipe, burning the occasional hole in his shirt, and the steam from the kettle curled all around him. Every day at four o'clock he had one shot of whiskey, downed in one gulp right out of the shot glass. Aunt Clara gave the chair to the Indians when he went to the home the next spring.

* * *

This, the last summer that my grandfather lived in the house in Balder, was also the summer I was consumed with admiration for my cousin Lyle. He was four years older than me, the son of Uncle Maurice, my mother's youngest brother, and Aunt Fay, and he was always in trouble. That whole segment of the family, in fact, was always going through trouble of one kind or another. Their youngest daughter, Charleen, who was my age, skipped school and stole men's magazines from the drugstore. Their oldest daughter, Roxanne, who was sixteen, kept running away to Winnipeg with various young men. Until she got pregnant, and then she kept running further away to Saskatchewan with the same young man, who nobody ever referred to by name, but only as "the father". I thought Roxanne was romantically rebellious and defended her in family discussions for years afterwards.

They all lived on a farm just outside of Balder. Lyle always said, "I'm bored with this crummy place," but he made the best of it. On the farm they had fifty head of cattle, a lethargic Saint Bernard who eventually turned vicious and had to be put away, and dozens of angry white chickens who were everywhere, pecking and shitting.

Lyle knew that I liked him and so he showed me how to catch grasshoppers in a sealer jar. When the jar was half full, all legs and eyes and broken wings, Lyle produced the ball of string which he carried with him everywhere. He had me open the jar slowly while he reached in (I thought he was fearless) and pulled out one grasshopper, pinching it just behind the eyes. Sometimes the head popped right off but Lyle kept fishing around in the jar until he got one that held together. At this point, I was no longer expected to participate, but my presence as audience was essential.

Lyle stretched out a good length of string, looped and knotted it around the grasshopper's head. Then, standing on a bale of hay and balancing himself with one arm out, he tied the other end of the string to the clothesline. I could count the mosquito bites on his arm while he did this.

Once he had strung up a dozen or so grasshoppers, he moved the bale of hay underneath the pulley and sent the clothesline out across the yard and back and out and back. The grasshoppers flapped silently until their bodies dropped off, squirting out eggs or yellow juice. "Tobacco juice", my grandfather called it, laughing and spitting real tobacco juice across the yard. I thought it quite natural that Lyle was his favourite grandchild.

By the next summer my grandfather was in the home and I had decided that Lyle was a barbarian.

This was also the summer I had my first period. I'd been prepared for it by a short speech from my mother and a book, but neither one had mentioned that the blood would be so sudden, so red. Aunt Clara and my mother were excited, as though this were an accomplishment they could somehow take credit and responsibility for. Together, they rushed to the drugstore to get me "just what you need, dear" and would not let my father in on the excitement.

Up until this time, the drugstore, Lloyd's, had been my favourite place in Balder. I was always in there looking through the stacks of elementary and high school textbooks which were piled on a plywood table near the door. In Manitoba, you had to buy your own school books every year; in Ontario, they came with the territory.

The other books in the drugstore were Harlequin romances displayed on a revolving rack in the back corner. The women on the covers had perfect hair and there was always a dark man or a dark house lurking vaguely in the background. There were twelve new titles every month, which Aunt Clara bought, kept in a stack on her night table, read through in a rush, and then circulated among the other female relatives.

At the front of the drugstore, next to the door, were the postcards, local landmarks in black-and-white at five cents apiece. I bought the same ones every summer. The fire station, the new Bank of Montreal, three different views of the Anglican Church where Aunt Clara sang in the choir and belonged to the Women's Auxiliary (which meant going to meetings twice a month and making aprons and pies for their annual bazaar — and every year, cross-stitching, she said, "I don't know why that Liddie MacAllister even bothers. All she ever brings is a pound cake and they're so plain . . . I just don't see it!"). There were also two postcard views of Main Street, one looking west, the other east, down a line of clean cars angle-parked on both sides of the street (for years I thought the signs said "*Angel* Parking Only" and this was one of the great mysteries of Manitoba which did not occur in Ontario).

After my mother and Aunt Clara rushed back to the house with their (my) box of Kotex wrapped in brown paper, I could think of the drugstore only as an embarrassing place where you went to buy "Sundries". I thought this was the polite adult word for Kotex.

I was angry and I said, "I bet the Queen doesn't have this!", gesturing wildly at my lower abdomen.

My mother laughed indulgently and said, "You're a woman now." I thought this was ridiculous but didn't say so. For the first time in my life, I realized there were things about myself that were supposed to be kept hidden.

* * *

Just back from the home one day in July, Aunt Clara said, "He's losing ground." She arranged herself at the kitchen table with her mending basket and a cup of tea. She spread my green-flowered blouse, the one with the ripped armpit, in her lap. "This'll just take me a minute," she said to me.

That day, which was my birthday, my grandfather, despite the nurses' assurances, had seemed much worse. I had complained about going to see him on my birthday — it wasn't my idea of a suitable celebration. My mother said I was being selfish: "You might never see him again, you know." This was some kind of threat. I wasn't sure why it worked but it did.

He didn't recognize any of us that day and his eyes seemed to have grown more opaque, covered with a shiny scum that made me think of a raw egg oozing over a white tile floor. He was very pale, even his lips were white. My mother told me this was because your blood gets thinner when you get old. He had been in the home for almost four years.

When we got back to Balder, we had the birthday cake. As usual, we looked and looked for the candles. Aunt Clara always put them away in a safe place. This time we found them in the cupboard above the stove. They were all bent out of shape by the heat and stood at odd angles around the cake in all the customary colours: pastel pink, blue, green, and white like nurses' uniforms or bathroom walls. My father lit the candles and then, after I blew them out, my mother cut the cake.

Aunt Clara dished out the pieces as we arranged ourselves around the kitchen table in the heat. I was wearing my new short-shorts, a present from Aunt Clara, who said I had the legs to pull it off. My thighs stuck to the chair and I thought about the drive across the prairie all the way to Aunt Clara's. I was stuck to the seat then too and I kept putting my arm straight out the window, feeling the wind. My mother, when she caught me, said this was a dangerous thing to do because the force of the air would suck me right out the window. I thought this was ridiculous and said so. She said, "Don't be cheeky with me, young lady."

The birthday cake was my favourite kind: chocolate layer with boiled white icing. It was growing dark while we ate and mosquitoes made sounds like pins dropping on the window screens. Moths flickered around the outside light.

Looking out the corner windows, I saw a drunk Indian coming up the sidewalk, weaving but stepping on every crack with some determination. Step on a crack, break your mother's back. There were still some angry days when I jumped fiercely on the cracks with both feet, seeking revenge.

I looked away from the window with a curdled feeling in my stomach. Maybe if I asked for more cake, no one else would notice him. I knew that the mere sight of him would provoke instant anger in my mother and Aunt Clara. They would sigh and be disgusted and then they would compete grimly with each other for the worst Indian story, the most outraged sensibilities. I was at an age where I could not bear dissension: it made me want to throw up. I was afraid of all kinds of anger. I wanted everyone in the world to get along. I was always running around intervening in other people's, adults', arguments. I thought I could control everybody if only I worked at it.

He was still coming closer to the house. He stopped right in front, right where the lawn had been cleverly sloped, carefully landscaped to furnish the family with both aesthetic pleasure and good drainage. His back was towards me now, I could see just the edge of his white underwear above his pants. He kept tugging at the waist of his jeans, he had no belt, no hips to hold them up — had drunk them all away, lost them in a back alley somewhere on the other side of town, or maybe in the all-night truck stop out on the highway. My mother wouldn't let me go there because she said that's where all the Indians went to drink coffee and try and sober up, which, she said, was impossible.

He lay down on the lawn, pillowing his head on one arm. I thought he might have to spend all night there. Maybe he belonged to one of the families who lived across the highway in abandoned cars with dangling headlights and no tires.

Aunt Clara came up behind me. "Bastards!" she said, so close to my ear that I jumped.

In a minute, she was gone from behind me and then she was out in the front yard too. She thrashed one arm at a swarm of mosquitoes and carried the broom in the other. Her mouth was moving but I couldn't hear what she was saying, not through that double layer of safe suburban glass. Like watching the late-night movie with the sound turned off. She poked at him with the broom. He looked up at her stupidly. It was dark now, there was heat lightning in the west, and I couldn't see the expression on his face, only the quizzical canary tilt of his head.

Trying to stand up, he stumbled and Aunt Clara almost put out a hand to help him. But she caught herself in time and snatched it back. Her knuckles were white around the broom handle. He was moving away.

Aunt Clara came back into the kitchen, squeezing a sliver out of her thumb. She put the broom back in the corner. She and my mother shook their heads together. He had been some kind of threat to them, but his power did not extend to my father who was in the living room now, reading the paper and having a drink of rum. Aunt Clara said, "There's more of them every year, they keep moving in from the reserve, we're losing ground."

When the phone rang about an hour later, Aunt Clara and my mother were at the sink, doing up the dishes. My mother was drying, Aunt Clara was washing and saying, "I'll do them, Iris, there's only a few, you go and sit down." But my mother kept hold of the tea towel on which was printed a map of Manitoba with a calendar inside it. She stood her ground and kept on drying the little plates which were painted with blue roses and a trim of gold leaves. I was moving between the kitchen and the living room, not sure whether I wanted to be with my father, who was still reading, or with Aunt Clara and my mother, who were talking about some woman I didn't know. Aunt Clara was saying, "She may be a breed but you'd never know it to look at her wash . . . so white, just beautiful." My mother was agreeing that the state of a woman's washing was very significant.

When the phone rang, we all turned and looked at it. It was nearly midnight. Drying her hands on her apron, Aunt Clara said, "Now who can that be at this hour?" I heard my father in the living room shake his paper and mutter, "Well, answer it and find out."

We watched Aunt Clara who was listening into the receiver and nodding.

She hung up and said, "Grandpa died in his sleep, not a heart attack or anything, he just died. The night nurse found him on her rounds."

Everybody was quiet at first and then they said it was a blessing really.

We went to the nursing home once more after that. We had to gather up his things, sign some papers which would make his death official and legal.

When we went in past the front desk, the matron was flipping through papers in a manila file folder. She didn't look up but smiled automatically at the sound of our feet on the linoleum.

Harold was still there and my grandfather's bed was already being used by another old man who was asleep in a lump. Harold, who knew something about everybody, said his name was Jack Manywounds and he had been an unsuccessful rodeo cowboy. "Not much fun any more though," Harold said.

No one said anything about Jack being an Indian. I supposed there was either something about this place or something about being old and asleep that removed all that, made everyone equally harmless.

When we left, Harold said he was sorry we wouldn't be coming back.

* * *

Summers at Aunt Clara's continued and there were still pilgrimages to be made. We went to the Balder Cemetery now. We went more frequently to the cemetery than we had to the home — these visits were less demanding — no conversation, no diplomacy, no peppermints.

The names on the headstones were unfamiliar at first but Aunt Clara, like Harold, knew something about everybody and I soon learned most of the names. There was one family who'd lost five children, all of them stillborn. They had five white headstones set in a row, with little sculptured lambs on top. There were also half a dozen suicides, unofficial of course, but Aunt Clara always knew what had really happened. My grandfather's grave was sealed with cement to prevent erosion and gopher holes. Aunt Clara planted peonies at the headstone.

The Indian graveyard was at the north end of the cemetery. The grass there had never been mowed and most of it had gone to seed. It looked like wheat. There were no headstones in the Indian graveyard, only the occasional white wooden cross heaved out of place by the frost. In some places, where the grass was thin, you could see that the ground had sunk down two or three inches where the bodies were.

Nobody tended the Indian graveyard and nobody ever came around. They knew that none of their dead kin would get away. They didn't have to keep making that weekly bed-check like we did, coming back for reassurance. There were no flowers on the Indian graves. I kept wanting to lie down in the long grass where I imagined I would be hidden and ignored, sweet-smelling.

STRANGER THAN FICTION

Any number of people will tell you that truth is stranger than fiction. They will usually tell you this as a preface to the story of how their Aunt Maude was frightened by a bald albino juggler at the East Azilda Fall Fair when she was six months pregnant (the juggler, himself frightened by a disoriented cow that had wandered into the ring, lost control of five airborne bowling pins, and one of them hit poor old Maude square in the back of the head) and later she gave birth to a bald brown-eyed baby, Donalda, who was allergic to milk and her hair grew in so blonde it looked white and now she's unhappily married to a man who owns a bowling alley in downtown Orlando.

Or they will tell it to you as an afterword to the story of how Rita Moreno appeared to their best friend Leona's first cousin Fritz in a dream, doing the Chiquita Banana routine and feeding the fruit off her hat to a donkey, and sure enough, the next day, Fritz, who was an unemployed actor, got his big TV break doing a commercial for Fruit of the Loom underwear and he was the grapes.

Oh sure, lots of people will tell you, and with very little provocation too, that truth is stranger than fiction. But I, now I have got THE PROOF.

★ ★ ★

I was writing a story about a woman named Sheila. Apropos of nothing, the name Sheila, I discovered, is an Irish form of Cecilia, from the Latin, meaning "blind". In the story, Sheila was thirty-two years old, slim, attractive, and intelligent with blue eyes and straight blonde waist-length hair. (I often give my fictional characters blue eyes and blonde hair because I have brown eyes and brown hair and I don't want anyone to think my work is autobiographical. Also, my hair is naturally curly, short.)

Sheila was married to a handsome brown-haired man named Roger, a bank manager, and they lived in a ranch-style bungalow in Tuxedo Park. Sheila amused herself by taking aerobics one afternoon a week, doing volunteer work at the senior citizens' home, and having long lunches a lot with her friends. She and Roger got along well enough, although every once in a while Sheila would remember that they hadn't had a meaningful conversation in four years. They lived an easy life, gliding gracefully and politely around each other like ice-dancers.

So then I made Sheila unhappy in her heart of hearts: because what's a good story without a little angst?

The thing was, Sheila wanted to be someone else. Sheila wanted to be a Country-and-Western singer. She knew all the words to all the best songs, which she practised by singing along with the compact disc player while Roger was away all day at the bank. She had a special secret wardrobe stashed in the back of her walk-in closet off the master bathroom. On the cover of her first album, she wanted to see a picture of herself astride a white horse in her chaps in the wind. Having never been much bothered by either self-doubt or self-examination, it did not even occur to her that she might very well be crazy or untalented.

Then she met a man named Carlos in a specialty record store called Country Cousins. Carlos bore a startling resemblance to Johnny Cash in his younger days. Of course they hit it off right away because they were both looking for that old Patsy Cline album with "I Fall To Pieces" on it. They went for a beer at The Hitching Post, a nearby country bar where, as it turned out, Carlos's band, The Red Rock Ramblers, was playing. They were only in town for the week, having just spent two months on the road, and now they were heading home to Saskatoon. Feeling gently homesick, Carlos talked a lot about the prairies, which Sheila had never seen, about the way they'll change colour in a thunderstorm or a dangerous wind, the way they'll make you think of things you've never thought before because you can see them forever and they have no limits. So by the time he got around to also telling her he had a wife and three kids out there, it was too late to turn back now, because he already had his hand on her thigh and his tongue in her ear.

I was having a bit of a time of it in my own life right then. Three and a half weeks earlier I had fallen in love with a man named Nathan who was from Winnipeg and also married. This was in July and it was hot, humid, and hazy; it was hard to concentrate. I was downtown Friday night having a drink at The Red Herring, which is an outdoor patio bar with a magnolia tree, orange poppies, handsome waiters, and blue metal tables sprouting red-and-white umbrellas advertising Alfa Romeo, Noilly Prat, and OV. The regular clientele consists largely of writers, painters, and jazz piano players who are just taking a little break in the sun. Nobody ever really gets drunk at The Red Herring: they just relax, recharge, have pleasant informed conversations about postmodernism, Chinese astrology, and free trade. They are intense and innocent.

Nathan was drinking alone and so was I, leaning against the stand-up bar inside. I'm not even sure now how we first got talking but, lo and behold, the next thing you know, he's telling me that he's a writer too! Well, you can just imagine my joy at discovering we had the whole world in common. He wrote poetry, mind you, whereas I write fiction, but I was willing, for the most part, to overlook this minor discrepancy. He was in town for a weekend workshop at the university. He was dynamic, sensitive, intelligent, funny, clean-shaven, tall, fairly well-off, very supportive, unhappy in his marriage, and he'd even read my books. So what else could I do? (Caught now in the act of recollection, I recognize how flimsy all this sounds, but at the time it was compelling.)

We found a table on the patio and drank a bottle of expensive white wine while talking about our favourite writers, books, and movies, our favourite foods, colours, and seasons, and the worst reviews our respective books had ever received. We congratulated ourselves on being so much alike and ordered another bottle of wine.

He did not talk about his wife, except to say that she wasn't fond of wine, and her name was never mentioned. (I already knew from Sheila that a married man who does not call his wife by her name is pretty well ripe for the picking.) So it was easy enough, sad to say, to keep forgetting about her.

I forgot about her as we walked back to my house arm in arm at midnight, singing a slow country song, and he was the slide guitar. I did remember her as he undressed me in the living room, but I forgot about her again as he took me in his arms and his skin was so cool. I remembered her when he sighed in his sleep, but I forgot about her again in the morning when we had a shower, some coffee, and he read to me from *The Norton Anthology of English Literature*.

Then I read him the story of Sheila so far and he said he really loved it. I took this to mean that he loved me too.

Afterwards, he told me about his teacher one summer at a writers' workshop years ago in Edmonton and this teacher was a big influence on him, always telling him, "Life ain't art." I wasn't sure how to apply this apparent truism to my own life/work but I agreed eagerly, as if it were something I'd known all along.

It was shortly after this that Carlos in the story began to look less like Johnny Cash and more like the young George Gordon, Lord Byron. He admitted that when he retired from the music business, he might take up writing. Sheila recalled, but did not relate, the story she'd heard of a writer and a doctor chatting at a cocktail party and the doctor said, "When I retire and have nothing else to do, I think I'll take up writing," so the writer said, "That's a good idea! When I retire and have nothing else to do, I think I'll take up brain surgery."

Carlos told Sheila that everybody has a book in them somewhere just waiting to be written and Sheila wondered, briefly, where the book in her might be right now: lodged behind some major organ perhaps, her liver, her lungs? She had this recurring dull ache, sometimes in her left breast, sometimes in her right. It worried her occasionally, usually late at night, and then she would lie in bed beside Roger, feeling her breasts through her pink cotton nightie, looking for lumps, holding her breath. Roger, who, she was convinced, could have slept through Armageddon, sighed dreamily and draped his left arm straight across her breasts by accident, so that she lay there pinned and pleading with God. She had come to think of this pain as her "heartache" but now she wondered if it might just be a book trying to get out.

I told Nathan this pink cotton nightie of mine had once belonged to my mother who was dead now, of lung cancer, though she'd never smoked a day in her life. He said he understood my not liking to sleep in the nude and I was relieved, as this is a point some men get funny about, as if it were an insult to intimacy or their masculinity. I told him that I might like to write a book about my mother someday, as she had led an interesting life, and he assured me that everybody has a story worth telling and I'd have no trouble finding a market for that sort of human-interest thing.

I told him how my first boyfriend had convinced himself that he would die young, tragically, in great pain, and alone. His name was Cornell and he suffered from migraines and whole days during which he could not climb out from under this escalating burden of impending doom. I felt guilty for dumping him but I could not let go of my own romantic fantasy of growing old beside my one true love and we would bring each other freshly fluffed pillows and cups of weak tea as the time drew near.

Sheila touched her breasts and felt nothing. Roger in the morning was always cheerful and animated, so she never told

him about the pain and the sad certainty of something that
would come to her at five in the morning when the earth shifts
imperceptibly on its axis and everything changes or begins to
be the same all over again. When she told this to Carlos between
sets at the bar, he said how his six-year-old daughter often woke
screaming from nightmares in which she was afraid of everything and then he would lie beside her all night while she sighed
and foundered feverishly.

At five in the morning on Sunday, Nathan got up to catch a
plane and I kissed him quietly goodbye without asking how
old his children were.

I am comfortable enough with the derivative aspects of Sheila's story in relation to my own. I am accustomed by now to
this habit fiction has of assuming the guise of reality. I am no
longer surprised to go out one night for New York steak with
baked potato (medium-rare, sour cream, and bacon bits) and
the next day my characters are enjoying the very same meal
(well-done, mind you, hold the bacon bits, yes, I'll have the
cheesecake please). I no longer find it unsettling to see the
woman beside me in a bookstore leafing through a paperback
called *How To Live With A Schizophrenic* and when I get home,
the next thing you know, there's a schizophrenic in my story
and that book is really coming in handy.

So the whole time I was putting Sheila through her paces, I
was also thinking, with some other side of my brain, about
Nathan. I wasn't seriously expecting a letter or anything as
incriminating as that. I did hope that he might get very drunk
some time and call me up in the middle of the night, begging
and reciting love poems. I knew this wasn't something he ever
could or would (considering his wife, his kids, the prairies and
all) do sober. This just shows you how little I wanted, how
little it would have taken, how very little I was asking for.

But then again, in a different mood (more confident, more
optimistic, very nearly jaunty), I was also thinking: Well, why
not? Why couldn't he, after sleeping with me just that one
weekend, go back to his bungalow in Winnipeg, pack up his

word processor, leave his wife, his kids, the dog, and the algae-eater, and come back to me with tears in his eyes and a lump of love in his throat? I would pick him up at the airport of course (all good romantic fantasies should incorporate at least one airport scene or maybe a bus station at midnight, or rain, high winds, a blizzard, a taxi at the very least, with a surly, silent driver and the meter running), where we would float across the mezzanine and fall into each other's well-dressed tingling arms while all around us dark-skinned foreign families wept on each other and tried to catch their luggage on that stupid whirligig.

Well? Why not?

Stranger things have happened. Which is another of those truisms that people will present you with just before they tell you about the time they picked up a hitch-hiker on the highway halfway between Thunder Bay and Winnipeg and he turned out to be from Wabigoon where their friends, the Jacobsens, used to live and he didn't really know them but he'd heard of them and he'd seen the same flying saucer they'd seen in 1975, August 17, 11:38 p.m.

Many of these stranger things are duly documented in the weekly tabloids which I buy occasionally at the A&P when I think no one is noticing. I take solace from the headlines, tell them to my friends, and we all laugh, comforted to know that:

MICHAEL JACKSON WAS THE ELEPHANT MAN IN HIS PAST LIFE
FLEA CIRCUS GOES WILD WITH HUNGER AND ATTACKS
TRAINER
MARRIAGE LASTS FOUR HOURS — GROOM WANTED TO WEAR
THE WEDDING GOWN
TERRIFIED TELEPHONE OPERATOR CLAIMS, MY HUSBAND
TRAINED ROACHES TO ATTACK ME
HUBBY WHO GAVE KIDNEY TO WIFE WANTS IT BACK IN
DIVORCE BATTLE
MEN FIGHT DUEL FOR GIRL'S LOVE WITH SAUSAGES.

So yes, stranger things have happened in the past. And the future, on a good day, extends eternally the promise of more.

About the time I got Sheila to the point in the story where she was actually going to get up on stage at The Hitching Post (Roger thought she was at a Tupperware party) and sing ''I Fall To Pieces'' (she had her satin shirt on, her fringed buckskin jacket, her cowboy boots, and everything), I accidentally thought of a girl named Sheila Shirley Harkness who was in my grade nine History class. She was not a friend of mine. In fact, I avoided her, because the one time we did have lunch together in the cafeteria, she ate half my French fries right off my plate and told me the story of how her Uncle Norman had killed himself by slamming his head in the car door. Sheila Shirley Harkness was older than the rest of us because she'd failed grade eight twice. Her mother was that woman who walked around the neighbourhood in her curlers and a mangy fur coat, twirling a baton, singing to herself, and waving her free hand like a flag. My mother said she should be ashamed of herself, acting like that in public, as if this bizarre behaviour were something we all secretly wanted to exhibit but we knew better.

Sheila Shirley Harkness was so fat that she had to sit in a special desk. And she smelled, although this was something we girls never discussed amongst ourselves because maybe we were afraid that we smelled too.

Sheila Shirley Harkness gave birth to a six-pound baby boy eight days before final exams. She was one of those girls sometimes written up in the tabloids who say they never knew they were pregnant: she thought she had something wrong with her, cancer, gas, or a blocked intestine. When the baby's head came out in the bathroom at three in the afternoon, she thought she was dying, turning inside out before her very own horrified eyes. She dropped out of school then, out of sight, and kept the baby, Brian, at home. There was surprisingly little speculation as to who the father might be. It was not unimportant;

rather, it was unimaginable. Immaculate conception seemed more likely than Sheila in bed with a boy, any boy, moaning.

This first Sheila (or this *second* Sheila, according to your perspective on such matters as fact/fiction, life/lies, and the boundaries or dependencies like veils hung between them) has receded fairly fuzzily into my memory now and so was probably not quite the girl I remembered anyway, was probably less frightening, less doomed, might well be working at this very minute as a high-level executive for a major advertising firm, living in a harbourfront condo with an original Matisse in the loft, brass end tables, and a marble Jacuzzi, rather than lying around all day in her underwear (yellowed or grey, the elastic shot), eating maple-walnut ice cream and watching *I Love Lucy* reruns while her mother bangs her head against the wall in the basement and her illegitimate children run rampant through the neighbourhood in their dirty diapers, as we all, in the grip of our mutually hard-hearted shiny-haired adolescence, assumed she would end up.

Either way, the first Sheila was not at all like the second, like *my* Sheila, as I had come to think of her. *My* Sheila was, among other things, friendly, cheerful, clever, clear-skinned, well-educated, long-legged, ambitious, and sweet-smelling. Her last name was Gustafson and her middle name was Mary, although neither of these names actually appeared in the story. Her parents, for the sake of simplicity, were either dead or living on Ellesmere Island and so didn't bother her much any more.

Being a fictional character, my Sheila was not obliged to explain herself to anyone or to divulge her darkest fondest secrets to total strangers. Unlike myself (with my disarming or disturbing tendency to spill my guts, to tell the worst about myself to anyone who will listen), unlike myself (me having yet to accurately determine the difference between revealing and defending yourself), unlike myself (me having only recently figured out that most people don't tell the truth about themselves, not even *to* themselves, because they don't know it, like it, or remember it), Sheila knew when to keep her mouth shut.

Nevertheless, my Sheila started to subtly change. She started feeling sluggish all the time. She wore the same old dress three days in a row. She bought a baton. She ate two cheeseburgers, a large fries, and an order of chili and toast at one sitting in a greasy spoon in a bad neighbourhood. For a minute there, she questioned the meaning of life, if there even was one, if there even *should* be one. She sniffed her armpits in public. She was on the verge of a transformation, threatening to rewrite her whole life, not to mention the story. I was having none of this.

It is for fear of exactly this sort of thing that I try never to call my fictional characters by the names of people I have really known, even just in passing. So I tried to change her name in the middle of the story. First I tried to call her Janet, then Beth, then Brenda, Delores, and Laura.

But no. None of the new names would do:

Janet was too responsible.

Beth was too timid and kept threatening to die of scarlet fever.

Brenda was too easily satisfied.

Delores was the name of my friend Susan's Irish setter bitch and her hair was red.

Laura was the woman who came to demonstrate a talented but over-priced vacuum cleaner all over my living room for an hour and a half one Wednesday afternoon and she was sorry she'd never heard of me but she didn't get much time to read any more what with this new job and her two-year-old twins, not to mention her husband, Hal, and did I know Danielle Steel personally, and when I said I didn't have $2,000 to spend on anything, let alone a stupid vacuum cleaner, she said, "Now that's funny, I thought all writers were rich."

So Sheila stayed Sheila and I struggled to keep her on the right track, would not give her permission to gain weight, pick her nose, or stay in bed with her head covered up till three in the afternoon. I would not allow her, much as she tried, to dream about babies born in bathtubs, buses, or a 747 cruising over Greenland at an altitude of 22,000 feet. Against my better judgement, I did allow her one nightmare about her mother having joined a marching band, playing the bagpipes with a sound like a cat being squeezed, and the parade stretched from one end of the country to the other, but at the very last minute her mother turned into Tammy Wynette and everything worked out all right.

Sheila got a little surly with me sometimes but that was understandable, considering her situation, her frustration, and human nature being what it is.

One Friday afternoon, when I'd manoeuvred Sheila around to the place in her life where she either had to shit or get off the pot, I decided to go down to The Red Herring for a drink instead. Sheila had been a big hit at The Hitching Post. Carlos had professed his love and offered her a job with the band. She hadn't vacuumed the house all week and Roger hadn't even noticed. Two things remained unclear: what was Carlos going to do about his family back in Saskatoon and why was Roger so dense? Now Sheila either had to pack up her buckskin and join the band (Carlos was waiting outside in a cab with the meter running, off to the airport any minute now) or go home and cook a tuna casserole for Roger (who was stuck in rush-hour traffic at the bridge, fuming, sweating, and listening to the stock-market report on the car radio). To the naked eye, this would seem like a simple choice, but Sheila didn't know what she wanted to do and neither did I. I wanted to make her live happily ever after (if only because I thought this would bode well for Nathan and me), but happy endings have fallen out of favour these days — modern (or should I say postmodern?) readers being what they are (that is, intelligent, discerning, and slightly cynical), they find them just too hard to believe, too much to hope for, fake. Could I really hope to convince any of them that stranger things have happened?

I was tense and thought a drink or two might do the trick. Going to The Red Herring in the afternoon is not like going down to, say, The Sunset Hotel, where they have table-danc-ing, four shows a day, and the regulars, in the manner of serious drinkers, gaze deeply into their glasses of draft between mouth-fuls, dredging there for answers or hope because they don't know where else to look. Some woman in gold glitter high-heels and pink short-shorts is dancing by herself and the old guy in the back booth is sleeping with his head on his arms, having just wet himself or thrown up under the table.

The Red Herring, on the other hand, is a classy place, and having a drink or even two or three there in the afternoon, especially on a Friday, is an acceptable enough thing for a real writer, even a female one, to do. I imagined that as I sat there sipping, my writer's block would be hanging off me with a certain attractive, highly intelligent sheen.

I mean, what can you expect of writers anyway when they are prone to sitting around all day with their heads full of events that never happened to people who never existed while con-ducting conversations that never took place in carefully deco-rated rooms that will never be built?

Besides, it was at The Red Herring where I first met Nathan, so that was another good enough reason to go there. If I am fortunate enough to get the same table (towards the back, to the left), I can imagine that he is sitting across from me, we are drinking dry white wine and smiling, holding hands, and making plans. In this fantasy, his wife is not, as you might expect, dead, confined to a sanatorium, or cheerfully giving him a divorce — she has simply vanished, vaporized, dropped off the face of the earth like rain. She might even be alive and well on another planet, having assumed a whole new identity with the papers to prove it, living out her life like a pseudonym.

So I fix my eyes on the empty chair and construct long loving conversations with Nathan, who is always wearing the same navy T-shirt and white cotton pants because that's all I ever knew him in. Sometimes I get carried away and catch myself nodding and moving my lips, smiling away to beat the band. I can only hope that the other patrons, on seeing this, take me for one of those independent strong-minded women who is always inordinately pleased with her own company. But then I remember that Ann Landers column where someone complained about always being told to smile and Ann reminded her that people who walk around smiling all the time for no reason are often followed by unsmiling men in white coats.

No such luck that day though — the only empty table was one to the right just beneath the magnolia tree. Our table was occupied by four cheerful young women in straw hats and lacy sundresses. They were eating elaborate beautiful salads and toasting the glorious day with Perrier and lime. I had no reason to resent, dislike, or envy them, but I did anyway.

I ordered a peach schnapps with orange juice which is called a Fuzzy Navel, so of course the waiter and I had a chummy little chuckle over that. Then I sat back to nurse my drink and read an article in *Harper's Magazine* called ''The Credible Word'' by John Berger.

At the very beginning, he said: ''Today the discredit of words is very great.''

And in the middle: ''A scarf may demand more space than a cloud.''

And finally: ''The pages burning were like ideal pages being written.''

I took this to be a validation of sorts and flipped through the rest of the magazine feeling light-hearted, encouraged, and close to inspired. (It is, I have frequently found, much easier to feel inspired in a nice restaurant, facing up to all that good cutlery, fine china, fresh pasta, and crisp lettuce, than it is in my office, facing up finally to the typewriter and all that blank paper.)

Skimming next through the ''Harper's Index'', I could not help but feel secure and confirmed in the knowledge that the number of brands of bottled water sold in the United States is 535, the number of fish per day that a Vermonter may shoot in season is 10, the price of an order of sushi at Dodger Stadium is only $4.50, and the number of Soviets in Petrozavodsk who were crushed to death in liquor-store line-ups last year was 3.

I felt myself to be having, after all, one of those dizzying days in which everything can be connected, all ideas can be conjugated and then consumed whole, sense and significance are dropped into your lap like gifts, and the very cast and camber of the air on your cheek is meaningful.

Stranger things, yes.

I ordered another drink and an appetizer, the liver pâté and some French bread.

I eavesdropped intermittently on the couple at the next table who were talking about their old dog, Shep, who was going blind, poor thing, about their new vacuum cleaner, and a misguided woman named Lisa who was looking for trouble and she was sure going to get it this time, couldn't she see that guy was no damn good?

I felt a tap on my right shoulder. I was feeling so happy and self-absorbed that I thought, without wonder, that it must be Nathan or God. It was a woman in a pale pink pantsuit, carrying one small grocery bag and a white wicker purse. She looked to be in her sixties. She said, "Please may I join you? There's nowhere to sit."

What could I do? I nodded as she took the chair beside me. She ordered a screwdriver and some escargots in mushroom caps. She said, "I like a long lunch with my friends."

I could see right away there was something *good* about her, something motherly and kind. A pair of bifocals lay on her chest, hung from a golden chain, and she'd put a blue rinse in her white waved hair. I thought of my own mother once saying that sometimes all she really wanted was a place to lay her head but why was it so hard to put it down there in the first place? This was after my father had left her for a younger woman.

I was glad enough for the company of a stranger. As opposed to family and friends, strangers will believe anything you tell them and they are less likely to ask you what's wrong right when you thought you were doing just fine. They will not tell you that you look tired on a day when you thought you felt terrific. A stranger will tell you any story as if it were true. Often I have envied total strangers on the street: just the inscrutable look of them makes it obvious that their lives are better than mine, more normal, more simple, and perfect, yes, perfect . . . perfect strangers.

"Hello," the woman said, "my name is Sheila."

I, rendered helpless in the face of coincidence, said, "Hello." It was the kind of thing that if you put it in a story, nobody would believe it. I recovered myself quickly enough because, after all, what possible harm could there be in exchanging pleasantries on a pleasant afternoon with a kind woman who happened to be, through no fault of her own, named Sheila?

It made little difference that I'm no good at small talk because this third Sheila (or was she, chronologically speaking, because of her age rather than her advent, the *first* Sheila?) proved to be exceedingly talkative. In the course of the conversation, I had to tell her very little about myself, virtually nothing in fact, except to say once, when her momentum was interrupted by the arrival of dessert (chocolate almond cheesecake) and her story was stalled, that I was a writer, single, no children, said to be successful.

She told me with detailed delight about a recent trip to the mountains she'd made with her younger sister, Serena, who had the glaucoma, and how you see things differently, more clearly, more brilliantly, bright, when you have to describe and explain them to somebody else, the blind or a child.

She confided that one of the hardest things about getting older was the feeling that your body was turning on you, falling to pieces one thing at a time, and also the hair, which got thinner and thinner and she never ever wanted to become one of those sad old ladies that you can see through to their pathetic pink scalp. In high school, she said, she had been much envied for her hair which was long and lustrous, a deep burnished red, and when she marched in the school parade twirling her silver baton, her hair swung and bounced, beautiful in the soft sun.

She talked about her children, three of them, two boys and a girl, who were all grown up now and living in other cities. She understood that but still, she missed them.

Mostly she talked about her husband, Victor, who had died tragically in a car crash in a snowstorm in December 1963, four days after they'd bought their first home, a brick bungalow on Addison Street downtown. She still lived in that house and every day she thought about her Victor, wondered if he'd have liked the new wallpaper in the bedroom, the beige shag carpet in the front room, the placemats, the blue towels, the new tuna casserole recipe, the microwave.

No, she'd never remarried. Things were different in those days: a new husband had never occurred to her. With her Victor gone, she just figured she'd had all she was ever going to get of or from love, for better or worse. She was satisfied, she said. She'd lived a lovely life, she said. For some things, yes, she agreed, yes, it was too late now. It was too late now to turn back. It was too late now to turn her back on what she had created: three children, the house, those long-felt heart-held memories of her Victor who, like all the young dead, had never aged, never betrayed her, never ever broke her heart again. Why would she want to change anything after all?

Why indeed? Why did I find all this so hard to believe: me with my constant chronic longing, my searching, my secret sadness at those moments when I should have been happy, me with this annoying ache always stuck in my heart or my head? "Why create trouble where there isn't any?" I'd asked myself often, asked myself now.

"Now I have this pain," she said unexpectedly. "This funny pain, *here*," she said, pressing the palm of her hand to her breast, which was draped with a silk scarf dramatically patterned with bright large tigers in various predatory poses.

My own hand twitched with wanting to reach across and touch her but I was afraid there would be nothing there . . .

. . . no woman
. . . no breast
. . . no scarf
. . . no tigers
. . . just air

. . . the palpable eloquent air pushing down from the swollen storm clouds which were gathering above us.

The patio was emptying quickly under the threat of rain. All around us, women were scooping up their purses and packages like prizes, gaily preparing to just disappear.

I walked slowly back to my car in the underground parkade where I'd left it.

I was tired suddenly and rested my head for a minute on my arms wrapped round the steering wheel. I thought of a morning not long ago when a navy-blue Oldsmobile had pulled up suddenly in front of my house while I sat at the breakfast table in my nightie, hovering over my third cup of black coffee. The driver, a stranger, a bearded young man in a plaid shirt, sat there for a full five minutes with his head like this on the wheel. Then he drove slowly away, leaving me alone again, alone again to speculate in the dappled moted sunlight.

I hesitated as I left the parkade, not sure which way I wanted to turn, which route home I wanted to take. A man in a baseball cap in a brown van behind me leaned so hard on his horn that my eyes filled in an instant with angry insulted tears.

I turned left into the rush-hour traffic and drove on.

Sometimes on my way home from The Red Herring these days, I can imagine a car (red with black interior, air scoop, chrome, shining) running the red light at 100 kph, rocketing through the intersection, hitting my car on the driver's side so that I am flung up and over, flying, then finally coming down face-first on the asphalt, so mutilated that no one will be able to identify me. I can imagine this so clearly that unconsciously I brace myself for the impact, for the sound of ripping metal and breaking glass, as I roll through each intersection.

Sometimes I imagine that I am one of the poor pedestrians in the crosswalk at the time. I am mowed down right alongside the rest of them . . .

. . . strangers

. . . young woman, Wendy, pushing baby in stroller, pulling toddler in harness, has a headache and hates the way her hair looks like straw in this heat

. . . bank teller, Jane, on lunch, carrying roast beef on rye with pickle and cheese in small white bag while worrying about varicose veins, humming sad song about cheating and hearts

. . . old man, Ed, with white cane and dog, wishing he was dead or his wife was still alive or his children, at least, would call

. . . businessman, Martin, with briefcase, nice teeth, green tie, has not a thought in his head, no reason to suspect that anyone else has either

. . . stranger things have happened.

Sometimes I imagine that I am the driver of the car, with the radio on and my foot to the floor, and the bodies scatter from me like pages or petals, unleashed. Or then they are not bodies at all but balloons, of all colours, full of wonder, words, and hot air, bobbing up and away, bouncing off asphalt, the rooftops, the pain, and a cloud.

RAILROADING

Or:

TWELVE SMALL STORIES WITH THE WORD "TRAIN" IN THE TITLE

Love Train

For a long time after Lesley and Cliff broke up, Cliff was always sending her things.

Flowers.

Red roses by the dramatic dozen.

Delicate frilly carnations dyed turquoise at the edges (which reminded Lesley of a tradition they'd observed at her elementary school on Mother's Day when each child had to wear a carnation, red if your mother was alive, white if she was dead — there were only two kids in the whole school whose mothers were dead — and what then, she wondered, was turquoise meant to signify?)

A single white orchid nestled in tissue paper in a gold box, as if they had a big date for a formal dance.

Cards. Funny cards:

"I thought you'd like to know that I've decided to start dating seals again, and . . . oh yes, my umbilical cord has grown back!"

Sentimental cards:

"I love wearing the smile . . . you put on my face!"

Funny sentimental cards:

"You You You You You You You You You You You You . . . These are a few of my favourite things!"

Apology cards:

"Please forgive me . . . my mouth is bigger than my brain!"

and:

"I'm sorry, I was wrong . . . Well, not as wrong as you, but sorrier!"

Pretty picture cards to say:

"Happy Thanksgiving!"
"Happy Hallowe'en!"
"I'm just thinking of you!"
"I'm always thinking of you!"
"I'm still thinking of you!"

Letters. Mostly letters.
Often Cliff would call during the day and leave a message on Lesley's answering machine, apologizing for having both-

ered her with another card or letter when she'd already told him, in no uncertain terms, that she needed some space. Then he would call right back and leave another message to apologize for having left the first one when she'd already told him to leave her alone.

He did not send the letters through the mail in the conventional way, but delivered them by hand in the middle of the night. Lesley never did catch him in the act, but she could just picture him parking his car halfway down the block, sneaking up her driveway in the dark or the rain, depositing another white envelope in her black mailbox. Where she would find it first thing in the morning.

At first it gave Lesley the creeps to think of Cliff tippy-toeing around out there while she was inside sleeping, but then she got used to hearing from him in this way. She took to checking the mailbox every morning before she put the coffee on. Waiting in her housecoat and slippers for the toast to pop and the eggs to poach, she would study the envelope first. Sometimes he put her full name on it, first and last; sometimes her first name only; once, just her initials.

Inside, the letters were always neatly typewritten on expensive bond paper. They began with phrases like "Well no . . ." or "And yes . . ." or "But maybe . . .", as if Cliff were picking up a conversation (one-sided though it might be) right in the middle where they'd left off, or as if he still thought he could still read her mind.

One of the first letters was dense with scholarly historical quotes on the nature of war. Cliff had set these erudite excerpts carefully off from the rest of the text, single-spaced and indented:

> In quarrels between countries, as well as those between
> individuals, when they have risen to a certain height,
> the first cause of dissension is no longer remembered,
> the minds of the parties being wholly engaged in
> recollecting and resenting the mutual expressions of
> their dislike. When feuds have reached that fatal point,

all considerations of reason and equity vanish; a blind
fury governs, or rather, confounds all things. A people
no longer regards their interest, but rather the
gratification of their wrath. (John Dickson).

And later in the letter he wrote:

The strange thing about this crisis of August 1939 was
that the object between Germany and Poland was not
clearly defined, and could not therefore be expressed as
a concrete demand. It was a part of Hitler's nature to
avoid putting things in a concrete form; to him, differences of opinion were questions of power, and tests of
one's nerves and strength. (Ernst von Weizäcker).

Lesley could not imagine that Cliff actually had a repertoire
of such pedantic passages floating around inside his head, just
waiting for an opportunity to be called up. But she couldn't
imagine that he had really gone to the library and looked them
up in order to quote them at her either.

Still, this letter made her mad enough to call him. When she
said on the phone, "I don't take kindly to being compared to
Hitler, thank you very much," Cliff said, "Don't be ridiculous. That's not what I meant. You just don't understand."

And she said, "Well no . . . I guess not."

He apologized for making her mad, which was exactly the
opposite, he said, of what he was intending to do. But the more
he apologized, the madder she got. The more he assured her
that he loved her even though she was crabby, cantankerous,
strangled and worried, hard, cynical and detached, mercenary,
unsympathetic, callous, and sarcastic — the more he assured
her that he loved her in spite of her *self* — the madder she got.
Until finally she hung up on him and all day she was still mad,
also feeling guilty, sorry, sad, simple-minded, and defeated.
She promised herself that she would send the next letter back
unopened, but of course there was little real chance of that.
She tried several times that afternoon to compose a letter in

answer to his repeated requests for one. But she got no further than saying:

> What it all comes down to is this: in the process of getting to know you, I realized that you were not the right person for me.

It should have been simple.

In the next letter, two mornings later, Cliff turned around and blamed himself for everything, saying:

> At least understand that all of this was only the result of my relentless devotion to you.

Lesley took a bath after breakfast and contemplated the incongruous conjunction of these two words.

Relentless.

Devotion.

After she'd dried her hair and cleaned the tub, she looked up "relentless" in the thesaurus. Much as she'd suspected, it was not an adjective that should be allowed to have much to do with love:

> **relentless,** *adj.* unyielding, unrelenting, implacable, unsparing; inexorable, remorseless, unflagging, dogged; undeviating, unswerving, persistent, persevering, undaunted; rigid, stern, strict, harsh, grim, austere; merciless, ruthless, unmerciful, pitiless, unpitying, unforgiving; unmitigable, inflexible, unbending, resisting, grudging; hard, imperious, obdurate, adamant, intransigent; uncompassionate, unfeeling, unsympathetic, intolerant.

The next letter was delivered on a windy Saturday night when Lesley was out on a date with somebody else. It was sitting there in the mailbox when she got home at midnight.

The weather had turned cold and her driveway was filling up suddenly with crispy yellow leaves. When she opened the back door, dozens of them swirled around her ankles and slipped inside. She imagined Cliff crunching through them on his way to the mailbox, worrying about the noise, which was amplified by the hour and the wind, then noticing that her car wasn't in the garage, and then worrying about that too.

In this letter, Cliff said:

I love you like ten thousand freight trains.

Lesley thought she rather liked this one, but then she wasn't sure. She thought she'd better think about it. She hung up her coat, poured herself a glass of white wine, and sat down in the dark kitchen to think. The oval of her face reflected in the window was distorted by the glass, so that her skin was pale, her eyes were holes, and her cheeks were sunken. She did not feel pale, hollow, or sunken. She felt just fine.

I love you like ten thousand freight trains.

This was like saying:

I love you to little bits.

Who wants to be loved to *little bits*?

This was like saying:

I love you to death.

Who wants to be loved to *death*?

I love you like ten thousand freight trains.

Who wants to be loved like or by *a freight train*?

The more she thought about it, the more she realized that she knew a thing or two about trains; railroading; relentlessness.

Dream Train

As a young girl growing up in Winnipeg, Lesley lived in an Insulbrick bungalow three doors down from the train tracks, a spur line leading to Genstar Feeds. Trains travelled the spur line so seldom that when one passed in the night, it would usually wake her up with its switching and shunting, its steel wheels squealing on the frozen rails. She would lie awake listening in her little trundle bed (it wasn't really a trundle bed, it was just an ordinary twin bed, but every night at eight o'clock her mother, Amelia, would say, "Come on, little one, time to tuck you into your little trundle bed.").

Lesley liked to imagine that the train outside was not a freight train but a *real* train, a passenger train: the Super Continental, carrying dignified wealthy people as carefully as if they were eggs clear across the country in its plush coaches, the conductors in their serious uniforms graciously bringing around drinks, pillows, and magazines. She imagined the silver coaches cruising slowly past, all lit up, the people inside riding backwards, eating, sleeping, playing cards with just their heads showing, laughing as if this were the most natural thing in the world. She imagined that the Super Continental could go all the way from Vancouver to St. John's (never mind the Gulf of St. Lawrence — there must be a way around it) without stopping once.

If the train on the spur line did not actually wake Lesley up, then it slid instead into her dreams, disguised as a shaggy behemoth with red eyes and silver hooves, shaking the snow from its curly brown fur as it pawed the rails and snorted steam.

Train Tracks

As a teenager, Lesley walked along the train tracks every morning to Glengarry Heights High School. On the way, she usually met up with a boy named Eric Henderson, who was two grades older and dressed all year round in faded blue jeans, a T-shirt, and a black leather jacket with studs. Occasionally he condescended to the cold weather by wearing a pair of black gloves.

After a couple of weeks, Eric took to waiting for Lesley on the tracks where they crossed her street. He would be leaning against the signal lights smoking when she came out her front door. They never walked home together at four o'clock because, even though Lesley sometimes loitered at her locker hoping, Eric was never around at that time, having, she assumed, other more interesting, more grown-up, things to do after school.

Every morning Lesley and Eric practised balancing on the rails with their arms outstretched, and they complained about the way the tar-coated ties were never spaced quite right for walking on. Lesley kept her ears open, looking over her shoulder every few minutes, just in case. Her mother, Amelia, had often warned her, "Don't get too close to a moving train or you'll get *sucked under*."

Sometimes Eric would line up bright pennies on the silver rails so the train would come and flatten them. Lesley would watch for the pennies on her way home from school, would gather them up and save them, thin as tinfoil, in a cigar box she kept under the bed. She never put pennies on the tracks herself because she was secretly afraid that they would cause a derailment and the train would come toppling off the tracks, exploding as it rolled down the embankment, demolishing her house and her neighbours' houses and everything in them. It was okay though when Eric did it, because somehow he could be both dangerous and charmed at the same time.

Every morning Eric told Lesley about what he'd done the night before. Lesley was not expected to reciprocate, which was just as well, since all she ever did in the evening was homework and dishes and talk on the phone.

One Monday morning Eric said he'd gone to the Gardens on Saturday night to see the Ike and Tina Turner Revue. He said Tina Turner was the sexiest woman in the world and the way she sang was like making love to the microphone right there on stage. He said he thought he'd die just watching her, and all the other guys went crazy too.

On the phone every night after supper, Lesley told her new best friend, Audrey, every little thing Eric had said to her that morning, especially the way he'd said, "I like your new haircut a lot,'' and then the way he'd winked at her in the hall between History and French.

"Do you think he likes me?" she asked Audrey over and over again.

"Of course he likes you, silly! He *adores* you!"

This went on all fall, all winter, all spring, until the raging crush which Lesley had on Eric Henderson could be nothing, it seemed, but true true love.

The week before final exams, Eric asked Audrey to the last school dance.

Lesley spent the night of the dance barricaded in her bedroom, lying on the floor with the record player blasting Tina Turner at top volume. She propped a chair against the door and would not let her parents in. She was mad at them too: at her father, Edward, because he'd laughed and said, "You'll get over it, pumpkin!''; and at her mother, Amelia, because she was old and married, probably happy, probably didn't even remember what love was *really* like, probably hadn't explained things properly in the first place, should have warned her about more than freight trains.

She would, Lesley promised herself savagely, spend the entire summer in her room, learning all the lyrics to Tina Turner's songs, and reading fat Russian novels which were all so satisfyingly melancholy, so clotted with complications and despair, and the characters had so many different, difficult names. Especially she would reread *Anna Karenina* and memorize the signal passage where Anna decides to take her own life:

> . . . And all at once she thought of the man crushed by the train the day she had first met Vronsky, and she knew what she had to do. . . .
> " . . . And I will punish him and escape from everyone and from myself. . . ."
> . . . And exactly at the moment when the space between the wheels came opposite her, she dropped the red bag,

and drawing her head back into her shoulders, fell on
her hands under the carriage, and lightly, as though she
would rise again at once, dropped on to her knees. . . .
. . . She tried to get up, to drop backwards: but
something huge and merciless struck her on the head
and rolled her on her back. . . .
. . . And the light by which she had read the book filled
with troubles, falsehoods, sorrow, and evil, flared up
more brightly than ever before, lighted up for her all
that had been in darkness, flickered, began to grow
dim, and was quenched forever.

And she would probably carve Eric Henderson's initials into
her thigh with a ballpoint pen, and she would probably not eat
anything either, except maybe unsalted soda crackers, and she
would not wash her hair more than once a week, and she would
stay in her pyjamas all day long. Yes she would. She would
LANGUISH. And for sure she would never ever ever ever fall
in love or have a best friend ever again so long as she lived, so
help her.

Night Train

When Lesley moved away from home at the age of twenty-one,
she took the train because there was an air strike that summer.
Her parents put her on the train in Winnipeg with a brown
paper bag full of tuna sandwiches and chocolate-chip cookies,
with the three-piece luggage set they'd bought her as a going-
away present, and a book of crossword puzzles to do on the
way. They were all weeping lightly, the three of them: her
parents, Lesley assumed, out of a simple sadness, and herself,
out of an intoxicating combination of excitement and anticipation, of new-found freedom, and, with it, fear. She was, she
felt, on the brink of everything important. She was moving
west to Alberta, which was booming.

Seated across the aisle of Coach Number 3003 (a good omen, Lesley thought, as she had long ago decided that three was her lucky number) was, by sheer coincidence, a young man named Arthur Hoop who'd given a lecture at the university in Winnipeg the night before. His topic was nuclear disarmament and Lesley had attended because peace was one of her most enduring interests.

After an hour or so, Lesley worked up enough courage to cross over to the empty seat beside him and say, "I really loved your lecture." Arthur Hoop seemed genuinely pleased and invited her to join him for lunch in the club car. Lesley stashed the brown-bag lunch under the seat in front of hers and followed Arthur, swaying and bobbing and grinning, down the whole length of the train.

Arthur Hoop, up close, was interesting, amiable, and affectionate, and his eyes were two different colours, the left one blue and the right one brown. Arthur was on his way back to Vancouver, where he lived with a woman named Laura who was sleeping with his best friend and he, Arthur, didn't know what he was going to do next. Whenever the train stopped at a station for more than five minutes, Arthur would get off and phone ahead to Vancouver, where Laura, on the other end, would either cry, yell, or hang up on him.

By the time the train pulled into Regina, Lesley and Arthur were holding hands, hugging, and having another beer in the club car, where the waiter said, "You two look so happy, you must be on your honeymoon!"

Lesley and Arthur giggled and giggled, and then, like fools or like children playing house, they shyly agreed. The next thing they knew, there was a red rose in a silver vase on their table and everyone in the car was buying them drinks and calling out, "Congratulations!" over the clicking of the train. Arthur kept hugging Lesley against him and winking, first with the brown eye, then with the blue.

They spent the dark hours back in Arthur's coach seat, snuggling under a scratchy grey blanket, kissing and touching and curling around each other like cats. Lesley was so wrapped up in her fantasy of how Arthur would get off the train with her in Calgary or how she would stay on the train with him all the way to Vancouver, and how, either way, her real life was about to begin, that she hardly noticed how brazen they were being until Arthur actually put it in, shuddered, and clutched her to him.

Lesley wept when she got off the train in Calgary and Arthur Hoop wept too, but he stayed on.

From her hotel room, Lesley wrote Arthur long sad letters and ordered up hamburgers and Chinese food from room service at odd hours of the day and night. On the fourth night, she called her mother collect in Winnipeg and cried into the phone because she felt afraid of everything and she wanted to come home. Her mother, wise Amelia, said, "Give it two weeks before you decide. You know we'll always take you back, pumpkin."

By the end of the two weeks, Lesley had a basement apartment in a small town called Ventura, just outside the city. She also had two job interviews, a kitten named Calypso, and a whole new outlook on life. She never did hear from Arthur Hoop and she wondered for a while what it was about trains, about men, the hypnotic rhythm of them, relentless, unremitting, and irresistible, the way they would go straight to your head, and when would she ever learn?

It wasn't long before she was laughing to herself over what Arthur must have told the other passengers when she left him flat like that, on their honeymoon no less.

Train Ticket

All the way home to Winnipeg to spend Christmas with her parents, Lesley drank lukewarm coffee out of Styrofoam cups, ate expensive dried-out pressed-chicken sandwiches, and tried to get comfortable in her maroon-upholstered seat with her purse as a pillow and her parka as a blanket. She tried to read but could not concentrate for long, could not keep herself from staring out the window at the passing scenery, which was as distracting as a flickering television set at the far end of the room. All the way across Saskatchewan, the train seemed to be miraculously ploughing its way through one endless snowbank, throwing up walls of white on either side of the tracks.

She didn't feel like talking to anyone and closed her eyes whenever the handsome young man across the rocking aisle looked her way hopefully. She had just started dating a man named Bruce back in Ventura and she did not like leaving him for Christmas. But this was her first Christmas since she'd moved away from home and the trip back for the holidays had been planned months ago. Once set in motion, the trip, it seemed, like the train once she had boarded it, could not be deflected. She was travelling now with a sorrowful but self-righteous sense of daughterly obligation that carried her inexorably eastward. For a time she'd believed that moving away from her parents' home would turn her instantly into a free, adult woman. But of course she was wrong.

She kept reaching into her purse, checking for her ticket. She memorized the messages printed on the back of it, as if they were a poem or a prayer:

RESERVATIONS: The enclosed ticket is of value. If your plans are altered, the ticket must be returned with the receipt coupon intact, for refund or credit. If you do not make the trip, please cancel your reservations.

ALCOHOLIC BEVERAGES: Alcoholic beverages purchased on board must be consumed in the premises where served. Provincial liquor laws prohibit the consumption of personal liquor on trains except in the confines of a bedroom or roomette.

BAGGAGE: Personal effects consisting of wearing apparel, toilet articles, and similar effects for the passenger's use, comfort, and convenience (except liquids and breakables) are accepted as baggage.

Explosive, combustible, corrosive, and inflammable
materials are prohibited by law.

The train trip took sixteen hours. The inside of Lesley's
mouth, after 1300 kilometres, tasted like a toxic combination
of diesel fuel and indoor-outdoor carpeting.

Her parents were there to meet her at the Winnipeg station,
her father, Edward, smiling and smiling, his shy kiss landing
somewhere near her left ear; her mother, Amelia, looking small
in her big winter coat with a Christmas corsage of plastic mis-
tletoe and tiny silver bells pinned to the lapel. The train pulled
away effortlessly in a cloud of steam and snow.

Freight Train

They had a saying in Ventura — when Lesley was still living
there with Bruce — a saying that was applied, with much laughter and lip-smacking, to people, usually women, who were less
than attractive.

"She looks like she's been kissing freight trains," one of the
boys in the bar would say, and the rest of them round the table
would howl and nod and slap their knees. Lesley would laugh
with them, even though she felt guilty for it, and sometimes,
calling up within herself noble notions of sisterhood, sympathy,
and such, she would sputter uselessly something in defence of
the poor woman they were picking on.

But she would always laugh too in the end, because she knew
she was pretty, she knew she was loved, she knew she was
exempt from their disgust and the disfiguring, inexorable
advent of trains.

Runaway Train

There was a story they told in Ventura — when Lesley was still
living there with Bruce — about the time Old Jim Jacobs stole

the train. It was back in the winter of 1972. Old Jim was a retired engineer who'd turned to drink in his later years. He sat in the Ventura Hotel day after day, night after night, ordering draft beer by the jug with two glasses, one for himself and one for his invisible friend. He would chat amiably for hours in an unintelligible language with the empty chair across from him, politely topping up the two glasses evenly and then drinking them both.

"At least he's never lonely," Bruce would always say.

On towards closing time, however, Old Jim or his invisible friend, or both, would start to get a little surly, and soon Old Jim would be jumping and cursing (in English), flinging himself around in the smoke-blue air of the bar.

"I hate you! I hate you!" he would cry.

"Let's step outside and settle this like men!" he would roar, hitching up his baggy pants and boxing in the air.

"So what then," Bruce would wonder, "is the point of having invisible friends, if you can't get along with them?"

Lesley knew Old Jim from when she worked in the grocery store and he'd be standing in the line-up in his old railway cap with a loaf of bread, a package of baloney, and some Kraft cheese slices. By the time he got to the cash register, he'd have made himself a sandwich and, wouldn't you know it, he must have left his wallet in his other pants — as if he even owned another pair of pants.

When he wasn't drinking or shopping, Old Jim was sitting in the long grass beside the CPR main line, counting boxcars, and waving at the engineers.

At the time of the great train robbery, he'd been bingeing, so they said, for eight days straight (this number could be adjusted, at the story-teller's discretion, to up to as many as ten days but never down to less than six) in Hawkesville, a nearby town twelve miles west of Ventura. He'd been barred for two weeks from the Ventura Hotel for sleeping on the pool table, which explained why he was drinking in Hawkesville in the first place. So Old Jim was getting to be a little homesick after all that time away from his old stamping grounds, and on the Friday night he decided it was high time to get back, seeing as how his two weeks were up on Saturday. But he was flat broke after his binge, pension cheque long gone, no money for a cab, and it was too damn cold to hitch-hike. So he decided to take the train.

So he hopped right in, so they said, to the first engine he found in the yard, fired her up, and off he went, hauling forty-seven empty boxcars behind him (this number too could be adjusted, interminably up, it seemed, because, after all, who was counting?). He made it back to Ventura without mishap, parked her up on the siding behind the Ventura Hotel so he'd be good and ready when they opened in the morning and he knew they'd give him credit for a day or two. He curled up in the caboose and went to sleep. Which was where the railway police and the RCMP found him when they surrounded the runaway train, guns drawn, sirens screaming, at 5:36 a.m. (the time of his legendary capture was unalterable, a part of the town's history which could not be tampered with).

"But what then," Bruce would wonder whenever he heard the story again, "is the point of stealing a train, when you can never take it off the tracks, when you can only go back and forth, back and forth, back and forth, and you can never really get away?"

Express Train

One summer Lesley and Bruce took the train up to Edmonton where his brother was getting married. Halfway there, they were stopped on a siding in the middle of nowhere, waiting for a freight train to pass. Bruce was getting impatient, sighing huge conspicuous sighs as he fidgeted and fussed in his seat, while Lesley beside him read on peacefully.

Spotting a white horse from the window, he said, "Sometimes simple things glimpsed in the distance can bring great comfort."

Train Trip East

All the way back to Winnipeg for her Uncle Mel's funeral, Lesley drank beer out of cans and wrote postcards to Bruce in Ventura. She bought the cards at various train stations along the way and then she mailed them at the next stop. She suspected that Bruce was on the brink of having an affair with a French-Canadian woman named Analise who was spending the summer in Ventura with her sister. All of this suspicion, sticky and time-consuming as it was, had left Lesley feeling sick and tired, a little bit crazy too. On the back of a green lake, she wrote:

> I tried to take pictures from the train, of a tree and some water, some sky, but they wouldn't hold still long enough.

On the back of a red maple tree:

> I saw a coyote running from the train, also white horses, brown cows, black birds, and a little girl in Maple Creek wearing a pink sunsuit with polka dots, running. All of them running away from the train.

Black city spotted with blue and white lights:

> There was a station wagon stopped at a crossing. It was filled with suitcases, babies, and basketballs. For a minute, I wanted to scream: "Stop! Stop! There's a train coming! We'll all be killed!" Then I remembered that I was the train and I didn't have to stop for anything. Trains are so safe from the inside.

Yellow field of wheat:

> What else is there to do on a train any more but remember? I thought of a witchy woman who lived on

the corner of Cross Street and Vine, in a wooden shack
with pigeons on the roof and chickens in the porch. She
watched me through the window when I walked by to
Sunday School. The winter I was eight she got hit by a
train. For a time I had nightmares . . .

Here she ran out of room on the card and finished up her
message on the next one. Purple mountain:

> . . . about arms and legs broken off like icicles, about a
> head rolling down a snowbank wearing a turquoise
> toque just like mine. Then I forgot all about her till
> now. I remember rocking my cousin, Gary, in his
> cradle, the way he couldn't hold his head up yet, and
> now he's the chef at a fancy French restaurant.

Sitting at her Aunt Helen's kitchen table in Winnipeg, surrounded by relatives, neighbours, warm casseroles, and frozen
pound cakes, she wrote on the back of a sympathy card:

> I've still got the sound of the train in my head. It makes
> it hard to think of anything but songs. Tomorrow.

War Train

In Lesley's parents' photo album, there was a picture of her
mother and her Aunt Helen seeing her father and her Uncle
Mel off at the train station. The women were waving and blowing kisses from the platform, stylish in their broad-shouldered
coats and little square hats with veils. The men were grinning
and walking away, handsome in their sleek uniforms and jaunty
caps. They were all very young then, and splendid. The silver
train was waiting behind them, its windows filled with the faces
of many other young men. They went away to the war and then
some of them came back again.

After her Uncle Mel's funeral, Lesley's father told her about the time he'd ridden the train all across France with Mel's head in his lap, Mel nearly dying of ptomaine poisoning from a Christmas turkey, but he didn't.

Train Trip West

All the way back to Ventura after her Uncle Mel's funeral, Lesley slept fitfully or looked out the train window and thought about how everything looks different when you are passing through it in the opposite direction. On this return journey, she was riding backwards, facing where she'd come from, as if she had eyes in the back of her head.

The train whistled through the backsides of a hundred anonymous towns, past old hotels of pink or beige stucco, past slaughterhouses, gas stations, trailer parks, and warehouses. Children and old men waved. Dogs barked, soundless, powerless, strangling themselves straining at their chains. White sheets tangled on backyard clotheslines and red tractors idled at unmarked crossings.

Lesley never knew where she was exactly: there are no mileage signs beside the train tracks the way there are on the highway. There is no way of knowing how far from, how far to. No way, on train time, of locating yourself accurately inside the continuum. You just have to keep on moving, forward and forward and forward, or back, trusting that wherever you are heading is still out there somewhere.

Horse and Train

One year for her birthday in Ventura (or could it have been Christmas . . . could it have been that same year when Lesley bought Bruce the guitar he'd been aching after, the Fender Stratocaster, and when she couldn't take the suspense a minute longer, she gave it to him on Christmas Eve instead of in the morning, just to see the look on his face, and then they stayed up all night playing music and singing, drinking eggnog till dawn . . . when Bruce took the guitar to bed with him and Lesley took a picture of him cuddling it under the puffy pink quilt her mother had sent, and then she kept him awake even longer, telling her theory that if men were the ones who had babies, then there would no more war . . . the best Christmas ever, it could have been then), Bruce gave Lesley a framed reproduction of the Alex Colville painting *Horse and Train*.

In the painting, a purple-black horse on the right is running headlong down the tracks towards an oncoming train on the left. The landscape around them is gravel and brown prairie grass. The ears of the horse are flattened, its tail is extended, and the white smoke from the black train is drifting across the brown prairie sky at dusk.

Bruce hung the painting over the couch in the tiny living room of their basement apartment and Lesley admired it every time she walked into the room.

After Bruce left Lesley and moved to Montreal with Analise, Lesley took the painting off the wall and smashed it on the cement floor, so that she was vacuuming up glass for an hour afterwards, weeping.

When Lesley moved back to Winnipeg a few months later and rented the little stucco bungalow on Harris Street, she had the painting reframed with new glass and hung it on her bedroom wall. She liked to look at it before she went to sleep at night.

She looked at it when she was lying in bed with Cliff, who had his hands behind his head and the ashtray balanced on his bare chest, who was talking and smoking and talking, so happy to be spending the night. She looked at it as she tried to concentrate and follow Cliff's train of thought, but really she was thinking about how they'd been seeing each other for three months now and it wasn't working out.

But really she was thinking about an article she'd read in a women's magazine years ago, and the writer, a marriage counsellor, said that in every romantic relationship there was one person who loved less and one who loved more. The important question then, which a person must face was: which would you rather be: the one who loves less or the one who loves more?

When Lesley asked Cliff this question, she already knew what his answer would be.

Which would you rather be: the one who loves less or the one who loves more?

This was like saying:

Which would you rather be: the horse or the train?

It should have been simple.

RED PLAID SHIRT

RED PLAID SHIRT

that your mother bought you one summer in Banff. It is 100%
Pure Virgin Wool, itchy but flattering against your pale skin,
your black hair. You got it in a store called Western Outfitters,
of the sort indigenous to the region, which stocked only *real*
(as opposed to designer) blue jeans, Stetson hats, and $300
hand-tooled cowboy boots with very pointy toes. There was a
saddle and a stuffed deer-head in the window.

Outside, the majestic mountains were sitting all around, mag-
nanimously letting their pictures be taken by ten thousand
tourists wielding Japanese cameras and eating ice-cream cones.
You had tricked your mother into leaving her camera in the
car so she wouldn't embarrass you, who lived there and were
supposed to be taking the scenery for granted by now.

You liked the red plaid shirt so much that she bought you two
more just like it, one plain green, the other chocolate brown.
But these two stayed shirts, never acquiring any particular
significance, eventually getting left unceremoniously behind in
a Salvation Army drop-box in a grocery-store parking lot somewhere along the way.

The red plaid shirt reminded you of your mother's gardening shirt, which was also plaid and which you rescued one winter when she was going to throw it away because the elbows were out. You picture her kneeling in the side garden where she grew only flowers — bleeding hearts, roses, peonies, poppies — and a small patch of strawberries. You picture her hair in a bright babushka, her hands in the black earth with her shirt-sleeves rolled up past the elbow. The honeysuckle hedge bloomed fragrantly behind her and the sweet peas curled interminably up the white trellis. You are sorry now for the way you always sulked and whined when she asked you to help, for the way you hated the dirt under your nails and the sweat running into your eyes, the sweat dripping down her shirt-front between her small breasts. You kept her old shirt in a bag in your closet for years, with a leather patch half-sewn onto the left sleeve, but now you can't find it.

You were wearing the red plaid shirt the night you met Daniel in the tavern where he was drinking beer with his buddies from the highway construction crew. You ended up living with him for the next five years. He was always calling it your ''magic shirt'', teasing you, saying how it was the shirt that made him fall in love with you in the first place. You would tease him back, saying how you'd better hang onto it then, in case you had to use it on somebody else. You've even worn it in that spirit a few times since, but the magic seems to have seeped out of it and you are hardly surprised.

You've gained a little weight since then or the shirt has shrunk, so you can't wear it any more, but you can't throw or give it away either.

RED: crimson carmine cochineal cinnabar sanguine
scarlet red ruby rouge my birthstone red and
blood-red brick-red beet-red bleeding hearts
Queen of fire god of war Mars the colour of
magic my magic the colour of iron flowers and

fruit the colour of meat dripping lobster cracking claws lips nipples blisters blood my blood and all power.

BLUE COTTON SWEATSHIRT

that says "Why Be Normal?" in a circle on the front. This is your comfort shirt, fleecy on the inside, soft from many washings, and three sizes too big so you can tuck your hands up inside the sleeves when they're shaking or cold. You like to sit on the couch with the curtains closed, wearing your comfort shirt, eating comfort food: vanilla ice cream, macaroni and cheese, white rice with butter and salt, white toast with CheezWhiz and peanut butter. Sometimes you even sleep in it.

This is the shirt you wore when you had the abortion three days before Christmas. They told you to be there at nine in the morning and then you didn't get into the operating room until nearly twelve-thirty. So you wore it in the waiting room with the other women also waiting, and the weight you had already gained was hidden beneath it while you pretended to read *Better Homes and Gardens* and they wouldn't let you smoke. After you came to, you put the shirt back on and waited in another waiting room for your friend Alice to come and pick you up because they said you weren't capable yet of going home alone. One of the other women was waiting there too, for her boyfriend, who was always late, and when he finally got there, first she yelled at him briefly and then they decided to go to McDonald's for a hamburger. At home, Alice pours you tea from the porcelain pot into white china cups like precious opaque stones.

None of this has diminished, as you feared it might, the comfort this shirt can give you when you need it. Alice always puts her arms around you whenever she sees you wearing it now. She has one just like it, only pink.

BLUE: azure aqua turquoise delft and navy-blue royal-
        blue cool cerulean peacock-blue indigo ultramar-
        ine cobalt-blue Prussian-blue cyan the sky and
        electric a space the colour of the firmament and
        sapphire sleeping silence the sea the blues my
        lover plays the saxophone cool blue he plays the
        blues.

PALE GREY TURTLENECK

that you bought when you were seeing Dwight, who said one
night for no apparent reason that grey is a mystical colour. You
took this judgement to heart because Dwight was more likely
to talk about hockey or carburetors and you were pleasantly
surprised to discover that he might also think about other
things. You spotted the turtleneck the very next day on sale at
Maggie's for $9.99.

You took to wearing it on Sundays because that was the day
Dwight was most likely to wander in, unannounced, on his
way to or from somewhere else. You wore it while you just
happened to put a bottle of good white wine into the fridge to
chill and a chicken, a roast, or a pan of spinach lasagna into
the oven to cook slowly just in case he showed up hungry. You
suppose now that this was pathetic, but at the time you were
thinking of yourself as patient and him as worth waiting for.

Three Sundays in a row you ended up passed out on the couch,
the wine bottle empty on the coffee table, the supper dried
out, and a black-and-white movie with violin music flickering
on the TV. In the coloured morning, the pattern of the upholstery was imprinted on your cheek and your whole head was
hurting. When Dwight finally did show up, it was a Wednesday and you were wearing your orange flannelette nightie with
all the buttons gone and a rip down the front, because it was
three in the morning, he was drunk, and you had been in bed
for hours. He just laughed and took you in his arms when you

told him to get lost. Until you said you were seeing someone else, which was a lie, but one that you both wanted to believe because it was an easy answer that let both of you gingerly off the hook.

You keep meaning to wear that turtleneck again sometime because you know it's juvenile to think it's a jinx, but then you keep forgetting to iron it.

Finally you get tough and wear it, wrinkled, grocery-shopping one Saturday afternoon. You career through the aisles like a crazed hamster, dodging toddlers, old ladies, and other carts, scooping up vegetables with both hands, eating an apple you haven't paid for, leaving the core in the dairy section. But nothing happens and no one notices your turtleneck: the colour or the wrinkles.

Sure enough, Dwight calls the next day, Sunday, at five o'clock. You say you can't talk now, you're just cooking supper: prime rib, wild rice, broccoli with Hollandaise. You have no trouble at all hanging quietly up on him while pouring the wine into the crystal goblet before setting the table for one with the Royal Albert china your mother left you in her will.

GREY: oyster pewter slate dull lead dove-grey pearl-
grey brain my brains silver or simple gone into
the mystic a cool grey day overcast with clouds
ashes concrete the aftermath of airplanes gun-
metal-grey granite and gossamer whales ele-
phants cats in the country the colour of
questions the best camouflage the opaque
elegance an oyster.

WHITE EMBROIDERED BLOUSE
that you bought for $80 to wear with your red-flowered skirt to a Christmas party with Peter, who was working as a pizza

cook until he could afford to play his sax full-time. You also bought a silken red belt with gold beads and tassels, a pair of red earrings with dragons on them, and ribbed red stockings which are too small but you wanted them anyway. This striking outfit involves you and Alice in a whole day of trudging around downtown in a snowstorm, holding accessories up in front of mirrors like talismans.

You spend an hour in the bathroom getting ready, drinking white wine, plucking your eyebrows, dancing like a dervish, and smiling seductively at yourself. Peter calls to say he has to work late but he'll meet you there at midnight.

By the time he arrives, you are having a complex anatomical conversation with an intern named Fernando who has spilled a glass of red wine down the front of your blouse. He is going to be a plastic surgeon. Your blouse is soaking in the bathtub and you are wearing only your white lace camisole. Fernando is feeding you green grapes and little squares of cheese, complimenting your cheekbones, and falling in love with your smooth forehead. You are having the time of your life and it's funny how you notice for the first time that Peter has an inferior bone structure.

WHITE: ivory alabaster magnolia milk the moon is full and chalk-white pure-white snow-white moon-stone limestone rime and clay marble many seashells and my bones are china bones precious porcelain lace white magic white feather the immaculate conception of white lies wax white wine as a virtue.

YELLOW EVENING GOWN
that you bought for your New Year's Eve date with Fernando. It has a plunging neckline and a dropped sash which flatteringly accentuates your hips. You wear it with black hoop earrings,

black lace stockings with seams, and black high-heels that Alice forced you to buy even though they hurt your toes and you are so uncoordinated that you expect you will have to spend the entire evening sitting down with your legs crossed, calves nicely flexed.

You spend an hour in the bathroom getting ready, drinking pink champagne, applying blusher with a fat brush according to a diagram in a women's magazine that shows you how to make the most of your face. You practise holding your chin up so it doesn't sag and look double. Alice French-braids your hair and teaches you how to waltz like a lady. Fernando calls to say he has to work late but he'll meet you there before midnight.

You go to the club with Alice instead. They seat you at a tiny table for two so that when you sit down, your knees touch hers. You are in the middle of a room full of candles, fresh flowers, lounge music, and well-groomed couples staring feverishly into each other's eyes. The meal is sumptuous: green salad, a whole lobster, home-made pasta, fresh asparagus, and warm buns wrapped in white linen in a wicker basket. You eat everything and then you get the hell out of there, leaving a message for Fernando.

You go down the street to a bar you know where they will let you in without a ticket even though it's New Year's Eve. In the lobby you meet Fernando in a tuxedo with his arm around a short homely woman in black who, when you ask, "Who the hell are you?", says, "His wife." In your black high-heels you are taller than both of them and you know your gown is gorgeous. When the wife says, "And who the hell are *you*?", you point a long finger at Fernando's nose and say, "Ask him." You stomp away with your chin up and your dropped sash swinging.

Out of sight, you take off your high-heels and walk home through the park and the snow with them in your hands, dangling. Alice follows in a cab. By the time you get there, your black lace stockings are in shreds and your feet are cut and you are laughing and crying, mostly laughing.

YELLOW: jonquil jasmine daffodil lemon and honey-coloured corn-coloured cornsilk canary crocus the egg yolk in the morning the colour of mustard bananas brass cadmium yellow is the colour of craving craven chicken cats' eyes I am faint-hearted weak-kneed lily-livered or the sun lucid luminous means caution or yield.

BLACK LEATHER JACKET

that you bought when you were seeing Ivan, who rode a red Harley-Davidson low-rider with a suicide shift, his black beard blowing in the wind. The jacket has rows of diagonal pleats at the yoke and a red leather collar and cuffs.

Ivan used to take you on weekend runs with his buddies and their old ladies to little bars in other towns where they were afraid of you: especially of Ivan's best friend, Spy, who had been hurt in a bike accident two years before and now his hands hung off his wrists at odd angles and he could not speak, could only make guttural growls, write obscene notes to the waitress on a serviette, and laugh at her like a madman, his eyes rolling back in his head, and you could see what was left of his tongue.

You would come riding up in a noisy pack with bugs in your teeth, dropping your black helmets like bowling balls on the floor, eating greasy burgers and pickled eggs, drinking draft beer by the jug, the foam running down your chin. Your legs, after the long ride, felt like a wishbone waiting to be sprung. If no one would rent you a room, you slept on picnic tables in the campground, the bikes pulled in around you like wagons, a case of beer and one sleeping bag between ten of you. In the early morning, there was dew on your jacket and your legs were numb with the weight of Ivan's head on them.

You never did get around to telling your mother you were dating a biker (she thought you said "baker"), which was just as well, since Ivan eventually got tired, sold his bike, and moved back to Manitoba to live with his mother, who was dying. He got a job in a hardware store and soon married his high school sweetheart, Betty, who was a dental hygienist. Spy was killed on the highway: drove his bike into the back of a tanker truck in broad daylight; there was nothing left of him.

You wear your leather jacket now when you need to feel tough. You wear it with your tight blue jeans and your cowboy boots. You strut slowly with your hands in your pockets. Your boots click on the concrete and you are a different person. You can handle anything and no one had better get in your way. You will take on the world if you have to. You will die young and in flames if you have to.

BLACK: ebon sable charcoal jet lamp-black blue-black bruises in a night sky ink-black soot-black the colour of my hair and burning rubber dirt the colour of infinite space speeding blackball blacklist black sheep blackberries ravens eat crow black as the ace of spades and black is black I want my baby back before midnight yes of course midnight that old black dog behind me.

BROWN CASHMERE SWEATER

that you were wearing the night you told Daniel you were leaving him. It was that week between Christmas and New Year's which is always a wasteland. Everyone was digging up recipes called Turkey-Grape Salad, Turkey Soufflé, and Turkey-Almond-Noodle Bake. You kept vacuuming up tinsel and pine needles, putting away presents one at a time from under the tree. You and Daniel sat at the kitchen table all afternoon, drinking hot rum toddies, munching on crackers and garlic sausage, playing Trivial Pursuit, asking each other questions like:

What's the most mountainous country in Europe?
Which is more tender, the left or right leg of a chicken?
What race of warriors burned off their right breasts in Greek legend?

Daniel was a poor loser and he thought that Europe was a country, maybe somewhere near Spain.

This night you have just come from a party at his friend Harold's house. You are sitting on the new couch, a loveseat, blue with white flowers, which was Daniel's Christmas present to you, and you can't help thinking of the year your father got your mother a coffee percolator when all she wanted was something personal: earrings, a necklace, a scarf for God's sake. She spent most of the day locked in their bedroom, crying noisily, coming out every hour or so to baste the turkey, white-lipped, tucking more Kleenex up her sleeve. You were on her side this time and wondered how your father, whom you had always secretly loved the most, could be so insensitive. It was the changing of the guard, your allegiance shifting like sand from one to the other.

You are sitting on the new couch eating cold pizza and trying to figure out why you didn't have a good time at the party. Daniel is accusing you alternately of looking down on his friends or sleeping with them. He is wearing the black leather vest you bought him for Christmas and he says you are a cheapskate.

When you tell him you are leaving (which is a decision you made months ago but it took you this long to figure out how you were going to manage it and it has nothing to do with the party, the couch, or the season), Daniel grips you by the shoulders and bangs your head against the wall until the picture hung there falls off. It is a photograph of the mountains on a pink spring morning, the ridges like ribs, the run-off like incisions or veins. There is glass flying everywhere in slices into your face, into your hands pressed over your eyes, and the front of your sweater is spotted and matted with blood.

On the way to the hospital, he says he will kill you if you tell them what he did to you. You promise him anything, you promise him that you will love him forever and that you will never leave.

The nurse takes you into the examining room. Daniel waits in the waiting room, reads magazines, buys a chocolate bar from the vending machine, then a Coke and a bag of ripple chips. You tell the nurse what happened and the police take him away in handcuffs with their guns drawn. In the car on the way to the station, he tells them he only did it because he loves you. The officer who takes down your report tells you this and he just keeps shaking his head and patting your arm. The police photographer takes pictures of your face, your broken fingers, your left breast which has purple bruises all over it where he grabbed it and twisted and twisted.

By the time you get to the women's shelter, it is morning and the blood on your sweater has dried, doesn't show. There is no way of knowing. There, the other women hold you, brush your hair, bring you coffee and cream-of-mushroom soup. The woman with the broken cheekbone has two canaries in a gold cage that she carries with her everywhere like a lamp. She shows you how the doors are steel, six inches thick, and the windows are bullet-proof. She shows you where you will sleep, in a room on the third floor with six other women, some of them lying now fully dressed on their little iron cots with their hands behind their heads, staring at the ceiling as if it were full of stars or clouds that drift slowly westward in the shape of camels, horses, or bears. She shows you how the canaries will sit on your finger if you hold very still and pretend you are a tree or a roof or another bird.

BROWN: ochre cinnamon coffee copper caramel the colour of my Christmas cake chocolate mocha walnut chestnuts raw sienna my suntan burnt umber burning toast fried fricasseed sautéed grilled I baste the turkey the colour of stupid cows smart horses brown bears brown shirt brown sugar apple brown betty brunette the colour of thought and sepia the colour of old photographs the old earth and wood.

GREEN SATIN QUILTED JACKET

in the Oriental style with mandarin collar and four red frogs down the front. This jacket is older than you are. It belonged to your mother, who bought it when she was the same age you are now. In the black-and-white photos from that time, the jacket is grey but shiny and your mother is pale but smooth-skinned, smiling with her hand on her hip or your father's thigh.

You were always pestering her to let you wear it to play dress-up, with her red high-heels and that white hat with the feathers and the little veil that covered your whole face. You wanted to wear it to a Hallowe'en party at school where all the other girls would be witches, ghosts, or princesses and you would be the only mandarin, with your eyes, you imagined, painted up slanty and two sticks through a bun in your hair. But she would never let you. She would just keep on cooking supper, bringing carrots, potatoes, cabbages up from the root cellar, taking peas, beans, broccoli out of the freezer in labelled dated parcels, humming, looking out through the slats of the Venetian blind at the black garden and the leafless rose bushes. Each year, at least one of them would be winter-killed no matter how hard she had tried to protect them. And she would dig it up in the spring by the dead roots and the thorns would get tangled in her hair, leave long bloody scratches all down her arms. And the green jacket stayed where it was, in the cedar chest with the hand-made lace doilies, her grey linen wedding suit, and the picture of your father as a small boy with blond ringlets.

After the funeral, you go through her clothes while your father is outside shovelling snow. You lay them out in piles on the bed: one for the Salvation Army, one for the second-hand store, one for yourself because your father wants you to take something home with you. You will take the green satin jacket, also a white mohair cardigan with multicoloured squares on the front, a black-and-white striped shirt you sent her for her birthday last year that she never wore, an imitation-pearl necklace for Alice, and a dozen unopened packages of pantyhose. There is a fourth pile for your father's friend Jack's new wife, Frances, whom your mother never liked, but your father says Jack and Frances have fallen on hard times on the farm since Jack got the emphysema, and Frances will be glad of some new clothes.

Jack and Frances drop by the next day with your Aunt Jeanne. You serve tea and the shortbread cookies Aunt Jeanne has brought. She makes them just the way your mother did, whipped, with a sliver of maraschino cherry on top. Jack, looking weather-beaten or embarrassed, sits on the edge of the couch with his baseball cap in his lap and marvels at how grown-up you've got to be. Frances is genuinely grateful for the two green garbage bags of clothes, which you carry out to the truck for her.

After they leave, you reminisce fondly with your father and Aunt Jeanne about taking the toboggan out to Jack's farm when you were small, tying it to the back of the car, your father driving slowly down the country lane, towing you on your stomach, clutching the front of the toboggan which curled like a wooden wave. You tell him for the first time how frightened you were of the black tires spinning the snow into your face, and he says he had no idea, he thought you were having fun. This was when Jack's first wife, Winnifred, was still alive. Your Aunt Jeanne, who knows everything, tells you that when Winnifred was killed in that car accident, it was Jack, driving drunk, who caused it. And now when he gets drunk, he beats Frances up, locks her out of the house in her bare feet, and she has to sleep in the barn, in the hay with the horses.

You are leaving in the morning. Aunt Jeanne helps you pack. You are anxious to get home but worried about leaving your father alone. Aunt Jeanne says she'll watch out for him.

The green satin jacket hangs in your front hall closet now, between your black leather jacket and your raincoat. You can still smell the cedar from the chest and the satin is always cool on your cheek like clean sheets or glass.

One day you think you will wear it downtown, where you are meeting a new man for lunch. You study yourself in the full-length mirror on the back of the bathroom door and you decide it makes you look like a different person: someone unconventional, unusual, and unconcerned. This new man, whom you met recently at an outdoor jazz festival, is a free spirit who eats health food, plays the dulcimer, paints well, writes well, sings well, and has just completed an independent study of eastern religions. He doesn't smoke, drink, or do drugs. He is pure and peaceful, perfect. He is teaching you how to garden, how to turn the black soil, how to plant the seeds, how to water them, weed them, watch them turn into lettuce, carrots, peas, beans, radishes, and pumpkins, how to get the kinks out of your back by stretching your brown arms right up to the sun. You haven't even told Alice about him yet because he is too good to be true. He is bound to love this green jacket, and you in it too.

You get in your car, drive around the block, go back inside because you forgot your cigarettes, and you leave the green jacket on the back of a kitchen chair because who are you trying to kid? More than anything, you want to be transparent. More than anything, you want to hold his hands across the table and then you will tell him you love him and it will all come true.

GREEN: viridian verdigris chlorophyll grass leafy jade mossy verdant apple-green pea-green lime-green sage-green sea-green bottle-green emeralds avocadoes olives all leaves the colour of Venus hope and jealousy the colour of mould mildew envy poison and pain and snakes the colour of everything that grows in my garden fertile nourishing sturdy sane and strong.

TRICK QUESTIONS

*Only the most naïve of questions are truly serious.
They are the questions with no answers. A question
with no answer is a barrier that cannot be breached.
In other words, it is questions with no answers that set
the limits of human possibilities, describe the boundaries of human existence.*

— Milan Kundera,
The Unbearable Lightness of Being

*The important thing about grass is that it is green. It
grows, and is tender, with a sweet grassy smell. But
the important thing about grass is that it is green.*

*The important thing about the sky is that it is always
there. It is true that it is blue, and high, and full of
clouds, and made of air. But the important thing
about the sky is that it is always there.*

— Margaret Wise Brown,
The Important Book

Sam was telling Janice an amusing anecdote from his recent
trip to a conference in Oslo. On the flight home, he had

been seated beside an obnoxious young man named Dirk, who,
Sam said, did not know his ass from his cranium and hadn't
the sense to shut up about it either. As they embarked on the
first leg of the transatlantic trip, Sam was trying to read, sleep,
or think with his eyes closed. But this Dirk was one of those
unfortunate seat-mates who simply cannot settle themselves.
He partook liberally of the free liquor served in first class,
flirted with the stewardess every time she came within range,
drummed his fingers maddeningly on the arm of his seat in
time to whatever juvenile rubbish was blaring through his head-
phones, and tried repeatedly to engage Sam in meaningless
conversation.

"Where are you from?"

"Where have you been?"

"What do you do for a living?"

Sam responded with vague one-word answers:

"Canada."

"Norway."

"Teach."

He kept his eyes closed and could only hope that the idiot
would get the hint eventually.

After the meal had been served and then cleared away again,
Dirk pulled a briefcase out from under his seat and placed it
on his lap. Sam thought thankfully that finally he was going to
get some peace and quiet.

But when the innocuous-looking briefcase had been sprung
open, Dirk pulled from it, with a flourish like that of a magician
pulling a rabbit from a hat, a contraption of tangled wires and
Styrofoam balls in different sizes and colours. He fussed with
it for a minute and then shoved it triumphantly under Sam's
nose. It was a planetary model, and a primitive one at that,
with the nine Styrofoam balls impaled upon the wires at various
intervals, waving now like insect antennae. Mars was painted
red, of course, and the rings of Saturn were shaped in gold foil.

"What's wrong with this model?" Dirk challenged Sam.

"Pluto should be three blocks away," Sam said.

"That's right!" Dirk cried. "How did you know that?"

"What do you think I am?" Sam said. "Stupid?"

Now, to Janice, Sam said, "It was a trick question. You can ask things like that of your friends, but not of a total stranger on an airplane." Janice laughed with what Sam took to be intelligent appreciation.

They were in the kitchen: Janice at the stove stirring the spaghetti sauce, Sam at the table having a drink of single-malt Scotch, their ten-month-old daughter, Celeste, in her play-pen in the middle of the room, flinging brightly coloured plastic blocks at her parents and crowing.

Technically, of course, Janice knew that Pluto was the most distant planet, placed at an educated guess of 6000 million kilometres from the sun. She could still recite the mnemonic device she'd learned in public school for remembering the planets in order: Man Very Early Made Jars Stand Up Nearly Perpendicular. It was only the M's, Mercury and Mars, that sometimes still got mixed up. She knew that Pluto had been found almost by accident in 1930 by Clyde Tombaugh and that it was believed to be a frozen world, totally encased in ice, possibly once a moon of Neptune that had somehow been flung out of its orbit, left to wander around the sun on its own.

But whenever they talked about Pluto, Janice pictured a grassy sweet-smelling planet populated by thousands of cartoon Pluto dogs, like the one from Mickey Mouse, with yellow fur, flapping black ears, and noses like black jelly beans. Lanky and clumsy with oversized feet and tangled-up legs, they went wiggling under white picket fences, tromping through pink flower beds, and tumbling headlong down soft green hillsides. So whenever they talked about Pluto (which was often enough in their household), Janice laughed.

Janice was Sam's second wife. Sam, a professor of astronomy at the university, was twenty-one years older than Janice, who was almost twenty-five. Sam had been divorced from his first wife, Solange, for only two months when he became involved with Janice.

The circumstances of their meeting and subsequent marriage were, as Sam put it, so trite that he had long ago begged

Janice to please stop telling the story to everyone they met. She
agreed. Guiltily. It was as if he knew (but how could he? he
was intelligent, yes, but hardly omnipotent) about that time
last fall on the crosstown bus when Janice, then six months
pregnant and very pleased with herself, had told the whole
story to the woman sitting next to her. She was a friendly,
motherly sort of woman who was, in fact, on her way to the
hospital to visit her daughter who had just given birth to twins.
She held on her lap a wicker basket of fruit with two pink bows
on top. She sat for ten whole minutes with her hand on Janice's
belly, waiting to feel the baby kick. She predicted that it would
be a girl because Janice was carrying high — or was it because
she was carrying low? Either way, she was right. And when she
got off at her stop, she gave Janice a big hug, an apple, and
two perfect pears.

The fact of it was that Janice had been Sam's student. She
had just returned then from an extended trek through Asia.
She had taken a year off from university, where she had been
studying a little bit of this, a little bit of that, in her first year:

English: When is *Beowulf* generally believed to have been
written and by whom?

French: Comment allez-vous?

Geography: What is the principal export of Surinam?

Art History: What group of French painters was most
intrigued by the science of light?

Developmental Psychology: At what age does a child normally realize that he is not the centre of the universe?

Like many people of her age and persuasions, Janice thought
that travelling to another continent would simultaneously
broaden her horizons and help her to focus, to *centre* herself.
But when she returned, she was more unsettled than ever. She
did not go back to university right away. Instead, she roamed
around the city in her beautiful Asian garments, her Nepalese
silver ankle bracelet tinkling its twelve tiny bells as she wandered in and out of specialty bookstores, Indian restaurants,
and eastern import shops, buying incense sticks, patchouli oil,
camel bells, and an annotated copy of *The Tibetan Book of the*

Dead. It seemed that everyone she'd ever known or cared about had moved away.

Janice had always been subject to bouts of depression, which had begun to escalate in both depth and frequency. But she had the kind of small perky face, apple-cheeked and bright-eyed, that always looked happy no matter how bad she felt. So that even when she was positively "beside herself" (as Janice sometimes thought of her condition, picturing a clone-like creature weeping and wailing and carrying on right alongside of her more ordinary self, which continued all the while to perform the necessary manoeuvres of daily life), nobody even seemed to notice. It was this sunny little face of hers which Janice blamed for the fact that no one seemed to consider her capable of sorrow or serious thought.

Janice's real problem, she had decided while travelling, was not that she wasn't serious; it was just that she had always had trouble distinguishing between what was meaning*ful* and what was meaning*less*. So that her problem was not a lack of seriousness, but rather, of not ever knowing what should be taken *seriously*.

Finally, in September, she took a job at the Farmers' Market and a night course called "Astronomy for Amateurs". Five days a week she stood behind a table under a green canvas awning, selling organically grown carrots, apples, and spinach, fragrant peaches, and living lettuce with its roots in a clump of wet dirt in a clear plastic bag. She also sold real maple syrup and free-range eggs. Two nights a week, Tuesday and Thursday, she went to Sam's class.

It began when she took to joining Sam and several of her classmates for a beer in the pub afterwards. Soon she and Sam were sneaking away from the group early, going to another bar where they could be alone together. By Christmas, they were lovers — by one of those romantic quantum leaps which afterwards left Janice, in her new-found happiness, unable to retrace the steps they'd taken, to reconstruct the decisions they made, unable to remember even the simplest things:

When did they first kiss?

How did they get that first time from the bar to her bedroom, from the car to her bedroom, from the kitchen to her bedroom?

Did they, that first time, take their own clothes off or each other's?

When did they fall in love, before or after?

When Janice discovered, less than six months later, that she was pregnant, Sam (much to everyone's surprise, including hers) up and married her.

* * *

Getting ready for another faculty dinner in the third month of her pregnancy, Janice stood naked in front of the full-length bathroom mirror. Sam was still in the shower behind her and the steam was welling up over the plastic curtain, so that Janice had to keep wiping the mirror clear with a towel.

She was twisting and turning supplely, trying to see herself from all possible angles. Was she showing yet? Finally she turned her back to the big mirror and looked into the tiny one in her eyeshadow case, positioning it so she could get a look at her behind.

Sam had always gloried in her slim young body, her tiny waist, her prettily protruding hip-bones. He liked to have her stretch out flat on the bed and hold her breath so he could count her ribs. Sometimes, when he drank too much Scotch at faculty parties (as he might well do tonight), he would point out the finer details of her figure to his friends.

Sam stepped out of the shower and wrapped himself in a blue bath sheet. To his reflection in the misty mirror, Janice said, "Will you still love me when I'm fat?"

Sam considered this carefully. He knew enough by now about pregnant women and their dazzling hormones to know that Janice was just feeling sensitive and insecure.

"Well," he said finally, caressing her damp back, "you won't be *fat* exactly — you'll just be pregnant."

"But what *if*," Janice countered, "what if I *do* get fat some-day? I mean, *real* fat. I mean, someday. Would you still love me then?"

Sam was cornered. "Well, no," he, being an honest man, felt he just had to admit. "No, I'm not sure I would."

While Janice lay face-down on the bed in her bathrobe and sobbed, she thought about a man she'd slept with in Tibet. His name was Gerry and he was yet another Canadian student on a tour of the east. She had first noticed him because the scars of adolescent acne on his cheeks and forehead were still so red and raised they looked painful. He had stringy greasy black hair and a scruffy goatee, but his brown eyes were soulful and kind. They undressed shyly on either side of the small foreign bed, having left the hostel where they'd met the week before and splurged on a real hotel room for the night. It was at that moment when Janice most betrayed herself for the sake of getting into bed with a man.

"Are you sure you want to do this?" she asked him. "I look really awful when I get up in the morning. Do you still want to sleep with me?"

Now she was crying even harder, hating herself in retrospect for having said it and for having been so grateful when Gerry laughed and hugged her and stayed.

Sam was ignoring her now, rummaging through the dresser drawers, wondering aloud why nobody wears cufflinks any more and humming. Janice went on crying and hating herself vigorously, also hating, for the first time, the fact that she was pregnant. She did not hate the baby, she hated the pregnancy.

She tried to console herself with the thought that for nine months at least, longer if she breast-fed, she wouldn't have to put up with having her period. That was an advantage, cer-tainly. But then she remembered the time, early in their affair, when she had apologized to Sam for not wanting to make love because she had her period.

Sam said, "I knew you had it. I can always tell. I can even tell two or three days before it comes."

"Am I that crabby?" she asked.

"No, no, it's nothing like that," he said and refused to explain.

For days she bugged him and bugged him to tell her how he knew. Could he smell it? she wondered with horror. Could he smell the blood, the useless blood, the decaying blood dripping from between her legs?

Finally Sam tired of her persistence and said, "It's just that your mouth tastes different when I kiss you at that time of the month."

Janice, embarrassed and self-conscious, had no proof of this, one way or the other. It was one of those things she never asked even her best friend about. The next month, when the time came, she took to brushing her teeth obsessively, gargling with Extra Strength Listerine, chewing mints and cinnamon-flavoured gum. Sam was amused but exasperated, said he wished he'd never mentioned it in the first place. It wasn't a bad taste, he assured her, it wasn't bad at all, just different. But Janice never forgave him.

★ ★ ★

Janice had always liked children, and the birth of Celeste in early December brought out all of her suppressed maternal instincts and set them in full glorious swing. She realized that she had been longing for years to have someone she could legitimately mother. She had often been accused of trying to mother everyone she knew, adults, mostly men, who lapped it up for a little while and then left because they felt suffocated. Mothering a real live baby was much more satisfying, she discovered, if only because a baby could never be loved too much.

After Celeste was born, Janice felt this part of her personality to be infinitely expandable and so, to indulge it even more, she set up an arrangement with several other mothers in the neighbourhood, forming a loose kind of baby-sitting exchange. When she and Sam had a dinner to attend or just needed an evening out once a month or so, one of these women would look after Celeste. Janice was always available to look after their children in return, often overnight. It was an unbalanced arrangement but Janice didn't mind.

Two or three nights a week, when Sam returned from the university, there would be a toddler or a half-grown child in the kitchen baking cookies with Janice and Celeste. Sometimes Sam would find them in the living room with the stereo turned up loud as they leapt and danced all around the coffee table and the bookcases, Janice leading the troupe at the top of her lungs with the turkey baster for a microphone and the soup-pot lid for a tambourine.

There had been no children in Sam's first marriage, to Solange, and so, at almost fifty years of age, he didn't really know whether he liked kids or not. They were certainly a rambunctious lot and their high-pitched voices seemed too often to become shrill and demanding. Their presence in the house seemed to fill every room at once with movement, bright noise and colours, projects and plans. Not to mention little trucks and wooden blocks that he was always tripping over. They hadn't been told in prenatal class about the way a baby would change every little thing in their previous serious lives. All they had been told was, "Breathe, breathe, breathe!" and that was certainly of no help to anyone now. He had trouble reconciling this constant commotion with his own intellectual preoccupations, with his image of himself as a bearded, learned man in a quiet book-lined room, smoking a pipe and nodding his large head with drowsy, dignified wisdom.

But he had to admit that he loved to watch Janice with the children: the way she would get down on her knees to talk to them, the way she could understand everything they said even though it all sounded like gibberish to him, the way she could not pass by any one of them without touching, patting, or hugging some part of their compact bodies, the way her love came spilling out all around her.

He worried occasionally though that Janice was neglecting her intellect. He deeply mistrusted the vacant milky look that came into her eyes whenever she put Celeste to one of her engorged leaking breasts. He suspected that she watched game shows and soap operas, maybe even *Sesame Street*, while he was at work. He tried leaving selected academic books and articles on the back of the toilet, on the top of the TV, on the pillow of their perpetually unmade bed. But by the time Janice picked them up, it was only because they'd been lying around for so long they were covered with dust and sticky little fingerprints. The only book she ever read with any dedication at all these days was called *The Womanly Art of Breastfeeding*. She went out and bought a three-volume set of child-care manuals which answered all her questions about teething, feeding, sleeping, and gross motor development. At the end of each chapter there was a growth chart showing what the child should be able to do at any given age. These charts listed such developmental achievements as:

"Looks in appropriate place when asked, 'Where is daddy? Where is the ball? Where is baby?' "

"Uses trial-and-error method to discover new solutions to problems."

"Pokes, bangs, pulls, turns, and twists everything within reach."

Over dinner Sam would try to engage Janice in meaningful discussion about Stephen Hawking's time concepts, the preposterous search for a tenth planet beyond Pluto, the quasar mystery, or the place of art in society. But Janice was always distracted, jumping up from the table to mash more carrots, get more milk, more apple juice, more ice cream. He tried once to tell Celeste that it was not necessary to scream bloody murder when one was hungry, because if that were the case, think what miserable places restaurants would be. But Celeste threw a forkful of zucchini at him and Janice just laughed indulgently and said, "Now you know why God made washing machines."

Of the neighbourhood children Janice looked after, Sam's favourite was an eight-year-old boy named Josh, who lived in a duplex at the end of the block. His parents were, as Sam put it, plain people: his father worked for the city, Public Works, and his mother was a salesclerk at Woolworth's downtown. Sam saw in young Josh an inquisitive, agile mind, hungering for all kinds of knowledge and much in need of guidance. Sam was secretly flattered by the fact that Josh seemed to prefer his company to Janice's patient nurturing.

While Janice cooked supper and tried to keep track of Celeste, who was just learning to walk, Sam and Josh would sit together in the living room or in Sam's study. Josh was a shy child, long-limbed and awkward, with bright brown eyes and a remarkably ugly haircut. He would sidle up to Sam and begin firing questions at him, one after the other, as if he'd been saving them up for days. And he listened to the answers too. Sam could barely conceal his delight as he pulled books from the shelves, flipped through back issues of scholarly journals, drew diagrams and charts, raising even more questions in his efforts to satisfy Josh's curiosity.

Sam treated even the simplest questions with the utmost seriousness. He understood that everything was equally important to Josh, who could not know yet the difference between trivia and truth, lightness and weight. There was an almost unbearable feeling of suspense around Josh as he waited for Sam's carefully considered answers.

"Why is the grass green?" Josh might ask.

"Why don't worms die when you cut them in half?"

"Why is Mars red?"

"Who invented ice cream?"

"How much does the Earth weigh?"

"Why is the sky blue?"

Janice in the kitchen had to laugh as she overheard Sam droning on in answer: "Not all skies are blue. The sky on Mars is pink. On the moon, it is black. Venus has a yellow sky. Sunlight is composed of a spectrum of colours. When it enters the Earth's atmosphere, it meets atoms and molecules of air. All of the colours except blue travel straight to the surface, but blue light bounces off these atoms and molecules. Because the blue bounces around, it eventually reaches us from all parts of the sky, not just straight from the sun, as the other colours do. Therefore, the sky looks blue. On the moon, there is no air, so the sky is black. Dust in the Martian atmosphere makes the sky pale orange or pink. Clouds on Venus make the sky yellow."

What, Janice wondered, did Sam expect a mere child to make of all this? There was plenty of room in a lifetime, she thought, to accumulate such information. Rather, it should be like telling them about the birds and the bees: you should only, as the child-care manuals advised, tell them as much as they could understand, otherwise they would be frightened and overwhelmed.

★ ★ ★

Which is not to say that life with Sam was a constant feast of intellectual stimulation or an endless barrage of braininess. Sometimes at dinner, instead of explaining (again!) how the weight of a planet might be measured or railing against a recent Letter to the Editor in the evening paper which tried to demonstrate the part witchcraft had played in the history of astronomy, sometimes Sam would just whine (yes, Janice had to admit it, he *whined*) about the petty politics of the department or the ungrateful illiterate ignoramuses passing themselves off as graduate students these days.

Sometimes whole evenings passed in which all the questions Sam asked were the same questions other men, other husbands, might well be asking other women, other wives, anywhere:

"Where are my socks?"

"What's for supper?"

"Why is the baby crying?"

"Why can't you make the baby stop crying?"

"Please, I'm so tired, would you please rub my back?"

★ ★ ★

Sam was still friends with his ex-wife, Solange. At first Janice found this unnatural and upsetting. She had never maintained a friendship with any of her former lovers because, once the romance was over, she invariably discovered that she didn't even *like* the guy, they had nothing in common (a discrepancy which could be overlooked in love perhaps, but certainly not in friendship), and in fact, she had to wince with embarrassment or outright revulsion whenever she thought about the time she'd wasted on the stupid guy or the look on his face as they climbed into bed.

But Solange was a gracious and generous woman who seemed to have nothing against Janice — after all, she and Sam were already divorced when Janice came along. But it was the layers of memory which Sam and Solange shared that Janice could not penetrate or duplicate. They did not deliberately exclude her from their reminiscences but she always felt left out. After Solange left, Janice would be petulant and childish (she knew she was being childish but could not stop herself), trying to trick Sam into saying that he loved her more than he'd ever loved Solange.

Eventually it occurred to Janice that it was hardly their fault for getting married the same year that she was born. And so what if they were off honeymooning in the Bahamas when she was cutting her top front teeth? So what if they were buying the limestone house when she was being potty-trained?

After Celeste was born, Solange confessed one afternoon to Janice that she had always wanted children but found she could not get pregnant. Janice decided she could afford to be sympathetic, and besides, Solange was even older than Sam and not very pretty. Janice vowed to try harder to rise above her own pettiness and, for the most part, she succeeded.

Solange came to their house once or twice a month and Janice no longer found it necessary to manufacture excuses to avoid her. Now, instead of having suddenly to go to the grocery store, visit a sick friend, or do the laundry in the basement, Janice was quite comfortable to sit and have coffee at the kitchen table with Sam and Solange. After twenty-three years of marriage, there were still many practical matters they needed to discuss.

The divorce had been amicable enough and, in the settlement, Solange got both the house and the car. The house was a hundred-year-old five-bedroom limestone building which

Janice thought of as a mansion, but she struggled to master her resentment over the fact that she and Sam lived in a small stucco bungalow with tiny dark rooms and a wet basement. She knew better than to ask what on earth Solange needed with five bedrooms, a sunroom, and a walk-in pantry the size of Janice's kitchen and living room put together.

Solange had recently retired, but for the years of their marriage, she too had worked at the university, a professor of philosophy. Being a true intellectual totally immersed in academia, Solange had never much troubled herself with the trivia of daily living. Now she found running the household, not to the mention the car too, a complicated and often overwhelming job. She came to Sam for help and advice. She could sit for hours at the kitchen table drinking coffee, asking questions, and taking notes.

"Should I buy radials or regular? Where should I buy them?"

"How often does the furnace need a new filter?"

"The toilet keeps running. Should I call a plumber?"

"What was the name of that piano tuner we always used to get?"

Janice would sit with them only half-listening, flipping through cookbooks and her recipe box, planning Sam's supper. Solange, as Sam often pointed out when she wasn't there and he and Janice were sitting down to yet another delicious and nutritious meal, was not much of a cook. Janice, on the other hand, was one of those enviable people who could throw any number of things together, toss in a little bit of this, a little bit of that, and produce a culinary delight night after night.

"Cooking, ah, cooking," Solange would sometimes sigh. She had already admitted that she went out for dinner almost every night, and when she did eat at home she favoured wieners and beans, Campbell's tomato soup, or those dehydrated dinners with a shelf life of two years.

She began to collect cooking hints from Janice and some recipes that were supposed to be quick and easy: Skillet Spaghetti, Quick Western Rarebit, Chicken Dinner Omelet.

But there were always so many details to worry about:
"What's the difference between dicing and chopping?"
"Does this mean fresh peas, frozen peas, or canned?"
"How much is a pinch?"
"How do you do it?" she would ask Janice with envy. "I just don't know how you do it."

* * *

In January, at Sam's suggestion, Janice enrolled in a painting course two nights a week. He said it would be good for her to get out of the house, to get away from Celeste sometimes. Janice could not make him understand that she didn't *want* to get away from Celeste. Even on a bad day, when Celeste was teething and fussing and crying, Janice could think of nothing else she'd rather do than be with her, cuddling her and giving her ice cubes to suck on or a raw carrot to chew on. Sam did not know how many afternoons, while Celeste was napping, Janice would sit on the floor beside her crib, just listening to her shallow sweet breaths, wishing she would wake up.

In the end, Janice took the painting class because she thought it would be good for Sam to have some time alone with Celeste. Maybe he would come to feel it too: the joy and the fear of loving her so much, the joy which suffused everything Janice did now, the fear which would strike suddenly, paralysing in its intensity, when she thought about Celeste getting sick, getting hurt, dying, when she heard on the radio stories of child abuse, Sudden Infant Death Syndrome, a two-year-old boy in Toronto whose mutilated body was found in a dumpster behind the corner store.

The painting instructor was a man named Réjean Simard who had earned a considerable reputation for himself with his oversized flamboyantly coloured still lifes of apples and oranges twelve inches across, wine bottles three feet high, salamis the size of torpedoes viewed through the glass window of a downtown deli so that they became mystical, pregnant, out of this world. He was most often described as an iconoclast, a compliment or an insult depending on who delivered it, a variable term of endearment, celebration, or disapproval.

During the first few classes, Janice found her mind wandering. She could not concentrate on the advantages and disadvantages of each medium which Réjean Simard enthusiastically explained to them. She could not get a grip on the differences between watercolour, oils, polymer, acrylics, pastels, and tempera, as he carefully and energetically demonstrated them. She was intimidated by her fellow classmates, who all seemed to know more about painting than she did. She felt just plain stupid. She could not think of anything that she wanted to paint. She was terrified when Réjean Simard said that the first question they must ask themselves was *why* they wanted to paint. He said the only way to find the answer was to look deep inside themselves, to uncover their own sensitivities, and then to train those sensitivities so that they became even stronger, even sharper, even more demanding. Then and only then could they hope to find their own true subject matter.

On class nights, Janice would lie awake afterwards in bed beside Sam with a sick feeling in her stomach and the growing certainty that she did not have a creative bone anywhere in her body. But she was too disappointed and embarrassed to admit it, even (or especially) to Sam. He could sleep through anything anyway and so had no idea of her recurring insomnia.

After Réjean Simard had covered the more mechanical aspects of the art form, he moved on to broader theoretical concepts which he called "the elements of art". He taught with a frenetic energy, always in motion, pacing dramatically and flinging his arms towards the back wall as if a gallery of great art hung there. He scrawled words and shapes across the blackboard so wildly that the chalk often broke in his fingers and bounced across the room. He pontificated in italics.

"Colour is *everywhere*," he said. "*We cannot escape it*. But what is it? *What is it?* Blue. *What is blue?* Green. *What is green?* It is not enough to know why the grass is green. *What is green?*"

"In nature," he said, "*there is no such thing as a line. Scientifically speaking, no such thing*. But *how can we possibly* recreate nature, how can we reproduce the world, without lines? *We cannot.* We must have the horizon in order to *survive.*"

"What does the word *texture* mean?" he asked. "Even the dictionary *does not know.* The dictionary *does not know* what you think of when I say gravel, a brick wall, newly mown grass, *skin.*"

"*Your paintings must have balance,*" he said. "How many white daisies does it take to balance the weight of *one black ball?* How much blue sky does it take to balance the weight of *three tall trees? How can a mountain equal the sun?*"

Janice, finally, was inspired. Now, when all the other students were nodding into their notebooks, she was riveted. One night at coffee break she overheard two women muttering to each other:

"What is all this airy-fairy stuff?" asked the first.

"Yeah, really," said the other. "We didn't come here to think, we came here to paint."

Now, on class nights, Janice lay awake afterwards with her head full of pictures while Sam slept on beside her, flat on his back, snoring.

They had stretched their canvases now and they had finally started to paint. Réjean Simard would flit among them, swooping down on one easel after another, exclaiming, adjusting, occasionally drawing the whole class around one painting to have a closer look.

Janice began with a painting of eggs, three white eggs submerged in a glass bowl of water. The perfectly oval eggs and the slightly cloudy water were rendered in an opaque shimmering light so that the total effect was one of otherworldliness, a submerged universe complete in itself, elliptical and promising.

If Janice's eggs were derivative of Réjean's own work, he didn't seem to mind. "These eggs," he said, "are *more than eggs.* These eggs, in the act of imagining them, have become *important.* These eggs are *the truth.*"

Janice suspected the successful picture was little more than a happy accident but she was encouraged by Réjean's admiration and began to see things in the painting that she hadn't known were there in the first place.

Each student was required to complete one major painting for the course. The rest of the class was painting landscapes, flowers, their mothers, their cats. Janice stretched another canvas, a larger one, and began. She painted nine pregnant women in various poses, sitting, standing, lying flat on their backs, so that their big bellies were like planets emitting pure light and their shiny faces were like reflecting moons.

Réjean was impressed. "Beautiful," he said. "*Beautiful. Perfect. Power.*" He wanted to know where her vision had come from, but Janice couldn't tell him, could not remember.

"Ah yes," Réjean said softly and rested his hand on her shoulder. Janice noticed for the first time his swarthy skin, his black flashing eyes, and the gentle strength of his broad shoulders inside his tight T-shirt.

When she took the painting home, Sam liked it too. Yes, he agreed, most definitely they must frame it and hang it in the living room. She was talented, yes, brilliant even, to have conceived of such a thing. "But," Sam said, "what does it mean?"

★ ★ ★

Josh's mother called to say she and her husband were going to a do at the Legion, one of his fellow employees was retiring, their other baby-sitter had come down with the flu, could Janice *please* keep Josh for the night? Janice agreed before she remembered that it was Wednesday, a class night. But she did not want to let Josh's parents down. They were such nice people. It took some convincing but finally Sam agreed that he was quite capable of looking after Celeste and Josh both for the evening. Yes, it would be all right, he finally conceded. There were some things he'd been researching anyway, for Josh, the questions he'd asked last week about the rings of Saturn.

"Did you know," Sam asked her, "that although the rings of Saturn stretch over 65 000 km, they are only a few kilometres thick?"

"Yes, I knew that," Janice said.

"Distant stars shine right through them," Sam said, but Janice wasn't listening. She was putting on her red coat, lacing up her black winter boots.

"What time will you be home?" he asked plaintively as she went out into the snowy night.

"Don't worry," she said. "I'll come right back. I'll be home by 9:30."

That night's class was especially stimulating. They were talking about composition now, how a painting when completed would have become more than the sum of its parts. Réjean used the analogy of human beings being more than the sum of their parts too, so that if you mixed together all those things that make up a person — water, blood, bone, and skin — you still wouldn't have a person, you'd only have a big mucky mess. Janice could see exactly what he meant and she was imbued all evening with that rarely reached sensation of everything falling into place, absolutely everything, so that all of her questions had answers and the whole world felt friendly.

When the others said they were going for a drink after class and Réjean made a special point of inviting her along, Janice changed her mind about going straight home and went to call Sam. Just for an hour, to go to the pub for just one hour, an hour and a half at the most, that's all she wanted, surely he wouldn't complain, she wasn't really asking for much.

Réjean and the others waited in the foyer while she stood at the bank of telephones and dialled. She could see the snow still falling outside, the night through the glass doors looking black and white at the same time. Réjean wore a black beret (of course!) and a red wool scarf wrapped twice around his neck. The phone was ringing, five times, six, seven, eight. She let it ring twenty times. She hung up and dialled again. No answer.

She rushed right past Réjean and the others still standing there smiling stupidly. "I can't come, I can't come!" she called as the snow fell on her face, her bare hands, down her naked neck.

She could not remember where she'd parked the car. She ran around the parking lot with the keys in her hand. There it was. The tires spun in the snow and then she fish-tailed away.

No answer. No answer. Where was Sam? Where were the children? The house was burning down. The house had burnt down to the ground. Someone was dead. They were all dead.

She hit the snow-covered caragana hedge as she skidded into the driveway. The house was still standing. The lights were on. Where were they? They were at the hospital. Someone was sick. Celeste was sick. Josh was sick. Someone was dead. They were all dead.

Sam was stretched out on the couch, flat on his back, snoring. The first thing Janice saw clearly was the bottoms of his feet propped up on the arm of the couch in those pathetic grey socks.

"Wake up, wake up! The children, the phone! If you couldn't even hear the phone, how could you hear the children if they cried? You stupid bastard, wake up!"

Sam stirred and grunted but did not open his eyes. "Sleeping," he muttered and started snoring again.

There was a half-empty glass of Scotch on the coffee table beside him. Janice grabbed it and threw it in his face. She sank to her knees and sobbed into her red coat still covered with snow which was melting now and dripping to the floor all around her.

"What the hell — " Sam sputtered, struggling to sit up. "What the hell is going on here?"

"What the hell is going on here?" Janice sobbed.

The children heard nothing, slept on.

In bed an hour later, Janice was calmer. She'd had a glass of Scotch and a hot bath. Sam had rubbed her back and told her she was overreacting. She was chastened, ashamed now of her own bad behaviour. She curled against Sam's back like a child in her white cotton nightgown, her hair on the cool pillow still damp from her bath. She tried to match her breathing to Sam's, which was already becoming deeper and slower. Breathe, breathe, breathe.

"Please, will you talk to me?" she asked.

"Mmm."

"Do you love me?" she asked.

"Yes, of course."

"Do you *still* love me?"

"Yes, of course." Sam patted her patiently and sighed.

"Why do you love me?"

She kept asking different questions and getting the same answer. The children slept on and knew nothing.

MASTERING EFFECTIVE ENGLISH

You tell me to close my mouth when we kiss. Think "man" in English, you say. In your language, it starts with the lips together and opens slowly the way love should begin.

— Linda Rogers, "Devouring"

Words describe features of the world judged stable. Something that appears to be a slice of cheese for a split part of a second, the tone of a violin for the next, then a prairie dog, a painting, a toothache, then the smell of garlic could not be given a name.

— J. T. Fraser, *Time, The Familiar Stranger*

A.   Pronouns

1.   She

The woman is named Naomi Smith, after her mother, her mother's mother, her great-aunt, her third cousin twice-removed, and so on. In fact, there are so many Naomis in her family that, in order to keep track of themselves, they call each other things like: Big Naomi, Little Naomi, Old Naomi, New Naomi, Naomi the Pianist, Naomi the Nurse, Naomi the Manicurist, and so on. This Naomi is Naomi the Teacher. She is young and strong, intelligent and honest, but she has never been very attractive to men. She has puzzled over this repeatedly. It must be her mouth, she thinks sometimes, which is too big and always open so that her silver fillings show. Or it could be her eyes, which are too small, too close together, and colourless, like the white eyes of those dogs which give many people the creeps. Either way, she is still a virgin. She suspects that's what the other Naomis call her behind her back, some saying it with pride, others with pity: "Here she comes, Naomi the Virgin!" Privately, she thinks of herself as Naomi the Anachronism.

She teaches grade ten English at an inner city high school with concrete-block walls and a barbed-wire fence around it. Every September she faces a new room full of thirty potential juvenile delinquents and warns them about the dangers of dangling participles, split infinitives, and the unforgivable incorrect usage of those tricky little words "which", "that", and "who". Even while she asks the class to write two pages, double-spaced, one side, on one of the following topics: butterflies, nuclear war, submarines, the etymology of the word "word", or "How I Spent My Summer Holidays", she is wondering why nobody ever falls madly in love with her.

At the age of thirty-two, she has had a sum total of two boyfriends. Neither of these romances was officially consummated. (When thinking along these lines, Naomi often mixes up the words "consummated" and "conjugated", and then she discovers that they really do amount to essentially the same thing.)

First there was Hector Addison, who was temporary head of her department for six months in 1983 when the regular head was away on maternity leave. The trouble with Hector, it turned out, was that he was just no fun. What attracted Hector to Naomi in the first place (her free spirit, he said, her

liveliness, her sense of humour, her penchant for wild dancing
and imported beer) was exactly what he tried to knock out of
her in the end. She should not dress so casually, he said. She
should not be so friendly. She should not drink, talk, or laugh
so much. She should not listen to that rock-and-roll music any
more because it was puerile and would probably damage her
morals, not to mention her eardrums. He was always correcting
her grammar, the more so when she said "Youse guys" on
purpose just to annoy him. Hector was, Naomi decided, too
smart for his own good.

And so her second boyfriend, two years later, was Billy
Lyons, a dump-truck driver she met in the laundromat. The
trouble with Billy, it turned out, was that he was just not serious
enough. And what attracted Billy to Naomi in the first place
(her brains, he said, her education, her good job, her informed
opinions on everything) was exactly what he tried to knock out
of her in the end. She read too much, he said. She didn't know
how to LIVE, really LIVE. She shouldn't think so much. She
should just LIGHTEN UP. Naomi was always correcting his colourful speech, especially when he said, "Right on, fuckin' A!"
Naomi was, Billy decided, too damn smart for her own damn
good.

Modern men, Naomi decided then and there, were a bunch
of malcontents. They wanted too much or too little, or they
wanted somebody else altogether. They thought women were
like empty rooms, just waiting to be redecorated. The wonderful women they had in their heads had little or nothing to
do with the ones they took to their beds. It was hardly her fault
that all she wanted, all she really wanted, was to be ADORED,
to be SWEPT AWAY by a man who thought she was perfect. She
decided she was tired of being disappointed. She would rather
be a cynic. She would rather give up on men than give in. And
they would all be sorry in the end.

Now, every summer, once school is out, Naomi takes herself
on an expensive vacation. She goes for a month or six weeks to
somewhere warm and exotic, tropical, preferably an island.
She has already worked her way through the more popular

tourist attractions: Hawaii, Barbados, Majorca, Jamaica, and the Virgin Islands (she's always had a good sense of humour, even in reference to herself, and is especially fond of irony). She now favours more remote destinations: tiny primitive islands which are difficult to get to, where the natives resemble those bare-breasted women and loin-clothed men frequently featured in *National Geographic*. These islands are the well-kept secrets of a certain travel agent who specializes in, as he puts it, off-beat vacations for unusual people and vice versa. Naomi likes to think of these islands as uncharted and unnamed, although she knows this is no longer possible in our shrinking world. But still, she finds comfort in putting herself in a place where no one would ever think to look for her, where no one will ever find her.

2. He

The man is named Iquito Hermes Honda Plato Mariscal Estigarribia. "Iquito," he says to everyone, "you can call me Iquito." But the truth is that he calls himself by different names on different days, depending on the weather, a whim, or a voice in a dream. On the day he met Naomi, he was thinking of himself as "Honda", but he said, automatically, "Iquito, you can call me Iquito." So she does, and sometimes he doesn't know who she's talking about.

Iquito has lived on this small island for his entire life, fishing mostly, and sleeping in the sun. He is, in English years, almost seventeen, but the island calculations for such quantitative definitions are complicated, akin to figuring a dog's real age by multiplying its people-years times seven or to converting Celsius to Fahrenheit by doubling and adding thirty-two. Chronological age, to the islanders, is either an approximation or a popular misconception.

Iquito works as a courier, delivering the island mail which arrives by boat every other Monday. His brown feet are muscular and sinewy from all the running around he must do. As part of his training for the courier job, Iquito has been to the missionary school to learn how to read, write, and speak English. When he delivers a letter, he reads it aloud to the recipient, who then dictates the response, which Iquito skilfully translates and transcribes and then carries back to the boat. Like most colonials, Iquito speaks English with a stilted precision, better than Naomi speaks it herself, so that he sounds thoughtful and genteel at all times, even when he is telling jokes or talking dirty. Iquito knows everything about everyone on the island and they all depend on him, with collective good faith and great respect. The grateful islanders reward him regularly with food, liquor, sex, and more secrets. On this island anyway, no one would dream of shooting the messenger.

The day he met Naomi, Iquito had just returned from a run to the eastern side of the island. He was feeling loose-limbed and nimble after all that exercise, and he was pumped-up too with pride, having just delivered and deciphered a complex letter from a lawyer on the mainland to a woman who was about to inherit a small fortune from a distant uncle she'd never heard of. The letter was dense with words and phrases like "forthwith", "hereto", "whereof", and "the party of the first part". The woman was so pleased with the good news (once Iquito had figured out that it was indeed good news) that she rewarded him with a bottle of home-made wine and a blow job.

Naomi, who had arrived on the island just three days before, was lying on the beach, her bare stomach flat on the hot white sand, her bathing-suit top unhooked so she wouldn't end up with tan-lines across her back. She was half-asleep, listening to the water lapping at the sand like a tongue. Iquito squatted down beside her and kissed the small of her back, where the sweat was gathering in a salty pool. Startled, she rolled over quickly and her bathing-suit top fell right off so that she lay there bare-breasted and blinking her little white eyes at him. "Iquito," he said, "you can call me Iquito."

In the language of love, as Naomi had learned it from her high school students, Iquito was "hot stuff". Much to her own surprise, she realized that she wanted nothing more or less than to lie him down and fuck his brains out for a whole week straight.

3. They

Naomi and Iquito have now known each other for three weeks and five days. They have been married for six and a half hours. For their honeymoon, they have travelled on horseback to the northern end of the island where there is a luxury hotel with one hundred air-conditioned rooms, two heated swimming pools in the shape of kidneys, and a restaurant specializing in French cuisine. It rises out of the humid green jungle like an oasis or a mirage, its copper-coated windows reflecting circling seagulls and clouds banked up in thunderheads to the west. Iquito and Naomi are the only visible guests. A uniformed valet leads the thirsty horse away and ties him up out back.

Iquito takes the unlikely presence of such a structure in such a place totally for granted. He cannot tell Naomi when it was built or why or by whom. He lives in a world of such perpetual wonderment that nothing surprises him. He never has got a grip on words like "incredible", "incongruous", or "imagine".

4. I

"I can hear what you're saying," Naomi says, "but I don't know what you mean." She is not exactly complaining.

5. You

"You must listen," Iquito says in his elegant English, "to the water instead of the words."

Naomi still doesn't know exactly what he means, but she's willing to give it a try. She figures it should be simple enough, something like listening to the ocean inside a seashell. She has to admit she's been getting a little fed up with words lately anyway, having spent her whole life (or so it seems in retrospect) surrounded by them, struggling with them, up to her ears in syllables and syntax. (Iquito, she has observed, has unusual ears, which remind her of gills. Maybe he is from the lost continent of Atlantis, washed up here by accident, waiting.)

She has suspected all along that there is a trick to words that she hasn't figured out yet: if you can just find the right ones and then string them together in the right order, it will all make sense. But there are so many of them, arbitrary and constantly shifting like sand beneath her feet. Sometimes she is overwhelmed by the sheer number of words in the world, by the sheer number of people flinging them around so freely, so certain that their words can mean something, DO something, CHANGE something: so that silence is no longer significant or socially acceptable.

6.   It

It is a question of mind over matter.

B.   Nouns

1.   Water

After a pretentious but delicious supper in the French restaurant, Naomi and Iquito take a stroll along the shoreline. They drag their bare feet through the wet sand and let the warm water wash them clean again. Naomi has never learned how to swim because she is afraid of the water. For somebody who spends so much time on islands, she realizes this is slightly ridiculous but she can't help herself. Mostly she is afraid to get her face wet. She is afraid of the way when you open your eyes underwater, everything around you is colourless, including the other swimmers, who look then like corpses, their stringy hair like seaweed, their arms and legs like driftwood. When they open their mouths, they look like bloated fish and only bubbles come out.

Iquito, who cannot imagine a world without water all around it, wades out deeper and deeper, until he is swimming parallel to Naomi who is still walking in the sand. She thinks of the time when she was twelve and her best friend, Lucy, nearly drowned. Lucy couldn't swim either, Lucy couldn't even float, and when she tried it, she sank silently out of sight into the water so deep it looked black. Naomi, who was perched on a rock on the shore, could do nothing but watch as the other girls, screaming and crying, dragged Lucy out by her hair and then pounded on her until the water and the mucus streamed like fish guts out of her mouth and her nose. Afterwards, they went back to the cottage where their unsuspecting parents were and they sat outside in the lawn chairs eating a whole watermelon, smearing the juice and the seeds all over each other, laughing hysterically, and flirting outrageously with Lucy's older brother and his friends, until finally somebody's mother turned the hose on them to calm them down and clean them off.

If Iquito drowns now, Naomi thinks, she will be a widow in her widow's weeds. She is not exactly sure what this phrase is supposed to mean but she imagines herself on this beach with green-black strings of seaweed draped over her face and bare shoulders like a veil, while the water-logged body of her new husband is plucked by the fishermen out of the sea.

If she was going to get wet at all, she would rather be in one of the kidney-shaped pools back at the hotel, where there is a lifeguard and blue water-wings. But swimming in a heated pool while in sight of the actual ocean strikes even her as an absurd thing to do, so she doesn't suggest it. She lets Iquito coax her out to him bit by bit until suddenly she is in past her waist. She is proud of herself for not panicking. Iquito swims slowly away just beneath the surface. When Naomi isn't looking, he circles back and grabs her from behind. He holds her head under the water with both hands.

She has always been afraid that once her head was under, the water would rush in through her ears and her nostrils, filling up her whole head, which would then either burst or stay like that, leaving her with water on the brain like her cousin who was born that way.

She remains absolutely still and nothing happens. Iquito lets go and she stays under for a few more seconds of her own free will. Her lungs are beginning to ache as she opens her eyes and there to the left is a car, a white car with the trunk, the hood, and all the windows open. A golden fish with large blue fins swims through it, undulating and unconcerned. Its gills seem to throb and its iridescent scales flicker through the milky sea like laughter or tiny hands in motion.

If the Eskimos have twenty different words for "snow" (and everybody says they do, although nobody seems to know what they are), the islanders have at least that many for "water". So that a glass of water, a body of water, and water under the bridge have virtually nothing to do with each other. There is even a different word for water when you are in it as opposed to water when you are only looking at it, thinking about it, or wishing for it. Naomi is coming to understand that this dislocation makes more sense than a lot of other things. Iquito has never had any reason to think otherwise.

2.   Angel

Back on the beach, Naomi lies down to dry off in the sinking sunlight. Her white cotton shirt and shorts stick to her skin like warm plastic. Iquito squats by her head and braids her long blonde hair which is stringy and gritty with sand.

She stretches out her arms and legs, moves them slowly back and forth, making an angel in the fine white sand. Iquito finds this hilarious and lies down beside her and makes one too. She tells him how the children in her country do this in the winter in the snow, how she used to do it too, in her red snowsuit with the bunny ears, flat on her back in the front yard at five o'clock on a January Saturday afternoon when it was already dark and the houses of her friends up and down the street were already receding into the night which was pressing down on her face like a pillow. She tells him how the tricky part is getting up again and jumping out of your angel without messing it up or leaving a trail of footprints which will give you away.

Iquito does it again and again all around her, until he can do it perfectly and there are sandy angels everywhere. He heard about angels at the missionary school, but he thought they had to be ethereal, airborne, and self-righteous. They were also chubby, and probably irritating, hanging around, as they did, at all the wrong times. He decided then and there that angels weren't for him. But he likes these ones better.

He has also heard about snow but has never been able to get it clear in his mind. He would like more information.

"What does it taste like?" he asks Naomi.

"Water," she says, which is not quite true.

"What does it smell like?" he asks.

"Nothing," she says, which is not true either. Snow smells like snow. There is no way around it.

They jump out of their angels and walk slowly on.

Iquito is no angel. He is an innocent, Naomi thinks, a reckless and remorseless innocent, who has no sense of sin and so no sense of the guilt which animates the remains of the real world.

3.   Monkey

As they walk beneath the smooth-faced cliffs, they meet a man with a monkey named Atimbo. The man is also named Atimbo. Both the man and the monkey are wizened, with leathery brown skin and no eyelashes.

"What a nice monkey," Naomi says politely.

"She is not just any monkey," the old man informs them proudly, "she is a talking monkey."

Iquito is very rude to the monkey, turns his face away and will not look the animal in the eye. The monkey snorts and spits at him. Iquito spits back at her. The old man doesn't seem to mind. "Say hello to the nice white lady," he tells the monkey, who makes a series of quick graceful motions with her black fingers, as if she were a magician about to pull a dove out of a handkerchief. She is talking with her hands. The old man rewards her with a kiss on the lips and a chocolate.

Iquito says to Naomi, "You're not white, you're pink."

The monkey squats square in front of him and makes the signs again, with a slight variation this time, poking herself in the chest with her right index finger. "I am nice white lady," the old man translates, laughing. "She is one funny monkey," he says.

"You're not white, you're brown," Iquito says scornfully.

"So are you," the monkey signs back.

Iquito stomps away. (Stomping away in bare feet, Naomi notes, is much less effective than stomping away in stiletto high heels or hiking boots.)

Iquito hates monkeys. He is convinced that they are really just funny-looking people who are only pretending they can't talk. He says they are evil incarnate. He swears by the story that his older sister, Komatsu, was kidnapped by a big black monkey who had stalked her for weeks and then this monkey forced her to live with him in a banana tree and bear his little black monkey babies. He swears by the story that, when these monkey babies grew up, they formed a gang and killed his sister and then they ate her all up.

Naomi thinks this sounds like a story straight out of the weekly tabloids back home: WOMAN GIVES BIRTH TO MONKEYS or MONKEYS EAT THE HANDS THAT FEED THEM. But she manages to be serious and reassuring for Iquito's sake. She tells him that in her country all the monkeys live in zoos or circuses, where they are kept on leashes, dressed in little red jackets and hats, forced to dance while an organ-grinder plays music for the audience which then drops pennies into the monkey's little silver cup. "Good idea," Iquito grumbles.

Naomi doesn't tell him that when all her friends were wanting ponies, she was longing for a cute little monkey of her very own. She would dress it up in doll clothes, she thought, with pink ruffles and a bonnet, and she would push it around town in a baby carriage. She would even teach it to talk, with its mouth, not its hands, and they would be best friends forever. But her parents wouldn't go for it and they got her a goldfish instead.

Naomi just nods now as Iquito tells her again about his stolen sister. She has never seen him angry about anything else and she doesn't know what to think.

4.   Fish

Goldfish, sunfish, swordfish, jellyfish, angelfish, devilfish, fish story, fishwife.

His tongue in her mouth flickers like a fish: tickling. The taste of her later on his lips is like fish: salty. His hands upon her face smell like fish: familiar. The major (indeed, the only) export of the island is fish: indispensable.

But even in the utopian ocean the fish must eat each other to survive.

5.   Time

Time passes. All time passes in its own good time.

Iquito does not think in hours.

At first, Naomi is always asking, "What time is it? What time is it now?"

Iquito gives her answers like, "It is time to eat. It is time to sleep. It is time to make love. The sun is shining. It is raining. It is dark. I am hungry. It is time to make love." Naomi would rather have a nice simple number to go by but Iquito cannot figure out how or when the number six might mean supper and what difference does it make if the sun comes up at seven, eight, or nine: it comes up anyway.

Eventually he teaches Naomi how to tell time by the sun and the stars, by the tides of the sea and of her own body. She stops asking stupid questions. She will also learn to navigate eventually.

No matter how you figure it, time is always passing and proving that everything changes, everything must move forward and forward and on. It is only when you think of it that time stands still.

C.   Verbs

1.   To Love

Iquito loves everything (except monkeys). He is always saying, "I love you. I love the sun. I love your left nipple. I love red bicycles. I love your yellow hair. I love all the stars and the full moon too. I love your teeth and your great big mouth. I love bananas. I love the way your belly button sticks out. I love raw meat."

Teasing him gently, Naomi says, "I love the way you love me and I love pizza too."

Iquito, who has never seen, let alone eaten, a pizza in his life, says, "Ah yes, that too."

2.   To Laugh

They laugh at each other with their eyes squeezed shut, their mouths wide-open and round. Their laughter is delicious, like that of mischievous children stuffed to bursting with secrets and plans.

3.　To Rain

Iquito wants to sleep on the beach. He does not trust the hotel. To him, all enclosures are an aberration. Naomi can suddenly see what he means.

They lie down in the sand with their legs entwined. Naomi nestles her head into the curving bowl below Iquito's left shoulder. She presses her ear to his moist brown skin. She can hear the blood inside of him (or is it her own blood?) like the ocean inside a seashell. The sound of the surf seems to come not from the sea but from the stars speckled above them. While they sleep, the clouds come in like ghost ships. The rain drops down on their skin like cool silver coins.

4.　To Sleep

The little green island feels like a boat, sealed up and salty, on the verge of becoming gladly and forever lost at sea. There is no telling what has become of the rest of the world.

In the dream, he asks, "What do you want?"

She says, "I want you to grovel." And in the dream he does it. With great delight. Prostrating himself before her on the sand, winding around her ankles, and whimpering like a slippery well-fed cat. She loves him so much in her sleep that she wakes up in the morning exhausted and covered with fine white sand and Iquito's elfin face sleeps on softly beside her.

D.　Conjunctions

1.　And

And the rain still falls silently into the sea.

2. Because

Because there is nothing to be said, there is nothing to be remembered or regretted.

In the dream there is no word for love.

In the silence, Iquito and Naomi are jumping out of their angels and swimming sleekly away.

3. But

But there is always the rest of the world out there, waiting to be acknowledged and appeased.

E.   Interjections

1. Oh

Oh never mind about that.

2. O

O to lie down in your arms and laugh.

THE LOOK OF THE LIGHTNING, THE SOUND OF THE BIRDS

You, who have lived your whole life believing
if you made enough plans
you wouldn't need to be afraid. . . .

— "Into the Midst of It",
Bronwen Wallace, *Common Magic*

Fear *is the general term for the anxiety and agitation*
felt at the presence of danger, **dread** *refers to the fear*
or depression felt in anticipating something dangerous
or disagreeable (to live in dread *of poverty);* **fright**
applies to a sudden, shocking, usually momentary fear
(the mouse gave her a fright*);* **alarm** *implies the fright*
felt at the sudden realization of danger (he felt alarm
at the sight of the pistol); **terror** *applies to an over-*
whelming, often paralyzing fear (the terror *of soldiers*
in combat); **panic** *refers to a frantic, unreasoning fear,*
often one that spreads quickly and leads to irrational,
aimless action (the cry of "fire!" created a panic.*).*

— *Webster's New World Dictionary*

An excessive secretion of adrenalin arising out of fear
eventually produces shock, a constriction of small
arterioles in the body, lowered blood pressure, loss of
blood fluid to the tissues, dehydration, increased heart
beat, and ultimate death.

— Kimble and Garmezy,
Principles of General Psychology

If a story is not to be about love, then I think it must be about fear.

I am meeting my friend Melody at Van's for lunch around noon. It's Friday and the relative humidity is 100 per cent, so that upon waking, I find the sheets wadded in a damp ball at the foot of my bed. On the clock radio, the weatherman is cheerfully promising another unbearably hot day and then they play "Summertime". I groan and try to remember how snow-flakes feel, falling on my face.

Melody and I made these arrangements earlier in the week on the telephone. I noted them in my appointment book and also on the calendar on the kitchen wall. I am fond of calendars and like to have one in every room. The one in the kitchen, under the clock, features, predictably, milk recipes. The one in the bathroom, over the white wicker clothes hamper, fea-tures classic cars in well-polished poses struck upon black asphalt, wet cobblestones, or circular driveways in front of cathedrals, wheat fields, or stately white mansions. The one in my bedroom, next to the vanity, features contemporary female artists, their paintings with names like *Cabbage in Bloom, Cher-nobyl and Navajo Medicine,* and *Apple Blossoms, 1987.*

Melody and I have lunch together at least once a month and we always meet at Van's on a Friday around noon. Melody, who is once again (or still) trying to lose that ten pounds she gained over the winter, will order the soup of the day and a small Caesar salad. I will have the chicken pasta and a side order of cheese-and-garlic bread. We will drink black coffee before, during, and after the meal.

When I have lunch with my other friends, we go to different places on different days. Ellen and I always go to the White Spot on a Wednesday. We both have the steak sandwich and a beer. Janie and I always go to the Burger King on a Saturday with our kids: my son, Andrew, and her twin daughters, Ashley and Kate. All of our children are three. At the Burger King, I have a Whopper, a large order of fries with gravy, and a chocolate milkshake. Andrew only eats the onion rings.

What I mean is: I cannot imagine being at the Burger King on Saturday afternoon on Princess Street with Melody.

At one time, close to ten years ago now, Melody and I were room-mates. We were best friends then. Now we are close, but no longer a conspiracy or a cartel.

At that time, Melody and I were both single and spent all of our evenings in bars. For three solid years we were drinking and partying like mad fiends. We were good-natured and resilient enough then to have hangovers which lasted for fifteen minutes at the most, rather than for two whole days the way they do now. We were going through a phase together: that was how I thought of it then. We were in disguise, playing at self-destruction. Or we had a new hobby. Or we had spring fever. We were generally pleased with ourselves, especially when we walked into our favourite tavern at The Belvedere Hotel and Billy the bartender would tease us, saying, "Here comes trouble!" We didn't even have to order, he knew what we wanted. He would let us write cheques if we got carried away and ran short of cash.

We sat around The Belvedere night after night, drinks and cigarettes in hand, talking about the time to come when we wouldn't be doing this any more. The bar would be filling up around us: there was a Country-and-Western band on stage, people dancing by themselves, minor altercations around the pool table, somebody sending us another pitcher of beer, and, over the twanging guitars, we could talk glibly about the future because the end of the pointless present was always firmly in sight. We were just waiting to get tired of it. We were going through our mid-life crises early or our adolescent rebellions late.

We were never in any real danger, or so we thought. There was always a part of us that didn't enter into it, that didn't get drunk. Much as I liked to drink, I always assumed that I would be sober when the time came: sober when my real life began. And now here we are.

Melody has no children. She does have a husband (his name is Ted) whereas I don't: this, however, is not a reason for anything and can hardly be construed as her fault. I did have one once, for a little while, and now I have Andrew.

Sometimes along about midnight or later on a Friday or Saturday night, I catch myself longing for those irresponsible old days, longing for a blast of loud brainless music, an elongated bloated beer drunk, a party all night with Richard falling into the stereo three times, Evelyn spilling a fish-bowl full of strawberry daiquiris into the piano, Donny dancing naked like he always did, his underwear like a bunny hat on his head. Then breakfast in the morning, the birds are already singing and we're all down to Smitty's at 6 a.m. where they were tolerant, the waitress was benign or blessed, the coffee pots were bottomless, and Melody, yelping at the sunrise coming pink all over the sky, said, "Wow! Wow! Wow! WOW!", and the construction workers ate bacon and eggs in their yellow hard-hats silently and Melody said, "Think of it, just think of it, all of these guys have been home, been to bed, been to sleep already and everything, and here we are!" I was poking at Hugh, who was falling asleep with his dreadlocks resting against the plate-glass window as if he were riding cross-country on a Greyhound in the rain.

I am no longer the woman who does these things. Perhaps I am no longer the woman who did them. I have become the woman who can always find, fix, or reach things.

This is from the hard-drinking days when new friendships were frequent, instant, emotional, and brief. I have no idea what became of these people who seemed so important, so bright, or so clever at the time, these people that I bought beer for, whose terrors and troubles I listened to, then decanted a few of my own, and sometimes the woman weeping by the window was me. They wouldn't know me if they knew me now. They are like the young dead, never changing, struck like statues back in time. I imagine them still drinking, still partying, in some other bar now, as if nothing ever happened, nothing ever changed. I think of them as witnesses, waiting and watching a woman who used to be me.

There were often near-strangers sleeping in our living room on Saturday morning: a man on the couch snoring, still wearing his jacket, his sunglasses, his pointy-toed shoes, or a woman fully clothed face-down on the carpet with her right elbow resting in an ashtray and her long red hair spread around her like a peacock's tail.

The residue of the night before would be spread through the entire apartment: beer bottles, caps, and cans covering the kitchen table, dirty ashtrays, empty album covers, and somebody's socks strewn around the living room, a dirty handprint on the bathroom wall, and long black hairs in the sink.

Even then, as I cleaned up the butts and the bottles while Melody vacuumed, I knew better than to mention the other residue, the disquieting dread which clung to me all the next day, which had something to do with staying up so late, then crawling to my bed while the party continued downstairs, the stereo raging, the bass notes crashing, the conversation flapping drunkenly around the room, me not drunk enough to stay awake, but not sober enough to sleep either, or was it the other way around? The anxiety hummed through me all day, striking a honed high note upon hearing, for instance, the news that a small plane had crashed into a bookstore in Atlanta, Georgia, and everyone on board was killed, everyone in the store too, those patient browsers swiftly incinerated while fondling crisp copies of *The Shining*, *The Velveteen Rabbit*, or *Six Memos for the Next Millennium*. I was certain then, in my spike-edged angst, that I too was bound to suffer heartbreak, loneliness, and terror forever, bound to be the victim of a random, ridiculous death, someday, somehow, soon.

The only thing to do then, it seemed to Melody and me, was to head back down to the bar where, if you got there early enough and helped put out the ashtrays, they'd give you the first round free. In the morning, we drank Bloody Caesars, which we called "seizures", our stomachs queasy, our furry tongues stinging with black pepper and tabasco sauce, my spirits lifting by increments until by noon it appeared that another day might actually be passed without panic or punishment. I was once again cushioned by that false sense of security, that expansive illusion of well-being you get on your third drink and then you have ten more trying to recapture the feeling and end up wondering why you're crying in your beer at 3 a.m.

It was there, at The Belvedere, that I met Andrew's father, who appeared to be a brown-eyed handsome man, gentle, polite, olive-skinned in a pink striped shirt. He was only unusual in the sense that he was nothing like the men I usually went for: the scruffy disreputable ones, unemployed, with a propensity for alcohol in large quantities. It was also there that Melody met Ted, who, unlike most men you meet in bars, turned out to be exactly what he seemed to be: kind, generous, and sane. The Belvedere is closed down now, bankrupt, scheduled for demolition in the fall.

That was a long time ago and now I understand about the comfort to be found in fear, also the power. Sometimes now I think it is the fear that keeps me safe; sometimes now I think the fear is *all* that keeps me safe. When I am scared of everything, the fear becomes a gauze bandage around me and I am convinced that if I stop being afraid, if I let my guard down for just one minute, all hell will break loose and fly apart in my face like a shattered windshield. On airplanes, I am so scared that I think if I relax and let myself enjoy the flight, the movie, the drinks, the conversation of the interesting woman beside me, we will crash for sure. It is my fear alone that keeps us airborne. All the other passengers can do whatever they damn well please: they have no responsibility and so no power.

I realize there is a pumped-up kind of vanity in this, a perverse delusion of grandeur in the belief that I could singlehandedly avert disaster and save these smug, stupid strangers, not to mention myself.

The power of fear lies in its conceit or the conceit of fear lies in its presumption of power.

Even as a child, I never thought that terrible tragedies could only happen to other people. I never acquired or accomplished this particular form of delusory armour with which most people gird themselves. I was a nervous child. I was quite confident that disasters could only happen, naturally enough, to me. Maybe it was selfish to be so afraid, but at a very young age I had stopped believing in protection, no longer expected to become safe, grown-up, or immortal. There were too many things to worry about: car accidents, plane crashes, kidnapping, fire, explosions, cancer, burglars, guns, knives, the bomb. The other girls at my school in their pastel angora sweaters and their A-line skirts, they didn't worry, I was sure of it. They didn't worry their pretty little heads about anything except their hair.

My flagrant fear, I figured, must single me out as the conspicuous choice for a catastrophe. The persistence of my fear was like a song stuck in your head first thing in the morning and it won't go away all day.

I did not tell this to anyone, knowing instinctively that fear was something to be ashamed of.

I was not afraid of monsters or magic: it was, I had decided early on, only people and thunderstorms that were seriously dangerous. One night at supper my mother was telling, with great amusement, the story of how her boss at the bank, Mr. E. Ingram, was on the toilet Tuesday night reading *Reader's Digest* in a thunderstorm when the lightning came in through the window and danced all around the sink while he just sat there, what else could he do? It was attracted by the water, my mother said.

This was the same summer that lightning struck the chimney of the Hatleys' house across the back lane and their television

exploded. When the fire trucks arrived, Mrs. Hatley was standing in our back yard with the heads of her three children buried
in her white nightgown, all of them crying. Water and chim-
neys, my mother said, electricity, lightning conductors.

After supper, she and my father went out (a rare occurrence
in itself and I can't think now where they might have gone)
and I was left in charge of cleaning up. The minute they left
the house, another storm blew in and the thunder began. I
roamed through the rooms of our suddenly flimsy frame house,
unplugging the electrical appliances and avoiding the windows.
I imagined my face flung down into the hot soapy dishwater
when the lightning came out of the ceiling and struck the sink
straight through the back of my head. I sat at the kitchen table
with my eyes closed for an hour, praying.

When my parents came home and found the dishes not done,
my mother slapped me across the face because I was too big to
spank. The humiliation of fear was inexcusable.

In my bed that night, I could not sleep and I lay there
contemplating my dolls, which were hung by their necks from
a pegboard on the far wall, me being too old to play with them
any more but not ready yet to give them away. Their plastic
eyes in the half-light were like those of an animal caught in the
headlights of a car on the highway. Their boneless legs were
still pink but useless. I could hear my father snoring wisely in
the next room but could no longer convince myself that he
would be, at any given moment, braver than me. He was afraid
of snakes and Ferris wheels: this was not comforting at all.

I used to know a woman who was afraid of moths, the pow-
dery-winged white ones my mother called "dusty millers",
and this woman had nightmares in which the moths flew up
her nose and suffocated her with their twitching trembling
wings.

Andrew's father was afraid of horses and pigs, although he
lied to me about this (he lied to me about many things, most
of them equally irrelevant) and said he loved animals of all
kinds, especially horses with their handsome legs and pigs with
their pink snuffling snouts.

In order to understand, it is not necessary to know that I am afraid of snowmobiles, needles, caterpillars (especially the furry black-and-yellow ones), down escalators, short blond men with beards, and other people's mothers. (And — not many people know this about me — I am also afraid of libraries.) It is only necessary to know that I am more afraid of pain than of death and sometimes this seems sensible.

Melody says she is not afraid of anything and I believe her. Melody does not think about things the way I do, which is probably why we were best friends then and are still close now. She is unsuspecting, unquestioning, and her conscience is clear. She has not heard that the unexamined life is not worth living and she thinks the aphorism "There is nothing to fear but fear itself" is actually true. Her clarity is contagious, and when I am with her, I too feel weightless.

While I have black coffee for breakfast and read last night's paper, Andrew is once again refusing to eat the meal I've made for him (oat bran, raisins, yogurt, cantaloupe, healthy, healthy, healthy: he'd rather have red licorice and a hot dog).

The newspaper headlines this morning are still about the pair of human legs discovered last week in a green garbage bag on the highway west of town. The severed legs were discovered at 7 a.m. Thursday by a man on his way to work who saw a foot lying in the middle of the road. Despite the fact that the limbs had been badly mutilated by predators, it has now been determined that they belonged to a twenty-five-year-old local woman named Donna Dafoe who had been missing for a week. They are looking for her estranged husband, Stuart Steven Dafoe, and for other body parts. The sergeant on the case has commented that it's like putting together a jigsaw puzzle.

Almost everyone I know is disturbed by this story in one way or another. It undermines the imagination. On the street, in the grocery store, the drugstore, the bank, everywhere I go all week, I overhear strangers discussing it. Their voices are soft, frightened, or outraged. They are all shaking their heads.

Two nights ago my boyfriend, Joe, came over after Andrew had gone to bed. We played three games of Scrabble and then we were watching the news and I said, "It's so sick," and Joe said, "Everybody's sick."

"Well, yes, probably," I said, "but not like that."

Joe said, "Yes, you're right."

But am I?

Right after the news, we got ready for bed and, while Joe was brushing his teeth, I put pot lids over all the ashtrays like I do every night.

Curled into his back in the bed, I said, "I smell something burning. Do you smell something burning?"

"You always think you smell something burning," he said, but not unkindly.

"I can't help it, I'm afraid of fire."

"I don't smell anything," he said. "There's nothing burning but your imagination."

"When I was a child, I always thought I could smell the gas," I started to say, but Joe was making that deflating endearing little sigh he always makes just as he's falling asleep, so I wrapped my arms and legs around him and hung on.

Now, as I get up for more coffee, Andrew dumps his breakfast on the floor. Feeling too defeated for the moment to be angry, I say, "You hurt my feelings when you do that," and he says, "Do you have feelings, Mommy?"

In the bathroom, putting on my makeup and trying to tame my hair which has gone completely out of control in this humidity, I see by my face there is no way of knowing. The black eye is long gone and the broken finger on my left hand, the one that had to be mended with a metal pin, only hurts now when I knit or the weather in winter turns damp. There is no way of knowing that, in what I think of as my former life, I was once thrown to the floor by a man I loved and while he kicked me in the head, I made a sound like a small animal with soft brown fur and beady eyes.

By the time I've located a clean pair of pantyhose without a run and Andrew has spilled his milk twice, we are both bitchy in the heat and I am yelling indiscriminately about the toys scattered everywhere and I keep tripping over them, about the cracker crumbs all over the floor and they are sticking to the bottoms of my bare feet, about his fear of flying insects which I think is foolish because he screams his head off every time we go out to work in the garden and I'm afraid of bumblebees but I haven't let it ruin my life and now there's no more milk.

Andrew says seriously, "I'm a person too you know."

I take him on my lap in the sticky morning and his hair smells like sleepy trees. His damp eyelashes on my naked neck flutter like butterfly wings or a baby bird scooped off the sidewalk, fallen out of its nest, and you hold it in your palm like a heart and you know it will die no matter what you do.

I want him so much that I weep.

I take him to the day care and then drive downtown. Going along Johnson Street, I see a pretty red-haired woman in a black jacket and grey pants coming out of the funeral home smiling as she steps around the hearse which is running. Her immunity is evident, even from across the street.

I get to work on time as usual. I am co-owner of an arts-and-crafts store called Hobby Heaven. We sell paint-by-number kits, model airplanes and cars, embroidery hoops, and the like. There is a large market for this sort of thing these days and the business is flourishing.

This morning I am unpacking three cartons of rug-hooking kits. As I stock the shelves, I hear a female voice behind me saying, "And then he pulled a gun on me." A second female voice sighs.

Looking around as discreetly as I can manage, I see two elderly women with carefully curled hair wearing polyester dresses, one beige and one navy blue, with matching square plastic purses hooked over their arms as they riffle through racks of knitting patterns for baby clothes. The woman in the beige dress has in her shopping basket several balls of baby-blue wool and a pair of size 12 needles. As I turn back to my rug-hooking kits, she is telling the woman in the navy dress about her new grandchild, her sixth, a boy who was breech, 9 pounds, 9 ounces, and they named him Hamish, of all things.

The morning passes slowly.

As usual, I am the first to arrive at the restaurant. Melody, who is a medical secretary, has the day off and so is coming from the other side of town where she and Ted have recently rented a two-bedroom apartment in a building on Driscoll Street: it is the kind of squat flat-topped yellow brick building with black iron balconies deemed modern by builders in the fifties. But Melody has a flair for decorating and so, inside, their apartment is strikingly cluttered with coloured cushions, wicker baskets, and fresh-cut flowers.

Eighteen months ago, a woman was murdered in that apartment. This is not the sort of thing that would bother Melody, but every time I go over there, I think I can see faint brownish stains on the carpet in the hallway leading to the bathroom. This is where, according to the newspaper reports, the murder took place, the woman stabbed twenty-seven times by her husband while her two children slept. The police took the children out past the body with blankets over their heads. The woman's name was Janice Labelle. Why do I remember her age, the date, the number of wounds? Why did I cut the articles out of the newspaper and save them in a big brown envelope? I didn't even know her.

I imagine Melody and Ted living out their lives in that apartment, cooking meals, reading magazines, listening to music, making love, taking a bath, and they would never notice how even the fresh-cut flowers smell sinister sometimes.

Van's is always busy on Friday but I have arrived early enough to get a table by the window overlooking Lewis Avenue. The restaurant, with its white furniture, pale-green walls, and the air conditioning on full-blast, is an oasis. I order a coffee, with lemonade on the side. It is fresh-squeezed and comes with a pink umbrella in a frosted glass.

I've brought along some new product-information pamphlets to read while I wait for Melody, who would be late even if she lived next door — I am both irritated by and envious of this because it seems to me to embody a carefree attitude which I know I will never be able to muster.

I pretend to be reading while I watch the people going in and out of the building across the street, a highrise with copper-tinted windows which houses the offices of various insurance companies, lawyers, travel agents, and architects. Most of these people are women, stylishly dressed in pastel summer suits and white sandals. They come out of the building in confident clumps, chatting and smiling, making their lunch-time plans. Even from across the street, I can see how clear-eyed and fresh-faced they all are — there is no way of knowing anything else about them.

The people at the next table, two women and a man, are talking about the severed legs. The one woman, it seems, the one wearing the diamond jewellery, knows someone who knows someone who knew the Dafoes when they were still married. There were signs, she is saying, there were signs all along. Someone turns the music up and I cannot hear her clearly any more. She is saying something about jealousy, alcohol, arguments, death threats, jail. The other woman and the man are nodding seriously, satisfied somehow, ordering another coffee, another glass of wine. Is this how it is done then — sorting through the past to find premonitions, portents, and signs, until you have convinced yourself that you knew what was going to happen all along, until you can say, I knew it, I just knew it. But then of course you didn't really know it, couldn't, were too far away, too busy, too tired, asleep.

I feel the fear come winding around me again. Maybe there *were* signs, maybe I just wasn't paying attention at the time, maybe there were signs all along and I missed them.

Melody arrives at 12:17 p.m. and does not apologize. She has brought me a bouquet of daisies. The waitress brings us a big glass of water to put them in.

Melody orders the soup of the day, which is cucumber with yogurt, and a small Caesar salad. I order the chicken pasta with cheese-and-garlic bread.

I am feeling jumpy, but try to match my mood to hers. We talk about her husband, Ted, and his promotion at the lumberyard. We talk about my boyfriend, Joe, and how good he is with Andrew. We talk about the new words Andrew is learning and how he is almost tall enough now to pee standing up.

I try to remember Melody, drinking beer at The Belvedere, dancing and flirting with strangers, one time climbing up on a table to sing the National Anthem just for fun. But it does not seem possible that she ever did those things. She is attended now by a blissful aura of amnesia which renders the past innocuous and the future bright.

When the food arrives, we fall silent except for occasional sighs and murmurs of appreciation. The people at the next table are leaving now, laughing and flashing their charge cards around in the cheerful argument over who will pay the bill this week.

After the coffee arrives, I try to talk to Melody about the severed legs. She's not sure at first what I mean. I tell her the whole story as far as I know it, including what the woman with the diamonds said about signs, there were signs all along.

Melody says, "Don't think about it. You just can't think about things like that."

I want to say, How can you not, how can I stop? But she has already launched into the story of a woman named Martha, a patient at the clinic where she works. Martha is a young woman, pregnant with her first child and also dying of cancer. She does not cry. She goes out and buys baby clothes, a crib, a teddy bear named Tex. She is knitting a yellow baby blanket and a green sweater set, which she works on in the waiting room until her turn comes. There is no way of knowing if she will live long enough to deliver, but, to look at her, there is no way of knowing that she is dying either. She does not cry but sometimes, as she's leaving the office after her weekly examination, she grins and shakes her fist at the sky.

Saying goodbye in the parking lot, Melody and I make plans to get together next weekend. Joe and I will go over to their apartment for a game of Scrabble and a pizza. Then she hugs me and brushes her soft cheek against mine and I too am weightless again.

The afternoon passes quickly and I am friendly to all the customers, even the ones who will not look me in the eye.

After work I pick Andrew up at the day care. He has had a pretty good day, having only had to stand in the corner once, for calling one of the other kids "shithead", one of his new words.

We are both in good spirits and, as I wind through the rush-hour traffic along Montreal Street, I am humming "Summer-time" and Andrew too is singing in fits and starts: "Old Mac-Donald had a farm" or, his own version, "Old MacDonald had a hamburger". We are pointing out the passing sights to each other: "truck", "bus", "dog", "smoke". I tell him that tomorrow we are going to meet Janie and the twins at the Burger King. I imagine that he too likes to have something to look forward to.

We idle briefly at the red light at Railway Street and the man in the silver BMW in front of us is talking on his car phone, waving his hands, and picking his nose as if he were invisible. He's not paying attention when the light turns green and all the horns behind me start to honk.

A flock of fat glossy pigeons flies up from the roof of a yellow brick apartment building. Through my open car window, the sound of their wings is like sheets on a clothesline, drying in the wind.

Andrew, excited, cries, "Birds, birds, birds!", reaching his arms up as if to catch them.

I drive around a running shoe lying like a dead animal in the middle of the intersection and I think about those severed legs and pray that Andrew will never be hurt or unhappy. There is no way of knowing, there is nothing I can do. For the first time I fully understand that having given birth to him guarantees nothing, gives me no power, no shelter, no peace save that to be found in the sound of the birds.

If a story is not to be about love or fear, then I think it must be about anger.